Beneath the Radar

S.M. Carson

A catalogue record for this book is available from the National Library of Australia

Linellen Press
265 Boomerang Road
Oldbury, Western Australia
www.linellenpress.com.au

Dedication

Dearest Lullah & Hamish,

Thank you for inspiring me to become a better person.

'Love and compassion are necessities, not luxuries. Without them, humanity cannot survive.'

Dalai Lama

'The more people read fiction, the easier they find it to empathise with other people'

Joseph Campbell

Disclaimer

This story is a work of fiction. The characters, locations and events are from the author's imagination. Any resemblance to actual persons, living or dead, or actual events is purely coincidental.

Contents

1 Connor

The damp, coldness beneath him nudged him from his sleep. The waft of urine confirmed that his sister had peed the bed again. He jabbed her on the leg. She did nothing, however, to suggest that she felt it, just curled herself up into an even tighter ball. He wondered what to do next as the wetness was preventing him from finding sleep again.

The television blared from the front room where his mum lay in comatose. Pointless trying to wake her. He knew the score. No amount of trying would rouse her from her slumber. Cursing his sister and her pathetic bladder, he dragged his shivering body out from beneath the covers and went to the bathroom.

Early morning light crept through the frosted window, allowing him to make out the mound of a discarded towel on the floor. It had been left abandoned, amongst the other detritus that had found a home on the patchy linoleum. Stupidly, he brought it to his nose and the dankness detonated his nostrils. His hope of finding a clean towel stripped away. He turned carefully in the small space, his unappreciated find just touching his two fingers. Repulsion flooded his face as he slunk back to the room. Laying it down as best he could, he tried to create a barrier between himself and the wetness. Twisting awkwardly, he contorted himself onto the dry space left at the bottom of the bed.

Sleep was nowhere near. Breathing through his mouth, he tilted his head back, elongating his neck to avoid the waves of sourness that floated over his new sleeping spot.

The position reminded him of the headlock Chris from his old school had forced upon him after he'd thumped him on the back. He thought his head was going to be ripped off. Never did he think he would have to inflict a similar measure on himself in order to get some kip.

Now that he was more fully awake, the blare from the television rapidly made his temper worse. The strained laughter from whatever pathetic television re-run was fuelling his fire. Made his blood boil. The pillow made a lousy barricade.

There was nothing to laugh about in this house and making matters worse was thinking about the new school he was supposed to go to in a few hours.

Another new school.

Another new teacher to tell him he couldn't read.

Another new heidy to tell him that his behaviour was unacceptable.

Another new bunch of weans he had to try and get on with.

Another load of lies and stories to tell until the next move.

His opened mouth would have screamed if he, Connor, had allowed it to. But just like he refused to let the brimming tears fall, he kept his sounds of despair entombed. There was just no fucking point.

2 Helen

"Time for a quick cuppa before the bell goes I think?"

"Always time, Helen. This is the most important cup of the day. We should really be issued with free caffeine injections in order to cope with our little darlings," Linda responded.

"Oh, did Mrs B catch you in the corridor?"

"No, I didn't see her. What was she wanting?" Helen asked as her face automatically scrunched up in a I'm-not-going-to-like-what-you-say-look.

"Not one hundred per cent sure, but think I may have heard her murmuring something about a new pupil …"

"What? When? Today? That is all that class is needing … on a Monday too." Helen's disheartened tone made her thoughts of a new pupil evident to all within earshot.

The jolt and jiggle of the wobbly metal fixture that belonged to the staffroom door stopped their chatter as they waited to see who was responsible for the interruption.

Appearing slowly from behind the door was Kate, the classroom assistant. Her glistening eyes and bouncing, enthusiastic nature was the antithesis to those who sat, fervently hoping that their caffeine fix would help them off their chairs to the standing position.

"Morning all. Did you all have a good weekend? Oh, hi, Helen; heard you're getting a new pupil today. Aren't you the lucky one?" Kate machine gunned out.

Hearing this whipped Helen into a grumpy weekend come down retort. "It seems like I'm the last to know., I mean it's not that important to tell the class teacher, is it? I'm off to find the source and see if perhaps I can be told what is happening in *my class.*"

Pushing past Kate, Helen marched off to find the headteacher or, probably more reliably, the secretary.

"Oops, looks like I may have put my foot in it. I thought it was common knowledge," Kate tried to reason, her facing taking the hue of a well-skelped arse.

"Common knowledge to everyone, apart from those that need to know more like it," Linda replied knowingly, after having been on the receiving end of such last-minute news too often.

After fumbling in the cupboard and finding nothing, Kate made a hasty retreat.

"Poor Helen," Ted remarked. "She really doesn't need any more characters in her class. Maybe she will be blessed with a gifted pupil that will be an asset, rather than a headache."

Just before Linda could make a snarky reply, the dreaded shrill of the bell went. Last swigs of coffee were hastily swilled down gullets before the teachers left the haven of their sanctuary to face the day ahead.

Helen hadn't got far on her mission before it was brought to a standstill by two well-known culprits deciding to have a brawl in the middle of the corridor. The pair had snuck in to use the toilet. That had somehow turned into a re-enactment of bucking broncos. And that had turned into fighting. Helen had quite literally stumbled upon them as the two tore into each other. Managing to steady herself on the wall before flattening them, Helen yanked one by the arm and put her body in front of the other, prising them apart. As it slowly dawned on them that they were in the presence of a teacher, they reduced their wrestling to pushes, then eventually put their arms by their sides and hung their heads awaiting their fate as the continuous glare from Helen bore into them. Helen's face emitted enough warning for them to take heed and not to mess.

"Both of you find your way out to the lines peacefully please; you have been saved by the bell," Helen shouted as she struggled to be heard over the shrillness of the punctual, ubiquitous timepiece. Fighting was forbidden in school, but the rigmarole of going through procedures today wasn't high on Helen's agenda. They never made a difference anyway, she thought, as she recalled the countless times she had acted as referee to this pair.

"Yes, Miss Kane," the boys grumbled under their breath, very aware they had just been granted a huge reprieve.

Beaten by the bell, Helen changed her trajectory and headed to her class in order to receive her little cherubs. Sighing, she carefully splayed her hand against the wooden door so the chipped paint didn't sneak beneath her fingernails and strode straight to her desk, the door allowed to reverberate noisily against the doorstop. Behind her, she could hear the penetrating voices of her class as they jostled with each other in the corridor, hanging their coats up before attempting the seemingly impossible task of standing one behind the other.

Taking a deep breath, she turned to the window that looked out over the sea, and drank in the view. She could almost hear the waves crashing and banging thunderously down onto the shore. The sun stole a space through the clouds, flickering on the sea below.

Having briefly realigned her senses, she turned to the open door and ushered her class inside, 'smiling' face on, teacher voice activated. "Morning, Chloe, a good weekend?"

"Aye, no bad, Miss. I went to the park with my papa and I saw Nicola there too. Didn't I, Nicola?"

"Not aye, but yes, Chloe," Helen gently corrected, while Nicola nodded in agreement.

"Morning, John, how was your weekend?"

"Ok."

"Two whole days off school and it was just ok?" Helen joked.

"Maybe we should make the school week seven days then?"

A collective groan erupted. Morning pleasantries were extended to the other kids as they filed into class.

Helen organised homework books as the kids scraped their chairs out from under their desks all the while chatting to their neighbour. The busyness of their weekends caused them to be more subdued than normal. The tinkling of the class chimes alerted the class to be quiet and after a few stragglers finally cottoned on to the expectations of their teacher, Helen began her teaching.

As they discussed the plan for their day, a knock came on the door. Helen saw Mrs Barr float in, her skirt brushing the floor as she entered. It often crossed her mind that her esteemed Head could probably be wandering around barefoot as it was rare you ever got to see anything beneath her floor-skimming skirts. The no foot attire would actually suit her bohemian exterior to a tee. With her bangles jangling, Mrs Barr ushered a girl who looked utterly terrified through the door, confirming the staffroom gossip. The child's long, brown hair hung over her face like a veil. Her fingers made desperate attempts at shielding her face from the attention she was receiving. Helen could see her body visibly shaking with fear. The girl's eyes stared resolutely at the green, plastic squares at her feet.

No uniform, Helen noted. Nothing new there, but her clothes looked far too small. Her skirt was indecently short for an eight-year-old, and the shirt looked more like a t-shirt, it covered so little of her forearm. First impressions didn't hold much hope for the new child being the gifted, talented, good all-rounder the class so badly needed. Helen felt her heart sink as her mind raced through all the possible problems another child with 'issues' would bring to her over-loaded class.

"Good morning, Primary Four," boomed Mrs Barr to the class.

"Good morning, Mrs Barr," they chanted back, staring at the new girl, shamelessly pointing their fingers at the newcomer in their midst.

"Now, Miss Kane, girls and boys, I am delighted to introduce a lovely new girl to your class. Her name is Lucy Jackson and I've been telling Lucy what a wonderful class this is and how lucky she is to be joining you. I hope that you make her feel very welcome."

"Welcome to Primary Four, Lucy. It's lovely to have a new pupil. Now let me see where you can sit."

Helen glanced quickly round the room. Children were squeezed in at every table, bags hanging on the backs of chairs jostled for what little space was left. A sea of expectant faces followed Helen's movements, as if waiting to see some magic trick produce more space. A bit lost as to where to put her, Helen sighed for the second time that morning. Just as she was about to start rearranging the class, Jane, her little class helper piped up: "Miss, I could move my chair over and she could share a table with me?"

"Jane, how kind. What a wonderful idea. Bring a chair over from the reading table please. Lucy, come in and join us. Jane will look after you. If you are not sure of anything, she will keep you right."

"Good, good. Right, I will leave you, Lucy, in the capable hands of Primary Four."

Mrs Barr bustled out the door leaving the musky scent of patchouli hanging in the air as she left to attend to other business. Very good, thought Helen, leave me with this child I don't know, while you go and sip some herbal concoction in your office. Helen kicked the table in front of her out of frustration and, if it wasn't for all the kids sitting listening to her every word, she would have used a torrent of swear words.

"Ok, boys and girls, let's get down to business, spelling games out, look at your new words on the board and get started. Green group your words are flavour, favour ..."

As she explained the classwork, Helen became aware of some pointing and whispering going on. Trying to ignore the fuss in the hope it would blow over, she continued: "Savour ..." but the whispering began to spread like wildfire around the class, along with sniggers and 'gads' comments, all at the expense it seemed of the new girl. Helen's teacher instinct kicked in as she saw the other kids pointing to Lucy's hair. Someone must have spied a head louse and was ensuring the rest of the class knew.

"Excuse me, can I have some manners please?" Helen demanded of her class. "Lucy is going to think we don't know how to behave in Primary Four. Talking and sniggering when the teacher is talking ... how rude!"

"But, Miss, there are ..." Ryan began.

"But Miss nothing. You know the rules: if someone is talking you are all quiet, so I will begin again for I am sure the green group didn't hear what I was saying. And if anyone else wants to interrupt me then they can spend break time with me, understood?"

"Yes, Miss Kane," they reluctantly replied.

Helen nonchalantly wandered over to Lucy's table on the premise of giving out jotters, casting her eyes over to Lucy's direction. Nothing was going to prepare her for what she saw, however. The poor child's head was crawling with the little creatures. Hair strands being used as a climbing rope as they moved up and down, causing Helen to give her own head an involuntary scratch. The little white eggs were scattered over her head like confetti. Helen couldn't believe she herself had missed it. Even worse, she thought, that her headteacher would allow a child in such a state into her classroom. Then her thoughts turned to what kind of parent would allow their child's hair to get into such a state.

3 Lucy

Lucy froze when she saw the teacher coming in her direction. She ducked her head down and pulled her hair over her eyes. Her heart raced and her palms felt sweaty. A fear of not belonging and for somehow being in the wrong, rose from the pit of her stomach. She clenched her buttocks as her stomach churned and the sudden urge to go to the bathroom came upon her. This was it. Now the teacher was going to shout at her in front of the whole class. She could feel it. She wasn't quite sure why all the kids had been whispering and laughing. But it was probably something to do with her. It usually was. Even her own brother had started off the day by laughing at her calling her pishy pants as she hadn't made it to the toilet during the night. It wasn't her fault she had got so scared and couldn't get out of bed. She didn't know what scary monsters were hiding in their new house.

She would no doubt find out soon enough.

Connor had snapped at her to get up that morning as it was a school day, and if she wanted something to eat then she had better go.

He had looked at her with that scowl in his eyes that dared her to argue back. She never did. And he knew it. His anger zapped through her, slapping deep inside her belly, like a gong. The thundering, rippling waves of fear washed all around, swishing and sloshing. Then they slowed to a persistent lapping, back and forth, just so she didn't forget.

She had risen and had done her best to get herself dressed into what she could find that resembled school clothes. Mum had been so tired she hadn't woken up no matter how many times she had tried to wake her.

Everything would have been so much better if mum had brought her to school and been with her instead of having to meet all these grownups with just Connor. She had no reply to the many questions they asked her. Connor wasn't much help as his sullen mood had reduced his responses to grunts.

Now the teacher was coming to get her and she needed the toilet, and why was her head always so itchy? Her legs began to take on a life of their own as they shook beneath the table, rattling the empty tray beneath her desk. A large audible sob escaped from somewhere deep within and she dropped her head onto the table and covered her head with her hands, waiting for the roar from the teacher.

Instead, she felt the gentle pressure of a hand on her back, rubbing up and down like her mum used to do. Surprised by this she began to sob.

"You poor wee thing. Jane, go and get my hankies. Everyone continue with your work. If you finish or get stuck, get out a quiet job from your tray. Lucy, come with me, and let's see if we can make you feel better."

Lucy, so shocked by the kindness being shown to her, followed the teacher obediently outside the classroom, ensuring her head stayed embraced beneath the warmth of her arm.

4 Helen

The tiny frame beneath Helen relaxed a little as her arm carefully guided the wee soul out the door, quickly flicking her hair off her shoulder away from the loaded head as she went.

"Ok," Helen gently spoke, "You seem really upset. It's a big thing coming to a new school and getting to know everyone, but you're ok. We're here to help."

The girl cowered beneath Helen's arm and said nothing.

"If you don't want to talk I need you to nod your head so I know that you've heard me."

Lucy made a slight up and down gesture with her head, her eyes remaining fixed to the floor.

"Ok, good. Now, why don't you go to the bathroom and get yourself sorted out. Then when you come back we'll get you organised, ok? Remember I need a nod if there are no words."

Lucy made another small movement with her head but remained stuck to the spot.

"Do you not want to go to the toilet? Do you know where it is?"

Lucy shook her head.

"Ok, wait a minute."

Opening the door to the class, Helen caught Jane's attention and motioned to her to come towards her. "Jane, can you do me a huge favour and show Lucy where the toilets are and then bring her back please?"

"Yes, Miss Kane." Jane shot out, desperate to please her teacher and even happier to have an excuse not to do her spelling.

Helen returned to her class to try and get the morning's

lessons underway without any further interruptions.

The staffroom quickly filled after the bell went for morning break. The noisy corridors quietened as the kids escaped the confines of the class for fifteen minutes. They ran around like pool balls smashed on a billiards table.

"Another new, wee, bloody, wide mouth, dumped in my class this morning. He has done nothing, but smirk ... oh, and claw at his head, which only means one thing. The mother didn't even have the decency to bring the weans to school on their first day. Another lovely family. We seem to get them all at Stanwell. I tell you, I'm fed up with it. Is there not a sister in your class. Helen? I bet she's just the same," Irene quipped.

Helen bristled as Irene spouted forth about a kid, her words spat out with the empathy of a medieval dentist. Refusing to be sucked into the derogatory commentary, she said very little before trying to change the subject.

"Yes, it sounds as though I do have the sister. Jackson the surname?"

"Aye, that's it. God I'm shocked – two siblings with the same surname. Do you think they have the same father? Wonders will never cease in this place," she cackled sarcastically at her own wit.

"Anyone see the 'Sound' at the weekend? That wee girl from Sheffield was amazing!"

Helen pointedly ignored Irene's last comment. She didn't have the energy to have another battle about the basic humanitarian rights of every child, no human on this earth; it was like talking to a brick wall. Ted quickly picked up on Helen's efforts to change the subject and lighten the tone of the staffroom.

"I did, Helen. She was a wee cracker, voice of an angel." His Irish lilt resounded around the staffroom.

All too quickly after a natter about the weekend's television viewing, it was time for round two.

Despite not uttering a word the entire time between interval and lunch, Lucy seemed a lot more relaxed and was not shielding herself with her hair quite as often. Helen caught her at least twice looking up at her while she was talking. *Definite need for a softly, softly approach here*, Helen noted to herself. The kids seemed to have settled and accepted her a little better too. It wasn't as if they hadn't seen head lice before – it was a common occurrence in her class, unfortunately, with each kid having their turn – though the evidence was not quite as obvious as it was on this wee one's head. Helen couldn't understand why the child's mother hadn't done something about it. Helen inwardly shuddered and gave her head another scratch. She would have to do a little investigative work at lunchtime to see what the story was.

5 Lucy

Lucy sat listening to the teacher and decided there and then that she actually liked this teacher. Not just because she hadn't shouted the entire time she had been in the class, but because she had been so kind to her. Never before had a teacher given her a playtime snack. That put her way up in her books. Not finding anything to eat for breakfast, she and Connor had shared a packet of crisps they had bought on the way to school, the lion's share being inhaled by Connor.

Her stomach grumbled audibly again and, just as she was wondering when lunch was, the bell went.

"Right, come on, Lucy. I'll take you to the dinner hall. You can sit beside me and Anna if you like?" Jane was enjoying her job as chief school guide.

Lucy nodded in agreement.

"You don't say much do you?" Jane could talk for Scotland and the fact that her new pal was quieter than the proverbial church mouse was just perfect.

Jane's chatter mode suited Lucy too, because when she didn't answer, Jane just answered for her.

"Ok, Lucy, we line up here with your tray, then Elsa will ask you what you want. Now you can't take too much time or she will get ratty with you. So today is mince and tatties or a cheese toastie, so have a think of what you want," Jane advised.

Lucy managed to communicate with Elsa her desire for mince and tatties without talking. She wolfed down the food in front of her in no time. This did not go unnoticed. Kate, the classroom assistant, watched intently as the wee girl consumed her plateful in no time.

"Do you want a second helping, Lucy?" Kate asked, "There's plenty." Kate took Lucy's hand and helped her get seconds, which were quickly scoffed again.

6 Connor

After what seemed like an eternity, the home bell went. Connor dragged his feet across the concrete of the playground, scuffing his battered trainers, his teacher's voice still ringing in his ears. Bitch telling him to make sure his mother checks his head before he returns to school tomorrow. *Fat chance of that happening.*

Kids ran past him shouting at each other as they ran free from school for another day, racing to meet their parents at the front gate. Connor gazed up at the old Victorian building with its huge arched windows. He bent down and picked up a stone and threw it in the air, considering the fun he might have later with a much bigger stone. He was snapped out of his reverie as a younger kid bolted into him from behind, sending him flying. Connor turned and shot the wee one a look that sent him fleeing in the opposite direction, muttering an apology as he went. Scowling, he made his way up to the school gate and saw Lucy standing waiting for him. *What the hell did she have to smile about?* he thought. He grunted at her as he neared. She scurried up to him and smiled, then tried to keep up with him as they made their way home.

"See you tomorrow, Lucy," a wee girl shouted.

He guessed she must have been in Lucy's class. Lucy looked up and waved at the girl.

"That's no like you to have a pal. You no going to speak to her? Cat got your tongue again?" he chided.

Lucy put her head down and Connor caught her smiling. Her happiness made him feel even more pissed off. *How can she have a pal, when she canny even talk?* He'd had a shite day moping around by himself as everyone else ran away with their best buds.

They wandered down the tenement-lined street, eyes down to ensure their feet didn't become splattered with new shades of brown from the dog shit that was smeared on every other paver. The warmth of the sun raised a glow from within their bones. It shone down victoriously from the rare, blue skies. Since early light, it had fought persistently with the clouds and now claimed its rightful position above.

Connor turned off the street and made his way along a bottle strewn alley, reminders of the youngsters that frequented the area with their carry-outs. The alley led to a playground at the top of the hill. Lucy faithfully followed her big brother, skipping every so often to keep up with his longer strides. Beyond the tops of the cruddy houses that littered the forgotten seaside town with its tormented inhabitants, the view of the sea was spectacular. The sunshine had transformed it into a magical scene of glittering waves that sparkled and danced. Yachts dotted the view as he looked out towards the nearby island. A glance to the south, however, revealed a dirty, oil tanker bobbing up and down on the gentle waves like a giant jobby floating in a pristine toilet bowl. Oblivious to this dichotomy, Connor made a run for the seesaw and energetically thumped up and down, the empty side banging with force off the cushioned tarmac below. Lucy perched herself onto a swing and gently began pushing herself forwards and backwards, dragging her feet through the mud left behind from a forgotten puddle.

They whiled their time away doing their own thing, no words required, both all too well aware there was not much to go home for. It wasn't like their mum would be looking for them. She probably wasn't even out of bed yet.

Their peace was broken by screeches and laughter travelling up the hill. Bit by bit, they saw the heads, then bodies, then legs of a group of kids making their way towards them. Connor recognised some of them from school. He turned his back to them and continued looking out to sea, his legs dangling over the side of the monkey bars. Lucy was still on the swing and once she had seen what the noise was had dropped her head back down.

The group of two boys and two girls confidently strode over to the playground. This was their patch.

"Look what we've got here, Gary: Itchy and Scratchy, and they're at our park!"

"I don't remember you saying they could come to our park, Tony," Gary chimed in.

"Look, Scratchy is trying to hide behind her nitty hair," shrieked Jenny.

The gang gave a snort of laughter, waiting to see what their ring leader was going to initiate.

Connor remained stonily quiet, pretending to ignore what was going on below. Clenching his fists, he could feel the sharpness of his finger nails as they dug into his palms as he tried to control his anger. Hawking phlegm noisily from the back of his throat, he used it to form a blob of spit in his mouth. He rolled it around his tongue before launching it out. The splat could be heard as it reached its landing on the ground below. Tony marched over to Connor and gazed up at him, squinting his eyes in the bright sun.

"I think you two flea bags better get back to where you came from. I don't want to catch no bugs off you," Tony challenged.

"Fuck off," Connor quietly, but firmly replied.

"Check the big man, Tony, telling you to fuck off." Gary loved a bit of drama and couldn't help but stir things up a bit, knowing full well that Tony would fall for it.

Jenny, desperate for a bit of the action, walked towards the swings Lucy occupied. "Aye, you too, you smelly wee cow. My maw is fed up combing they nits out ma head because of skanky folk like you. Go on, get off ma swing!" She yanked the chain attached to the swing, throwing Lucy off.

Lucy let out a yelp as she fell to the ground, the swing then deliberately pushed again so it whacked off her head, skelping the side of her face and causing her to scream.

Then all hell broke loose. Connor leapt from his eyrie and smacked Tony full force on the nose. Caught with such surprise, the boy fell to the ground, his nose gushing with blood. Jenny made to catch the swing again and push a returning blow but Hayley, a quiet bystander up until then, grabbed it before it skelped Lucy again.

Gary, not much of a fighter, and more there for the patter, stepped back and let his tongue do the work. "Holy fuck, man, what a punch! Tony, he took you out with one punch. Oh my god!"

The girls started screaming at the sight of blood spewing steadily from Tony's nose. Tony writhed in agony under the monkey bars. Wasting no time, Connor pulled his sister off the ground and swiftly transported her down the hill. Lucy, still dazed, being pulled like a rag doll to the bottom. Tears streaked down her face, not just at the pain caused, but also the injustice of it all. After her good day today, she hoped things in this new town were going to be different, but she was fast losing hope.

Once at the bottom of the hill and out of sight of the playground, Connor slowed to a quick walk and exhaled a noisy "Fuck". He looked at his wee sister and reckoned she would be ok. He gave her a quick hug once they were well out of sight and directed her with his hand at the small of her back towards the busy road. Edging out between two parked cars, Connor looked up and down the street, waiting for a break in the traffic. Seeing their chance, he grabbed his sister's hand and made a dash for it, making it to the other side with only one beep of the horn.

Slowing as they reached the entrance to the stairs, Connor pushed his sister in first then, glancing up and down the street and seeing no one he knew, entered himself. He groaned as he reached into his trouser pocket and found nothing, and kicked the door in frustration.

"Shit! I've left the key for the flat in my bag up the hill!"

Lucy looked up at him and the tears began to roll down her face, mixing with the snot that freely flowed from her nose.

"It's ok. I'll try and wake her up."

He rattled the door and flipped the letter box in quick succession so that the metal twanged noisily.

They waited.

Nothing.

He lifted the letterbox lid and hollered through it. "Muuuuum, Muuuuum, MUUUUM!" repeating this sequence over and over again.

Nothing.

The only one to take notice was the nosy neighbour from the landing above telling them to shut it. Connor slid his back down the door and hit his head off the door in despair. Lucy accidentally leaned against the handle of the door and it miraculously pushed open.

"Ya wee dancer!" Connor hugged his sister then pushed her in before closing the door behind them.

7 Helen

Sitting at her dining room table with a pile of marking in front of her, Helen couldn't concentrate enough to finish the last ten. Her mind kept wandering back to her new pupil. She pushed the jotters to the side and picked up her well-earned glass of red. *Who cares if it's only Monday?* she thought. Slinking down onto her couch, she recalled her fact-finding mission that lunchtime and sighed. Having first sought out her headteacher, Rosie, she was quickly redirected to Carol, the secretary. Apparently, the two kids had been registered on the Friday, by the mother who had turned up at 3:30 pm to do so.

"She was lucky I was still here," Helen replayed the conversation with Carol earlier that day. "I was rushing to get home as I was going out with the girls from work, so to be honest I didn't pay much attention to her. She was in her late thirties maybe. Hard to tell. Life definitely hasn't been kind to her. The boy had to help her as she had something wrong with her leg. Quiet, head down a bit like the daughter, but polite enough. She said she couldn't remember the name of the school the kids went to as they hadn't been there long. Said it was in Glasgow, East End. Neither of the kids could remember the name either, not that the girl uttered a single syllable the whole time she was in the office. That was probably the strangest thing … who doesn't remember the name of the school your kids go to? No name or contact for dad – nothing new there and nothing major on the health front. Oh, and those beasties in their heads were kept under wraps with hoods. It'd been a pishy wet day, so I never thought anything of it. I didn't see the infestation till later this morning. Poor, wee thing is covered."

Helen looped the story for another time. But regardless of the amount of replay, it still didn't make any sense. No recollection of the previous school's name? *Very unusual. Something to hide there?* The mother obviously knew about the head lice problem, but happily let her daughter come to school with her head resembling a prized breeding habitat. Not to mention the fact that the kid's clothes were more suited to kids of nursery age. There and then Helen decided that the next morning she would have to pester her head teacher in order to get some more information. Her gut was yelling at her with the ferocity of a machine gun on auto fire.

Pushing her thoughts and concerns to the side, she rose and put some music on. Settling back on the couch, she scrolled through her newsfeed, catching up on the day's gossip. After a few comments on new photographs of her friends from their weekend antics, she put her phone to one side, turned her music off and watched a bit of mind-numbing TV.

Yawning, she headed off to bed, ever hopeful her newfound problem child didn't keep her awake all night. Just as she was settling down to sleep, her mobile began to vibrate. Automatically Helen lifted it to see who the late-night caller was. It was John. Not having the energy required to speak to him, she let it go to Answer-phone, telling herself she would call him tomorrow. He no doubt just wanted to update her on his recent conquests and, quite frankly, tonight she could do without listening to the dramas of his love life. She triple-checked that her alarm was set at the unearthly time she needed to get up at, pulled her eye mask down and set off into a fitful slumber.

Helen was roused from her sleep with a commotion going on out in the street below. She peeked out the narrow slit at the bottom of her eye mask, not wanting to fully awaken herself needlessly. The flashes of blue light blinked through the slither between her two curtains. Her nose got the better of her and she flipped the eye mask over her head, letting out a cry as a tangle of blonde hair got stuck in the Velcro. She hurried to the window, stopping suddenly so her curtains didn't move too violently, giving her whereabouts away to anyone watching. That was the trouble living so close to the school where she worked, constantly feeling as though she was under supervision. If only she earned more money, she could live away from the midst of her pupil catchment area. Sneaking a peek out the not quite closed curtains, she saw an ambulance and two police cars at the tenement flat across the road. "Oh no," she groaned. "I bet he's done it good this time."

A crowd of onlookers stood round the nearby door, dressed in various forms of night-time attire from fluffy slippers and dressing gowns to joggy bottoms and bare feet. Helen then spied the guy with the mullet who lived down the road, clad in just his boxers, beer belly bulging over the top, with a fag hanging from his mouth and a mobile phone in his hand taking photos. No doubt the problems of her neighbour would be posted all over Facebook before the ambulance had left to go to the hospital.

Deciding that sleep probably wasn't going to happen, Helen went into her lounge, pulled a chair up to her dining table, that just happened to be by the window, and finished doing her marking. A short time later, she saw a seat stretcher being lifted out the tenement door and into the back of the ambulance. It looked as though it was Mrs Turner sitting in it with a bandage over her head, securely strapped into the chair so she couldn't tip out. Helen suspected her injury was sustained from the lovely Mr Turner. Confirming this suspicion, a rather vocal Mr Turner was then frog-marched out the building, hands cuffed behind his back before his head was forcefully bent so he'd fit into one of the police cars that had been abandoned out in the street. The crowds slowly dispersed.

Seeing it was nearly time for her alarm, Helen flicked on the kettle. It would be the first of many coffees she feared she would need to see her through what was going to be a long day, given this unexpected early morning start. A quiet 'fuck' crossed Helen's lips as she remembered the staff meeting at the end of the day. *Still*, Helen thought, *at least I'm not in hospital like poor Mrs Turner.*

8 Lucy

The bright sun streaked through the make-shift curtains, waking Lucy. Relief flooded her wee, tight body as she realised it was morning. By all accounts, she'd had a peaceful night.

Lucy had rushed to see her mum after getting into the house the previous evening and had stayed put for the rest of the night.

Lucy's mum stirred a little, whether due to the sunlight filtering through or being aware she was there, Lucy couldn't tell. Her closed eyes opened briefly and a smile flitted across her face. Lucy smiled back. Enjoying the closeness, Lucy snuggled further into her mum, nestling under her arm, wiping her snotty nose on her mum's t-shirt.

Watching her mum intently as she slept, Lucy began playing with her hair, mesmerised by the occasional grey that poked up between the dark, lank strands. Wiry, and more white than grey they contrasted against the dark strands like the moon against the night sky. Her fingers drifted down her face, feeling the contours of her eyes; the dips and ridges of the wrinkles that fanned out from the corners, to the hollows that sunk underneath like plastic bags half-filled with water, smooth and hard at the same time.

Her fingers travelled further down, tracing over the scar left from the other night. It had formed into a long, skittery thing. Unable to resist the crusty lid, she gave it a wee pick, trying to rid her mum of the rough incongruous mass that had formed. Flinching, her mum brushed Lucy's curious fingers away, turning her body at the same time so her fingers could no longer reach her face.

Thwarted, Lucy rolled onto her side and surveyed the room. Their few possessions were still housed in the hold-all they had hastily brought with them. It had all been such a rush that Lucy was still processing all that had happened. Thinking about it made her feel strange.

A hollowness deep within began to growl and rise through her stomach as she remembered her mum's screams. Being too afraid to replay the events of that night, she quickly shut her mind off and returned to studying the room she was in.

Her eyes rolled up to the ceiling and she let them follow the cracks in the plaster, pretending they were roads. The missing bits of plaster being holes she had to dodge round with her imaginary car. The large damp patch pooling round the centre where a light had once taken pride of place was a pond. The straggly wire that hung pathetically, gingerly holding the dangling light bulb, was a fishing line. Quietly she lay there playing her imaginary game, content with her own solitude. The dank, musty smell that pervaded the room went unnoticed. The rhythmic breathing and closeness of her mum was all she was aware of.

Like a riptide dragging everything back out to sea, her mind returned her to the events of the other night.

It flicked through the scenes it could cope with. Apart from the screams, it was the darkness that had terrified her most. She remembered desperately trying to escape the monsters she feared were lurking before her opened eyes by keeping her head locked firmly beneath the pillow and her eyes clammed shut. Connor had screamed at her to get up; he had yanked her roughly by the arm, dragged her down the stairs and shoved her into the taxi. Bravely stealing a glimpse out the window, she saw her mum running. Her black leggings would have concealed the whereabouts of her bottom half if they hadn't been let down by the boldness of her white trainers. She grappled with the bags that slowed her down as she fought to move her legs in a running fashion. Not even at the door of the taxi, she remembered her mum screaming at the driver, telling him to move. Blood dripped down the side of her face and Lucy watched as her mum hopelessly tried to stem it with a towel. Her straggly hair was determined to get in on the act and Lucy watched her mum clawing her hair out from under the makeshift bandage.

Lucy was inconsolable despite Connor's best attempts at comforting her. The taxi driver didn't bat an eyelid, just happy to have a fare on what had been a somewhat dull and long evening.

Lucy had drifted in and out of sleep during the rest of the journey, resting her head on Connor's shoulder. Not even he had the energy to complain about his sister using him as a pillow. She was occasionally aware of her mum making a frantic phone call – to whom she did not know – just aware of the desperate sound of her voice as she pleaded to whoever was at the other end of the phone for somewhere to stay. After what seemed like ages, they had ended up here at another new home. A lady mum seemed to know gave her keys after mum had exchanged more money than Lucy had ever seen before. Exhausted, they had all slumped onto the couch and Connor and Lucy had fallen fast asleep.

The excitement Lucy had felt on the first morning in their new home as her mum had not only got up and dressed but told them they were going out didn't last for long. After the trip to see their new school, and a brief trip to the corner shop to buy some essentials, her mum had set up a bed on the couch and hadn't moved since.

The gurgling noise erupting from Lucy's stomach brought her back to the here and now, reminding her it had been hours since her stomach had last been fed. Sliding off the couch, she slipped from beneath her mum's heavy arm and went in search of food.

Squeezing behind the couch, she bent down and rummaged beneath the sink, opening the cupboard. Her search revealed nothing except a few mismatched plates and cups. Water continued to drip from the tap, drumming onto the steel sink.

Lucy saw a plastic carrier lying amongst the strewn clothes on the floor that looked more hopeful. Stepping over the mess, she poked her hand into the bag and found a packet of rice krispies. She stuck her hand into the box and felt them crinkle beneath her touch. Pulling her hand out, she held it above her tilted head and opened her clenched fist, dropping the little krispies into her mouth, brushing the missed ones off her well-worn clothes. Sitting on the floor repeating this action to try and quell her appetite, she didn't notice her brother standing in the doorway watching her.

"Lucky find? Is she awake?"

Lucy shook her head.

"I'm starving. I wonder if there is any money left in her purse? You seen it?"

Shaking her head again, Lucy continued eating. She watched as her brother began to poke at her mum in a bid to wake her. "Mum! Mum!" She didn't flinch.

He eventually gave up and searched round about for her purse. Kicking at the mess on the floor, he sent clothes and other bits and pieces flying across the room. Having a brainwave, Lucy stopped her krispies frenzy and quietly stood up, stepping over the detritus. She bent down and shuffled her hand under the cushion on the couch, splaying her fingers till they reached the hardness of her mum's purse. With some difficulty, she slid it out from beneath the still mass and handed it to her brother.

"Thought you said you didn't know where it was?"

Lucy just shrugged in a quiet response.

Snapping the purse open, he looked inside and counted out the few coins inside. "£2.35. Right, come on, let's go to the shop and get a sausage roll. Suppose we better get to the school today, at least we will get lunch there. Not that I can be arsed seeing that bitch teacher or those wee buggers fae last night," he ranted.

Lucy grimaced at her brother's decision, but Connor pushed

her towards the door, telling her not to worry. He was going to sort the wee bastards from yesterday out. Walking in front of her brother, she scratched her itchy head and winced. She must have been clawing at it all night and she could feel an open wound at the back of her ear. Connor watched helplessly as the blood trickled down her neck onto her once-white shirt. Not knowing what else to do, he grabbed her and they went out the door to buy some food to fill their empty bellies.

9 Helen

The staffroom buzzed with chatter and gossip. Helen pushed the door open, her hands straining under the weight of the marking she was returning, her eyes feeling as though they had been pierced by hot pokers as she struggled to smile and say 'morning' to everyone. Catching snippets of the 'hot off the press' chat, she realised they were talking about the drama that had unfolded in the Turner household the previous evening.

"Did you no see anything, hen?" Isa, the school cleaner, drilled. "Do you no stay right across the road?" she continued without waiting for an answer.

"I didn't see much. Just poor, wee Mrs Turner being stretchered out and put in the back of an ambulance," Helen eventually replied.

"I heard she's lost both eyes and he smashed her best crystal wedding glass right into her face, the bastard. I tell you I wouldn't be long in sorting him out. Such a tiny, wee woman. And there was six police cars there and it took eight police officers to put that evil bastard in the back of the motor as well."

Helen shook her head at the liberally strewn embellishments. This was Isa in her element, retelling stories that happened to others; making up what she didn't know and everyone hanging on her every word.

"I shudder to think what the three girls must have endured, staying under the same roof as him when he went off on a bender. It's such a shame: he was actually a really nice guy when he was sober. The demon drink just turned him into a monster," Ted commented.

"Ted, he is vermin scum and should be locked away for a long time," Irene spat out in return, her venomous roots rearing their ugly head as the words sneered off her tongue.

Helen, not wanting to listen to any more of the gossip that made the lives of many harder than they already were, did what she needed to do then set off on a mission to find her boss.

It was not even eight-thirty, but the short entrance outside the secretary's office was in full swing. Parents milled about waiting to hand over money or speak to the secretary. Helen smiled at the waiting parents, then excused herself as she pushed her way through to have a quick word with Carol.

"Morning, Carol. Busy already I see?"

Carol turned round and rolled her eyes, frowning at the queue of faces waiting to speak to her. She closed the glass partition that protected her from the throng of people so she could let off a little steam.

"Always the bloody same. I give them a letter, ask them to return it in their child's bag, but no … they feel they have to personally return it to me. Anyhow enough of my moaning. How are you today?"

"I'm good, although a little tired after the drama in my street last night."

"Oh, I've heard all about it, about ten times from everyone I've spoken to. About five different versions, from Mrs Turner being blinded in both eyes to her being almost dead. The truth will no doubt be in there somewhere. I even saw some sicko had posted pictures of poor Mrs Turner on Facebook."

"Oh, that would have been my mullet-headed neighbour, I bet. I spied him last night out with his mobile snapping away like it was a day at Disneyland. Some people have strange fascinations all right."

"What can I do you for this morning?" Carol asked.

"I was wondering if Rosie was free. I need to quiz her about a few things."

"Give me a minute and I'll buzz through. I'm sure she would rather talk to you than come out and get caught up with all these parents haranguing her about their nearest and dearest."

Helen waited as Carol spoke to Rosie and got the thumbs up to go through to the head teacher's office.

The floral peach wallpaper always seemed misplaced to Helen, reminding her more of a bedroom in an old people's home than an office where the lives of children were discussed. Thankfully it didn't smell the same. Rosie's alternative attire clashed violently with the tweeness left behind by the previous headteacher. Helen always reminded herself that the bohemian ways of Rosie were also far more preferable to the sergeant-major approach of their previous head. Although Helen had been dubious at first of the efficiency of Rosie, she had soon come to realise that her peace-loving head had more about her than just the whiff of incense and patchouli oil.

"Helen, what can I do for you this morning?" Rosie asked before going off on a tangent about some new breathing and meditation technique she'd been practising. Her bangles jangled together noisily as she used her hands to 'talk' and Helen found herself listening more to the rhythmic chime they made as they clattered off one another than to the hippy shit coming from her mouth. Being polite as ever, Helen nodded and smiled whilst sneaking glances down at her wrists and the music being played on them. Eventually, she stopped and Helen reddened as she had no idea what she had been talking about and stood awkwardly with her eyebrow raised unsure whether she had been asked a question or not. Rosie eventually put her out of her misery: "So, is there something I can help you with?"

"I'm hoping so,' Helen began, quickly trying to remedy her glaiketness. "It's the new pupil in my class, Lucy. I'm really concerned about her. There are some things just not adding up."

"Oh, she is a bit of a soul I agree," Rosie replied.

"Can I ask the mother in for a chat? I always feel you get a better understanding of what's going on once you meet the family."

"Yup, of course, go ahead, though you might not get very far. If she can't be bothered turning up for her children's first day at a new school, it's doubtful she'll come in."

"True, but I'd like to try. As far as I'm aware, Lucy didn't utter a single word to anyone yesterday. The psychologist may have to be involved if that continues. Also, you must have seen her head?"

"Her head? No, I didn't. Head lice rearing their ugly little selves again?"

Not believing for a second that even her airy-fairy head could have possibly missed the state of the girl's head, Helen continued, "Yes, but on mammoth proportions. I've never seen a case like it. It's bordering on abuse, not to mention her clothes. I'm thinking a call to social work wouldn't go amiss?"

"Let's get mum in first, see if anything unfurls from that. You know what social workers are like. They won't be interested unless the child is black and blue. Their caseloads are huge. They are completely snowed under."

"Ok, I'll get Carol to contact mum for a meeting as soon as possible. I just wanted to say how concerned I am – something definitely not right with this one."

"And all the others, Helen. We work in a difficult area in difficult times. So many of our children come from difficult backgrounds. We can only do so much."

"I know, but I really feel this child needs special help, Rosie, and I intend to do all I can to help."

"Ok, leave it with me and I'll see if there is anything I can find out. Start with the mum and we will take it from there."

Helen left a written note with Carol, asking her to phone Ms

Jackson and make an appointment with her. Helen could hardly see Carol as she went past her office. She was deluged in a pile of paperwork whilst answering phone calls and dealing with kids at her door.

Scooting down the corridor just as the bell went, Helen managed to get into her class just before the kids did. Quickly she changed the date on the whiteboard and put out some jotters before the masses descended. Helen went through her morning welcome routine. It always amazed her at how difficult kids found it to sit in a circle when they did it every day. She squeezed herself in next to Taylor and welcomed them all. She was so relieved to see that Lucy had returned, albeit wearing the same clothes she'd been wearing the day before. In fact, the more she looked at them the more she believed the girl had slept in them, they were so badly crumpled. The girl's little freeloaders were still climbing up and down her hair, making Helen start clawing at her own head again.

"Ok, everyone, I'm going to start us off." Helen began demonstrating. "Today I feel about a six because I didn't get very much sleep and I am super tired. So if you see me snoozing, give me a nudge." The kids giggled. "Ok, Taylor, you are next. And everyone remember the rules; you're only allowed to talk when it's your turn."

"I'm a ten," beamed Taylor, "'cause last night I went to McDonald's with my dad and it was brilliant."

Everyone obediently waited their turn and listened to their peer's comments. Helen was amazed that even her little chatterbox Greg had managed to stay so quiet, and wondered how this had happened. Searching for him she found him sitting next to Lucy completely mesmerised by the continuous movements of the head lice, keeping him entertained as he sat in the circle. Then it became Lucy's turn. Helen could feel the nerves emanating from her but gently encouraged her.

"Ok, Lucy, it's your turn." Helen looked hopefully over at Lucy, but her head remained hanging down staring at her battered shoes. "Ok, Lucy if you can't tell us how you feel, perhaps you could show us?"

Helen saw her wee body visibly relax at this offer of refuge. She lifted three fingers up keeping her head hung down between her shoulders.

"Oh, Lucy, three tells me that you're not feeling so great today. Maybe later you'll be able to tell me what's going on?"

"Miss, I think I might ken," piped up Jane. Without waiting to be asked, she rushed on. "Last night she was battered up the Cannon Hill by Jenny in Primary Seven."

"Aye that's right, Miss," a quartet of voices pitched in.

"And Tony White got an awffy beatin' from Lucy's big brother," a shocked Ross added.

Helen looked over to where Lucy sat, but she didn't show any signs of having heard what was being said. However, she could not have missed the excited voices, eager to share the news. Not wanting the morning to be spent figuring out whether or not the rumours were true, Helen swiftly moved the conversation on, deciding to investigate the matter later. Helen directed the class back to their tables and it was while this was happening that Helen caught a glimpse of the sore behind Lucy's ear. The poor child's skin was red raw and, by the looks of her shirt, it had been bleeding.

"Lucy, can you come outside a minute please, you're not in trouble. I just want to have a quick chat with you."

Lucy's eyes widened at the mention of her name and her cheeks flushed. Helen kicked herself for speaking to her like that. She had momentarily forgotten how fragile she was. Lucy walked to the door, reluctantly, flicking her brown eyes up at her teacher and back to the floor again.

"I'm sorry if I embarrassed you, Lucy, by calling you out, I didn't mean to. I just wanted to speak to you. I noticed that you have a really sore bit behind your ear. Do you know what happened?"

Lucy shook her head.

"Has it been very itchy?"

Lucy nodded.

"Do you think you might have been scratching lots?"

Lucy nodded again.

"Ok, I think you need to go and get it cleaned up so it doesn't get infected. How does that sound?"

Lucy didn't move.

"Remember our deal, Lucy? If you don't use words you need to tell me using your thumbs. Will I get Jane to take you along to Mrs Young's room and she can sort you out? It won't hurt and Mrs Young is really kind. I bet she even gives you a sticker." Helen tried her best to convince her. Lucy eventually nodded and Helen sent her along to the first aider's room with Jane and a note explaining the situation.

10 Connor

Connor watched Lucy walk past his classroom door. He was fed up listening to the teacher drone on. As far as he was concerned, it was just all utter shite spilling out between her dog-arsed-shaped lips. The sliver of action he had spied out the classroom door window was far more entertaining.

So far, he had watched two primary one boys try and carry a book between them. He watched them pulling it out of each other's hands, like a pair of dogs wrestling with a bone, their wee legs propelling them along the corridor to try and be first to reach their teacher. Next, he watched one of the classroom assistants putting up a display across from his room. Every time she fired the wall stapler into the wall he imagined it was a real gun. He conjured up his own wee war story involving his evil teacher and himself. The imaginary shooting skills he possessed took his teacher down and his heroic efforts were applauded by his classmates as he had saved them all from death by boredom.

His reverie was cut short as Lucy infiltrated his zone of vision. Lucy didn't see him – she was too busy watching her shoes as she traipsed along the corridor with her 'friend' who had acknowledged her the day before. Seeing her out there annoyed him. He felt trapped and began to get restless he was so bored.

Not wanting to be spotted by any of his classmates, he chanced a sneaky glance round this new curious mob of kids. He quickly assessed and analysed the groups found in every class; the brainy ones – always listening attentively, even when it was boring as shit – the cool ones – sitting with that air of 'I don't give a shit'. And finally, the misfits, like him, sitting looking like shit.

So far, he had managed to avoid Tony. Though he had earlier

shot a quick flick at him as they filed into class. He had two black eyes coming along nicely. There had been a bit of whispering and pushing going on out in the line, but Connor ignored it. He had more pressing things to concern himself with.

Forgetting where he was, Connor let out a rather loud and audible yawn that brought a few laughs from his class. Unfortunately, his teacher didn't have the same sense of humour.

"Keeping you awake, Mr Jackson? I'm so sorry. Maybe you should try getting yourself to bed at a reasonable hour at night time instead of creating havoc at the park," sneered Mrs Gallows.

Connor fidgeted on his chair and his face flushed.

"TURN ROUND when I am talking to you!" she roared. "Did your mother not teach you any manners? And while we are talking about your mum I hope you got your mother to check your head last night like I told you to. I don't want any bugs getting passed around my classroom!"

That last retort engulfed his fiery nature and he could feel his temper rising. The whole class had erupted with laughter at the reference to his itchy head. In a bid to appear nonchalant, he began swinging on his chair. His eyes averted from his teacher's stare in fear he would do something very regrettable. This was the wrong thing to do however.

"Is there something wrong with those lugs of yours? I told you to turn around and look at me!"

Connor continued to ignore his irate teacher and kept his eyes firmly planted on his escape route out of the class.

"It is so very obvious your mother never taught you very much, as you can't even sit on your chair properly. Put the four legs on the ground, now!" His teacher put down the pen in her hand, moved her hands to her hips and stared at the imposition in front of her. Through gritted teeth and a snarling face, she puffed out again, "Put the four legs on the ground, immediately!"

Connor continued to swing back and forth. No way was she

getting the satisfaction of seeing him do what she demanded. Out the corner of his eye, he saw her striding across the classroom towards him. Just before she reached his table, he stood up, forcefully pushing his chair behind him and stormed out the room, letting the door bang behind him. The class sat dumbstruck at his behaviour, and stock still, their jaws open. Not quite sure of what or where he was going, he began to wander up the corridor. Behind him, he heard his teacher opening the door.

"Get yourself along to the Head Teacher, you impudent boy!" she spluttered.

He turned his head and smirked at her. Her face was puce, which gave him some satisfaction. He heard the door being thrown shut and made the short walk to the Head Teacher's room last as long as possible. He carefully and meticulously perused the various pieces of children's work on the wall. On reaching the hub of the school, he tried to casually hang around, but it wasn't long before he was spotted loitering by Mrs Barr as she came out of her office.

"Connor what can I help you with? Did Mrs Gallows send you down for something?"

"Eh, aye," he mumbled at his feet.

"Well, what was it she asked you to get?"

"Eh, I dunno."

"What do you mean, you don't know? And when you are talking to an adult you look at them, Connor. Have you been sent down here because you are in trouble?"

"I dunno."

"Right, young man, I'm about to go and speak to Mrs Gallows. Do you want to tell me anything before I go?" Connor shook his head. "Right sit there until I get back."

Connor sat down as directed and waited to see what interesting punishment this headteacher had in store for him.

11 Helen

The two eyes staring back were more like piss holes in the snow. Splashing water over her face, she tried to shake the tiredness. Standing on her tiptoes to get a closer inspection, she felt a wave of depression wash over her, as the face looking back at her looked as though it had aged considerably. Her usual rosy pallor verged on grey, and wrinkles had crept upon her where none had been before. Feeling older than her thirty years, she sighed and was sure this job had something to do with her ageing. Contemplating her single status made her mood sink deeper. Flipping the lid on her gloss, she smudged the costly gloop across her lips, practising a half-hearted pout. Her heart jolted as someone tried the door and she remembered where she was and where she should be.

"God, I nearly shit myself there," she laughed at Linda as she opened the door and saw her friend waiting to get in.

"Well, you were in the right place. I'll be along in a minute, save me a seat."

"Will do. Take your time, I'm sure you won't miss anything," Helen joked back.

Helen quietly shuffled her way round the packed table to the remaining two seats at the back.

Irene had started off the meeting ranting about Connor Jackson and his behaviour. Helen couldn't help wondering what part her behaviour had played in making him behave the way he had. Her teaching style was definitely old school and if she could get away with using a belt, Helen was sure she would.

"I want him removed from my class until his head lice are

sorted out. He is putting me and all my other boys and girls at risk, not to mention his atrocious behaviour."

"Irene, I hear what you are saying, but unfortunately the child has a right to an education and his head lice are not his fault. I spoke to Freya Young, our first aider, and she was very concerned over Lucy's head. I have arranged for the school nurse to get involved and visit the family at home to help," Rosie advised the busy staff meeting.

"That is a great idea, Rosie. Hopefully, she will be able to fill us in on what the family situation is like," Helen commented.

Linda squeezed herself in beside Helen.

"Nice of you to join us, Linda," Rosie rather cheekily said.

"Sorry. There was a queue for the toilet."

Rosie continued the meeting, discussing at length all the other points on the agenda. Having been awake for so long, Helen felt her eyes glazing over and battled to keep focus. A nudge from Linda made her bolt up and a little bit of drool escaped from her mouth. Quickly wiping it away, she glanced round the table to see if anyone else had noticed, but all heads were down, mesmerised by the scintillating agenda. In a bid to keep herself awake, Helen covertly scrolled through the messages on her mobile. She saw one from John and kicked herself for not contacting him sooner as he sounded pissed off. She typed a quick message, keeping her hands well out of view of prying eyes, arranging to meet him in an hour at their favourite Bistro. He sent a thumbs up. Helen grinned at the thought of the stories he would no doubt have for her.

Feeling her phone vibrate, she stole a look down and saw a message from Linda, slagging her off for drooling. A giggle shook her shoulders and put a smile on her face and she sent Linda a rude gesture in return.

"What are you like?" Linda slagged Helen off as they walked out to their cars at the end of the day.

"I know. I can't believe I fell asleep through such an interesting meeting. Not! I'm off to the Bistro with John if you fancy coming?"

"Aw, I would love to, but I've got to take the kids swimming," Linda moaned.

"Next time then! And thanks for waking me up. Imagine if I had started snoring!"

"Ha, ha, no problem," laughed Linda.

John had already sunk half a bottle of red by the time Helen made it to the table. He sat with his back to the door watching the yachts out in the marina. Helen snuck up behind him, squeezed his shoulder and gave him a hug, her arms barely reaching round him. It was no wonder that all the ladies swooned over him, typical that he was only interested in men.

"How are you, doll? You're like the scarlet pimpernel. I've been trying to get in touch with you for ages. I have so much to tell you. Oh my god, I don't know where to start." He prattled on as he poured a large glass of red out for Helen. Helen pulled up a seat and settled down to listen to the stories John had to beguile her with. The wine slid down easily. The waitress took their order and John eventually stopped for breath. "What you having, doll?"

"Think I'll have the linguine. I need something to soak up all this wine. It's a school night you know."

"Aye, I know, you're a two can dan. Can't have you drunk on a school night. Make that two linguine. I hope you don't mind me saying, doll, but you look like shit."

"Thanks, John, I can always rely on you for some brutal honesty."

"Have you actually got any foundation on? I've just got this new one and it is fabulous – it would hide those carrier bags under your eyes nae bother. Hold on a wee minute." Helen sat sipping her wine as John scurried in his man bag looking for his wonder cream. She flicked a quick look at her reflection in the window for confirmation and sighed as she realised how right he was.

"Och, I don't think I've got it."

"Don't worry, John. What I need is a bag over my head, not just a bit of cream."

"Aw, doll, you know I'm only thinking of you. I'm worried about you. I'm no really meaning to be rude. Have those kids at school been giving you a hard time again?"

Helen sighed then poured out the story of her current headache pupil.

"Oh my god, no wonder you've no been sleeping and look like shit. That sounds just horrific. Poor, wee lamb. God, there's always some crazy drama going on with those kids. It must be mental working there."

"You know some days it is. The best way I can describe it is like being the only sober one at a nightclub when everyone else is going bonkers."

"Ha, now that is crazy!"

"Please don't say anything to anyone else. It's all meant to be strictly confidential. It's causing me so much stress seeing a child neglected so badly."

"You know me, hen, my lips are sealed," he said zipping his lips in a theatrical manner and throwing away the key.

Before they knew it, they were onto their second bottle of wine, and they oscillated between drowning their sorrows and letting go to hilarity at John's lewd stories.

"Shhh," Helen slurred as John told a funny story about the size of his latest boyfriend's appendage, "everyone can hear you."

"And what? They're just jealous they're no getting a bit. I tell you there is enough to go around."

Helen slapped John's arm and wine dribbled out the side of

her mouth as she tried to control her laughter.

An elderly couple sitting at the table in front of them were tutting and giving them looks of disgust at their conversation. Giggling, the pair wrestled over who was to pay the bill, then left the Bistro, bumping off the wall as they staggered out the door.

"I suppose I will be leaven ma motor here the night," Helen's teacher voice left her completely as the wine took full effect.

"Come on and I'll walk you home, hen."

Helen clung onto John as she lurched up the road, spewing rubbish from her mouth as she went.

"Aw, John, ma head is so fucking itchy. I cannae stop scratching it."

"Come tae think of it, you've done nothing, but scratch it all night. Here let me have a look."

He dragged her under the glow of a street light and started to part her hair, hunting for evidence of life amongst her locks. "Oh my god!" He began to fumble about her hair trying to grab something.

Helen screamed too. "Fuck, get it out for me. I cannae stand the thought of those wee things in ma head."

Dancing and screeching about the pavement shaking her head upside down to get rid of the beasties, John hugged the lamppost as he bent over double laughing hysterically at the sight of his friend's reaction.

"I'm ..." he gasped in between fits of laughter," joking, you silly cow, there is nothing there."

"Ya wee bastard!" Helen slapped him on the back, cursing him. "Fuck, are you sure you're sure?" Helen slurred.

"Aye, well as sure as I can be after a bottle of wine or two. I'm sure yer head will be fine. Come on, let's get you home, you've got all those weans tae see to in the morning."

"Arrh, don't remind me, I'm going tae look even worse after the night."

"Och, you'll be fine. Come on and stop your blethering."

John shoved his hand under her oxter and propelled her up the road. The short walk home took longer than the usual ten minutes as the duo waivered about the road as John attempted to keep Helen on the straight and narrow. On reaching Helen's tenement door, John said his goodbyes and left Helen to fumble with the lock. She tripped up the stairs, talking aloud to herself as she went. She went to put the key in her door and missed. Swearing loudly, she guided the key in with two hands and one eye. The door slammed behind her as she collapsed onto her bed fully dressed.

Sometime during the night, she woke up with a drouth and hauled her aching head off the pillow in search of water. "Fuck," she said to no one; she downed a pint of water and swallowed two painkillers. Tipping her bag upside down, she found her phone and set her alarm. Then she groaned, realising she only had two more hours sleep. She crashed back down onto her bed, managing to get beneath the duvet this time.

Getting out of bed the next morning proved difficult. The snooze button was put to good use. Eventually, Helen's brain made the connection that her drunken antics meant she would have to walk to work today. Her car had spent the night at the Bistro. She was far too hungover to drive anyway. Cursing her inability to refuse wine, she slowly lifted her dull head off the pillow and went for a shower in the hope it would sort her out. Continuing to berate herself in the shower, she vowed never to drink like that again … well at least on school nights.

Telling herself it was really John's fault, she dried off and quickly pulled on the only ironed outfit she could find, breathing in to fasten the button. Blaming the alcohol for the few extra pounds she had gained, she decided this was another good reason to stop drinking.

Stopping suddenly, she felt her heart racing as her mind

scoured through the events of the previous evening, double-checking with her hazy memory she didn't do anything too regrettable: she didn't find anything to be worried about. Relieved, she checked her mobile that she'd sent no dodgy texts. All she found was a message from John, checking her head wasn't too sore. Pouring an extra-strong coffee into her mug, she threw some random things into her bag, closed the door and gingerly went down the stairs, her feet echoing on the concrete floor.

She heard the rain falling before she stepped out onto the street and gave herself another beating for not being more prepared. Cars swooshed past, throwing arcs of dirty water her way, and she stepped back just in time to escape the worst of it, feeling only a few splashes against her ankles.

A newly created piece of graffiti jumped out at her as she neared the opposite side of the street, unfortunately not noticed for its artistic credibility. A derogatory remark made about the local gay couple who lived in the street spoke volumes about the mentality of some of the locals. It saddened Helen as her eyes skimmed over it – she couldn't understand why people couldn't let others be. Sipping her coffee, she tried to keep under whatever shelter the buildings gave her. This only worked so far, as every so often a cracked drainpipe released a torrent of water that caught her unawares.

As she neared the school, she noticed two figures huddling by the building and realised it was Lucy and Connor. Checking her watch in case she was really late, she saw that it was only 7:30.

12 Connor

Connor watched her as she jotted in towards the sides of the buildings before scurrying quickly over the side roads where there was no shelter. Her movements reminded him of a nature documentary he had once seen, where a mouse had tried to seek protection from its predators running and hiding between stretches of undergrowth.

He had known who it was as soon as she'd come into sight beyond the parked cars at the end of the street but, only now as she neared the school, did he say to his sister. "Is that no your teacher coming?"

Lucy lifted her head and nodded, and Connor saw a smile flit across her face.

As the teacher drew nearer, he noticed that her hair looked as bedraggled as theirs. Her wee jacket was as useful against the dreich morning as their jumpers were. Watching her, something began niggling the back of his mind. It was as a car drove along the street that it dawned on him; she was walking to school. In all the schools he'd ever been to he'd never seen a teacher walk. They'd all arrived by car. Except, he remembered, that one teacher who rode his bike, rain, hail or shine. But he was barmy and hairy and had eyebrows that warranted a personal hairstylist each. Connor thought back to the times he had successfully flicked boogies into them and got away with it. They were so thick and bushy a child could have easily got lost in them. Not at all like her. Miss Kane was young and sort of good looking for a teacher, Connor decided.

They watched her open the heavy gate. She had to shove it

twice to get it to move. She squelched up the path towards them, skiffing through the puddles that had drowned the path below.

The pair had sought out the driest place to stand, which happened to be next to the entrance of the school. Apart from the janitor who had shouted morning to them, this was the first staff member they had seen.

Connor shivered as a drop of rain found its way down his t-shirt and rolled down his back, stopping when it reached his waistband. He stuck his tongue out and licked, catching some drips that had fallen from somewhere above. He was so wet it was too hard to tell exactly where they came from.

Squirming at the sight of the teacher, he shuffled his feet and kept his head low. The 'drowned rat look' that he and his sister currently sported made him feel a little more self-conscious than usual. He'd had cabin fever earlier and had dragged his sister out of the flat not long after waking. Having lived in several shit holes since their escape, he couldn't understand why this new place made him feel so claustrophobic. He had a bed with a duvet, though who had slept on it before he chose not to dwell on. The toilet worked and the kitchen area was so small there was very little of it to be offended by. He hardly noticed the stains on the brown excuse of a carpet he and his sister had strewn their stuff all over the top of. There was just something about it that made Connor feel uneasy. His mum's moping didn't help matters.

He preferred to be outside. And that was fine when the weather was fine, but when it was grey and wet it made things a bit trickier. Then there was Lucy to consider. It wasn't always cool to have your wee sister hanging out with you, particularly a mute one. But he knew she was better off with him.

He knew it was early from the deserted streets and the absence of kids in uniforms walking to school, but he felt better just being away from the confines of the flat.

The pair had wandered down by the shore, the rain directing

them to seek shelter. They hopped under the broken pier finding a place amongst the empty and fading beer cans. Connor watched as Lucy gathered the cans up, then lined them along a flat rock according to their type. Quite a collection she had managed before a rat scurried past scaring the bejesus out of them both. The unwanted visitor having disturbed their peace, they had set off to find a new hang out.

Not knowing where to go next, they had found themselves drifting towards the school. Passing the local fisherman's pub, a rather merry fellow stumbled out after wrestling with the door, making them both jump. A waft of stench permeated the air after him – it was honking and made Connor gag – a similar smell, Connor thought, to some dodgy toilets he'd had to use as a matter of urgency.

Having nowhere else to go, he and Lucy had drudged to school and had been here ever since, just waiting. The silence drowned by the rain teaming down.

Looking up as the teacher drew even nearer, he spotted the seagulls busy drumming their feet on the grass, the only things in the vicinity that seemed happy in the pelting rain.

"Hi, you two. You guys are early."

"I thought it was time for school," Connor mumbled to the ground as his teeth chittered against one another.

"It's a bit wet and a bit too early to stand out here till school starts. Do you think you could help me organise some things in my class?"

Lucy's eyes lit up and she stared pleadingly at her brother; and tugged the sleeve of his jumper. He was a bit bemused by this offer and wasn't quite sure how to reply: this was the second time in less than twenty-four hours a teacher at this school had whipped the words that were usually quick to fall away from his mouth. He was still trying to process the actions of his headteacher from the previous day, or more accurately, the lack of actions.

Sitting awaiting his headteacher's return from the 'Gallows' room, the list of possible punishments or 'consequences' (his other teachers liked to call it), formed in his mind.

On her reappearance, Mrs Barr had sat down next to him; said next to nothing, except explaining the work he had to complete. Shocked by her lack of action, he tried his very best to finish what he could, before eventually giving it up as it was genuinely too difficult. Later, she had spoken to him about his behaviour and had been so understanding he had felt the tears prick the back of his eyes and his words stolen from him.

He again felt his words disappear, only managing an "Eh, aye, Miss Kane."

"Come on then, you can start by opening the door for me."

Connor rushed ahead and opened the door once the security buzzer beeped.

"You two go along to my room. I'll be along in a minute. Maybe you could sharpen the pencils in the middle of the desk? Lucy, you know where the sharpeners are, don't you?"

Lucy excitedly nodded and pulled her brother down the corridor, almost running as she went, and smiling with importance at the task she had been given. The squelch from their sodden trainers followed them up the corridor. Connor gazed round the class as his sister rushed off to find the things necessary to help Miss Kane.

The room had bright photographs of the kids on the wall and he quickly spotted his sister's, her eyes just peeking out behind her hair. Only two days at school and she was a fully-fledged class member. Connor felt a pang of jealousy rub at his insides. Every inch of the walls was plastered in the kid's work. Proudly displayed. It was in complete contrast to the class he was meant to be part of.

Connor continued his perusal of the room. Each area of the

class was clearly set out. He noted the abundance of paint and coloured paper stacked in the area next to the sink. A waft of glue came his way as he looked inside the unlidded tubs. The rough handles of the paintbrushes stuck out of the jar at jaunty angles having been hastily shoved in by children eager to get the chore of tidying up finished. Looking at the handles on the brushes made him squirm as he imagined his hands holding the rough, wood.

Next, he saw the funny cartoon posters in the class library that drew him over for a closer look. He ran his hand over the comfy chair in the library and tried the seat out for size. The back was squishy and he rocked back and forth using his feet to create the gentle swaying movement.

His eyes then caught a whole shelf of crazy looking cars that the kids must have made. He darted up finding his hands moving them back and forth. He marvelled at all the individual styles, pushing them up and down the crafted road they sat on. Taken back to a time when his life was not as complicated, Connor acted like a child half his age. Lost in play, he jumped when Miss Kane clanged the door open. Connor rushed over to his sister as though he had been caught in the act of doing something he shouldn't have been.

As she made her noisy and clumsy entrance, Connor realised her hands were juggling plates piled with bits of toast. The smell made his mouth water and he saw the familiar aroma had reached Lucy's nose too.

"I don't know about you guys, but I'm starving. Do you fancy helping me munch through this toast?"

Connor didn't need to be asked twice and he found his voice had thankfully returned. "Aye, I'm sure we could do that. Couldn't we, Lucy?"

His sister nodded furiously and he grinned as he saw the smile spread over her face.

"Well, what are you waiting for?"

The pair left the pencils and sharpenings that had drifted onto the floor and took a pew next to the toast. Munching greedily, they stuffed their faces.

Connor felt the toast slide down and somehow melt his insides, an unfamiliar feeling smoothing his interior. As he looked at this teacher he felt his face relax. The teacher smiled in return. He glanced at her blue eyes and felt that easiness intensify, a feeling he had not experienced in a long time and definitely not one he had enjoyed at school before.

Feeling relaxed, he studied Miss Kane as she took tiny bites out of her toast, nibbling her way round the crust before eating the soft doughy middle. She didn't really look that hungry, he thought. The buttery toast was the best breakfast he'd had in ages. He hardly noticed his sodden jumper clinging to him or the funny noise his squelchy feet made as he wriggled his toes.

Glancing up at the row of windows at the back of the room, he watched the rain streak down. The grey clouds blanketed the sky. Only the white tips of occasional waves peaking in the distance, made him aware that the sea was there, its dull colour mirroring the sky above perfectly.

"I totally slept in this morning and didn't get a chance for breakfast this morning?" Helen chatted.

Being so relaxed and happy, Connor chatted back on behalf of his sister and himself. "We never had anything either."

"No? You didn't sleep in though as you guys were super-duper early this morning."

"We had run out," Connor replied.

"That happens sometimes, doesn't it? Was mum working this morning?"

Connor stole a look at Lucy who stared with a look of "What are you going to say?" etched all over her face.

"Eh, no. She was eh really tired and was sleeping." His reply was slow as he desperately tried to think of a plausible excuse that wouldn't lead to more questions.

"Oh, I know how that feels. I had to hit the snooze button four times before I could get out of bed this morning. You know, I was just thinking about you guys. I used to work in a school in Glasgow. I wonder if it was the same one that you two went to."

Connor was relieved she had stopped talking about his lack of breakfast and his mum and let his breath out, unaware that he had been holding it.

"Was it a big school?" Connor asked.

"Yes, it was quite big. Was your school big?"

"Aye, it was huge and dead old like this one. It had two storeys and two gyms."

"Wow! That sounds massive. I just wish I could remember the name of the school in case it was the same one you went to. Old age makes you lose your memory you know."

Hearing Lucy giggle at her teacher's response made Connor laugh too. He had forgotten that her mouth could actually produce sound, it had been so long since she had spoken.

"You're not old miss. Our school was called Bruce Primary. Does that make you remember?"

"Oh no, it doesn't, but I know that school and it is huge!" Connor was none the wiser to the lies the teacher told. "Right, you two, now that you have helped me finish the toast, see if you can finish those pencils before you head outside for ten minutes until the bell rings."

"No problem," Connor beamed.

13 Helen

Helen practically skipped down to the office once the Jackson kids went out to line up. Her jubilant mood didn't go unnoticed and Linda laughed at her as she passed her in the corridor.

"Good night last night?"

"Aye, but an even better morning!"

"Oh, aye, how?"

"Tell you at break."

Despite her head still pounding from her overindulgence the previous evening, it was nulled somewhat with the scheming investigative work she'd opportunistically seized that morning. Seeing the pair standing out in the rain at a stupidly early o'clock started her mind whirring: why they were at school so early? Why were they dressed so inappropriately? What should she do? Thinking unusually quickly considering the state of her head and the shakes her body was emitting, Helen suddenly knew what she was going to do. She just had to hope the kids would follow her plan. However, her idea of 'buttering' them up with the toast worked hook, line and sinker. Armed with her newfound information, she was off to see if Carol could continue her investigative work with a phone call to Bruce Primary School.

As she neared the office, she saw Rosie chatting to one of the parents. So many of their parents were as needy as their children and Helen admired the time Rosie tried to give each one. This parent was no different and knowing only half the background, Helen felt empathetic towards the mother.

Despite this, it didn't stop her from being bemused by the parent's dress sense. Did the mother really think it was perfectly ok to wear socks with her sandals? Did she not look in the mirror before she left the house? Or check the weather? Smiling, she went past the parent deep in conversation, obviously oblivious to her major fashion faux pas. Rosie was making all the right acknowledging sounds, nodding her head in return to the talking parent.

Finding Carol proved to be a wee bit trickier than she had anticipated as she wasn't in her usual hot seat. Helen went off on a search into the classroom assistant's room to see if she was there, to no avail, but she did bump into Freya.

"Morning, Freya, how are you?" Helen asked.

"I'm fine ... you look happy."

"That I am. Some investigative work I've been doing has paid off. I'm looking for Carol?"

"I've not seen her recently. I've been meaning to catch you though. That was some mess that girl's hair and ear was in."

"Tell me about it. I just wish we were allowed to comb them out for her. It must be hellish for her. I can't believe her mum isn't doing anything about it. The mother must have a headful too, they spread like wildfire."

"I was thinking the same thing. The wee soul stood there and never uttered a single cry as I cleaned and dressed the sore on her ear. I really struggled with all those creepy beasties all over her head. I was tempted myself to do a bit of combing, but Rosie made it clear that we're not allowed."

"It just doesn't seem right, does it? Though Rosie has got on it by sending the school nurse out to see the mum and kids at home. I'm desperate to hear what she finds on her visit. I'm sure she will find out some interesting things."

"Aye, you're not wrong there. If I see Carol I'll tell her you are looking for her."

"Thanks, Freya."

On her way back round to her class, Helen noticed that Rosie was edging her way back from the parent, indicating that she must be nearly finished her conversation. Deciding that it would be a good idea to tell the boss her new information, she hung around, pretending to read some bulletins on the news board.

"Morning, Miss." Tony, one of her former pupils, who was now in primary seven, walked past with his darn musical instrument. *It's Wednesday. Nightmare,* Helen thought as she began to think ahead to the two hours of torture coming her way. Two hours of a cacophony that made her ears bleed as noises that vaguely resembled music escaped from the music room as the older kids began their painful and arduous task of learning an instrument. Helen said a brief morning back to Tony. Only after he had passed did Helen remember the gossip from her class the previous day. Deciding to do a little probing, she called Tony back.

"Yes, Miss?" Immediately, Helen noticed the yellowing bruise beneath his eyes and used this as her way in.

"Tony, I've just noticed your eye. What on earth happened? It looks really sore." Helen smirked at how easy she could switch her theatrical skills on.

"Eh, I know. It is a bit sore. That new boy, Connor, did it, Miss."

"What, Connor Jackson?" Helen asked, feigning shock.

"Aye, him."

"That is awful. What happened? Did he just come up and wallop you?"

"Aye, more or less. There was me, Gary, Jenny and Hayley and we were just playing up the hill and he came up and smacked me."

"That doesn't sound good. I think we might need to get you all together to discuss this as we can't allow this to happen. Oh, I know what we could do. We could contact the police station and ask them to play the CCTV footage. When and where did you say it was?"

Helen noticed Tony turn red and start to fluster at the mention of police and CCTV. Having already got accounts from some of the other musketeers in his group she had a fair idea of what had happened and waited for him to spill a more accurate version.

"Well, eh, Jenny was being mean to his sister that cannae speak and I think I told him to go away."

"You just politely told him to go away? That doesn't sound like something you would do."

"Well, maybe no quite like that."

"I heard there was a bit of unsavoury language, a bit of provoking going on?"

"Eh, provokin?"

"Yes, wound up so that he was made angry?"

"Well, aye, maybe you could say that, but it was'nae me. It was more Jenny. She was bein' actually more than mean, she was wicked to his wee sister."

"And you had absolutely nothing to do with it?"

"Just a wee bit I suppose."

"Well, Tony, I happen to know that you are the very boy who hates people winding him up. Am I right?"

Tony darted his eyes everywhere except in the direction of Helen and replied, "Yes."

"Well, please in future, put that good brain of yours into action before you react with words that cannot be retracted. And also, if you see Miss Jenny getting wicked again, maybe you could try and stop her?"

"Yes, Miss. Can I go now?"

"Yes, off you go, but please remember. Oh, and do me a favour … send Jenny to my room as soon as you see her please. Before 9 am. I want a word with that young lady."

Tony nodded in return and walked briskly down the corridor glad to escape the interrogation.

Helen turned round and realised that Rosie and her parent had long finished conversing and Rosie had moved on to her next job. 'Fucking hell! I take my eyes off her for a minute and she vanishes,' Helen mumbled.

Walking back to the front of the school, she chapped the boss' door and got a positive result.

"Yes, come in," came the muffled reply. *Double bonus*, Helen thought as she saw Carol was in talking her boss through the daily diary.

"Good morning, Helen. You are looking bright-eyed and bushy-tailed this morning."

"Well, I've got some information that I'm rather excited about, regarding the Jackson kids."

"Well do tell," Rosie requested.

After explaining to the duo about finding the kids earlier that morning, she got onto the exciting part of finding out about the school.

"Well done. That was rather sneaky of you, though I dare say they were in need of breakfast. Carol, perhaps you could phone the school and see if they have any information they could share with us."

"Yes, not a problem."

"I was chatting with the boy yesterday. He seems to have been rubbing Irene up the wrong way and got into a bit of trouble. He seems a nice enough child one to one. Needs lots of TLC. He is also way behind academically. He looked so sad, like he had the weight of the world on his shoulders. I didn't have the heart to be too hard on him. We're going to have to get our heads together for this pair I think. Has Lucy spoken yet?"

"No, nothing, though she did laugh today, which is the most I've heard come out her mouth. I really felt as though I was connecting with Connor today and if I can, would like to try and build on it. I'm hopeful he answers more of my questions."

"Yes, I think that's a good idea. Perhaps there are some

lunchtime duties he could help you with?"

"That's a great idea, Rosie. I'll suggest it to him later."

Helen went off to complete her morning duties with a spring in her step. Little by little she felt she was making headway with her problem family.

At break, she decided to forego her much needed caffeine hit and see if Carol had got anywhere with her phone call.

14 Lucy

Lucy felt as though she was on cloud nine today and had indicated this to all her classmates during check-in that morning. She felt positively glowing as Miss Kane thanked her for all the work she had done earlier that morning. What a way to start the day, having breakfast with her lovely teacher. It was times like this she wished she could find her voice again. At break time, Lucy ran out of class straight into the playground, causing Jane to notice her abrupt change in behaviour.

"Look at you. Have you been eating ready break or something to give you all this energy?"

Lucy grabbed her friend's arm and spun her round before giving her a hug. Then she ran off again at full pelt, past the kids on the football pitch. Jane struggled to keep up and eventually stopped as she found she couldn't eat her crisps and run at the same time. At the end of the playground, Lucy found a puddle and ran through it, ignoring the shouts from the classroom assistants to stay out of it. She felt wild and free and nothing it seemed would dampen her spirits. Jane roared at her to come over and she dutifully did.

Sitting next to each other on the bench, the rain veiled them in a light mist. Seagulls hovered waiting to swoop on the leftovers. Jane offered Lucy a crisp, but Lucy refused by shaking her head.

"What you're no hungry? That is no like you!" Jane exclaimed.

Lucy pulled Jane up and dragged her over to the games box and pulled a pair of ropes out. The friends jumped together with the rope, giggling as they bumped into each other. All too soon they saw kids running to their lines. Dropping the ropes back in the box, they dashed quickly over there so they didn't incur a penalty, or worse: the wrath of one of the prefects. They made it just in time.

Realising that it was literacy time from now until lunch put another smile on Lucy's face. Being so special (Miss Kane had told her yesterday), she had her own special jobs and even had her very own special teacher to work with. Lucy had loved working with Mrs Brown the previous day. She had felt so relaxed in her private little room, just the two of them. Particularly when they shared a story together at the end. Not being able speak didn't seem to worry Mrs Brown. She hadn't shouted the whole time they had been together. Some of the work was tricky, but Lucy didn't get that scared feeling she used to get at her other school.

Lucy skipped along to Mrs Brown's room and chapped the door as she had been told to do.

"Well, good morning, Lucy. How are you today?"

Lucy put her thumbs up.

"Great, glad to hear it. Will we start with our writing?"

Lucy nodded and they set off to work. Listening intently to the instructions given and trying her hardest resulted in success, which pleased them both.

Then it was time for Lucy's favourite part, listening to Mrs Brown read her a story.

"Ok, Lucy, what story is it today?"

Lucy went over to the bookshelf and ran her fingers over the spines. Slowly, she pulled out books that caught her eye. Her favourites were about animals and she searched for something that took her fancy. Her fingers dipped between two books and grasped the back of a thin one that was hard to see. Interested to find out what was on the front, she prised the two bigger books apart and slowly eased the smaller one out. It had been worth the effort as on the cover was the most beautiful dog Lucy had ever seen. It had big, brown eyes and a mop of curly hair that floated down onto his nose. Opening the book, she flicked through the pages and decided that this was the book for her. She handed it to her teacher, who smiled.

"I had forgotten all about that book. It used to be a favourite of mine when I was about your age. Come on, let's go and sit in our comfy chairs."

Lucy sprang over to the orange chairs and made herself comfy by curling her legs beneath her and laying her head back onto the headrest. Mrs Brown opened the book and was just about to start reading when Lucy bolted upright and put her hand up to signal to her teacher. Surprised by this request, the teacher waited to see what Lucy was up to. As Lucy reached her hand down into the basket next to the chair a slow realisation came over her face.

"I forgot the blanket, didn't I? Silly me. I'm so glad you're here Lucy to keep me right."

Lucy put the blanket over both their knees and snuggled back to enjoy the story, rubbing the soft fabric between her fingers. She listened to the soothing sound of her teacher's voice tell the story of the lost puppy.

Lucy loved the way that, after everything seemed to be going so wrong for the puppy, it all turned out ok in the end. Unfortunately, the book finishing, was also the signal for the end of her time with Mrs Brown. Lucy folded the blanket up carefully, straightened the books then searched for something else she could do.

"Alright Lucy," Mrs Brown interrupted, "I will see you tomorrow at the same time, ok?"

Realising she could stall no longer, she made a thumbs up reply to Mrs Brown and made her way back to class.

She was in her own wee world as she wandered happily down the corridor. The tall, Victorian windows on her left allowed glimpses of the outside world. Stopping to look at the photographs on the birthday wall, she spotted Jane's face and smiled.

She felt the closeness of the body first, her personal space encroached. The voice came next, prickling the hairs on the back of her neck. Not wanting to move, she rolled her eyes round as far as they could go, but she already knew who it was. The voice just confirmed it.

"You better watch it, hen, you and your brother telling tales tae the teacher. Right?"

Jenny dunted the back of Lucy's knee, making her crumble to the floor, driving the message home. Jenny whipped off in a flash as Lucy yelped, then quickly got back to her feet, fears and worries flooding back into her mind. What was Jenny talking about? What did she do?

Shaken up, she made a hasty retreat to the safe haven of her class and quickly and quietly found her seat. She put her head down, worried someone would guess what had just happened. Her stomach churned as she replayed the events over in her mind. She wrapped her arms around herself as her body began to tremble and shake. Buried thoughts and fears bubbled to the surface. Lucy began to sink to dark places she struggled to make sense of. Her wailing was her siren, alerting others to the depths of her pain. Cocooned in her darkness and her noise, she felt safely squirrelled away, where no one could reach her.

15 Connor

As Jenny returned to the class, she shot Connor a sneering look. He scowled in return. His ears tuned into the snippet of noise that slid through the door as Jenny opened it. He immediately knew it was Lucy. His hand shot up desperate to reach his teacher's attention. Standing up at the front of the class pontificating, he knew she could see him.

"Miss, Miss," he interrupted. She droned on and he tried again, "Miss, Miss!"

"Are you so stupid that you don't know the class rules yet?" Mrs Gallows spat back. "When I'm speaking, you listen. It's not that hard really."

"But, Miss ..."

"But Miss nothing. You are in Primary Seven: you can just wait your turn and learn some manners."

By this point, the class resembled a domino rally with each kid nudging another as the noise rippled further. Fingers pointed out towards the door, mouthing "Who is that?"

Crying in the infant end of the school was common. But in the upper end of the school, it was unheard of. Their last headteacher, Mr Barker, had been a master that had ruled with fear, regularly reducing kids to tears. But Mrs Barr led with a whole new approach that negated the need for terrifying kids. This fact mystified the kids even more. Something really wrong must be going on.

Unable to sit and listen anymore, Connor rose from his seat and made his way to the door.

"Where and what do you think you are doing young man? Get back to your seat now!"

Ignoring the command, Connor opened the door and ran to his sister. Miss Kane had her arms around her, having managed to escort her out the door for a little more privacy. Lucy was trying to curl herself up into her ball of protection. Her body shook with the sobs that hiccupped from within.

"Connor, thank goodness you are here. I have no idea what is wrong with her. She had just come back from being with Mrs Brown, then this."

"She sometimes gets like this; don't worry." Connor heard his class door being yanked open and could sense the venom and hatred from his teacher before she even opened her mouth.

"Get back in here now, Connor Jackson. You do not have my permission to leave this classroom."

Connor kept his back to the screeching that fell from his teacher's mouth, and did his best to comfort his wee sister. He stole a glance at Miss Kane and caught her rolling her eyes.

"Sorry, Mrs Gallows. As you can see there is a bit of an incident going on with his sister and I could really do with Connor's assistance. I'm sure he will catch up with anything he is missing later," Miss Kane shouted back.

Shooting her a look, Mrs Gallows retreated back into her lair, the door falling heavily back into its frame.

By rubbing his sister's back and whispering into her ear, Lucy eventually calmed down, although she was still curled in a ball. She had however, stopped the incessant noise.

"Connor, I need to go back and see my class. Can I leave you for 5?"

"Aye, miss. She'll be ok, I'm sure. Something must have given her a fright or something."

"Will I get Mrs Young, the first aider, to come down?"

"No, no. She'll be fine. I'll tell her to go back into class in a minute."

"Ok, only if you are sure? There is no rush. Take your time.

Don't worry about Mrs Gallows. I will speak to her later for you. I was going to come and speak to you later anyway, Connor. I need some helpers at lunchtime and wondered if you and Lucy would like to help me once or twice a week? You both worked really hard today. Have a think and I'll get back to you."

Connor could feel his cheeks redden at Miss Kane's request. Unused to this type of offer, he was again lost for words and could only manage a nod. He knew instantly what his answer would be, however. *God, I'm beginning to get like Lucy with this constant loss of speech,* he thought. He heard the door to Lucy's class rattle as it closed and he slid down the wall, positioning himself next to his sister, his arm patting her back. A few kids walking to the toilet gawped and stared at the two of them as they walked past. Connor sent one of his classic looks and they soon clipped on their way. *This school is something else,* Connor thought. Never before had he been told he was helpful, usually all the 'jobs' went to the goody-two-shoes, but here he was being asked to do a really special job. If only Miss Kane was his teacher instead of that silly old cow he might actually learn something. Lucy began to sit up, indicating she was feeling better.

"What happened? You were screaming like a banshee. Someone try to murder you? I think the whole school heard you. You're so lucky you've got Miss Kane as a teacher otherwise you would have been sent off to the loony bin or something."

Lucy just sat and listened to her brother with a confused look on her face. Periodically, she wiped her face with the sleeve of her jumper, leaving snail trails of snot over the forearm. Connor watched her as she looked around as if checking new surroundings. She looked almost surprised at what she saw.

"You're at school, you silly cow. I sometimes wonder what goes through that head of yours. Do you no remember anything? You got carted out the class 'cause you were screaming. Did someone do something?"

Lucy turned her head as if she was trying to recall what had happened, but then looked back and shrugged her shoulders. Quick as a flash she jumped up, straightened her skirt, gave her nose another wipe then made off for her class.

"Is that it then?" Connor asked incredulously. "I come to your rescue like a knight in shining armour then you buggar off without so much as a thank you?"

Spinning on her heels, she bent down and gave her brother a hug.

"Off you go. Next time you feel like causing a scene try and keep the noise down, eh?"

Lucy smiled and went off to class wondering what all the fuss was about. Connor stayed on the floor contemplating what he should do next. He hadn't expected Lucy to feel better so soon, secretly hoping he wouldn't have to return to his class at least until after lunch. Beneath his jumper, he could feel his heart pound as he thought about going back into class. He could guess what type of reception he would receive from his cow-faced teacher. He feared the worse and he knew he wouldn't be able to slip back into his seat without some sort of retort being made by her. Not to mention all the slagging he would get from the kids in the class.

Having not made many, if any, allies he wasn't up to the job of defending his sister's wellbeing. He stood up and through the single pane of glass in Lucy's class door, he watched Miss Kane fussing over Lucy, handing her a hankie and saying something nice, then watched as Lucy's face beamed. Just at that moment, she looked up and caught Connor watching.

Making her way towards the door, Connor panicked knowing full well he should be back in his class by now. Instead of looking angry, however, he saw her smiling at him and relaxed a little and stood waiting to see what would happen, knowing that this would be a far preferable outcome to the one cow-face would provide for him.

"Connor, I don't know what you did, but she seems absolutely fine now. Did she say what happened?"

Connor shook his head, screwed his eyes and made his face form the shape that said 'of course not. Are you stupid?'

"God, that was a silly thing to say … she doesn't speak, does she? Has she ever spoken?"

"Yeah, she used to, but not for a long time."

"Listen, you don't need to worry about her. We've had a wee chat and she has agreed to use a wee card I gave her if she ever feels like that again, so I can try and help her before she gets into such a state. You know you are a really thoughtful big brother coming to help her like that. Not everyone would do that."

"Eh, yeah," creeping the words slowly out, Connor could feel his face flush yet again.

"Still, it must have been quite a shock for you. You look worse than Lucy now. Why don't you go along to Mrs Young's room? I'll send a note down telling her you need to lie down for a bit." Connor looked up towards his class and looked back again at Miss Kane. "Don't worry about Mrs Gallows. I will send a note to her too. It'll all be fine. You seriously don't look well."

"Thanks, Miss."

"No, thank you. Have you managed to have a think about my request for a helper?"

"Aye. I suppose I could do it a couple of days."

"Great. I was hoping you would say that. I just need to ask your sister now."

"Oh, I think she will be an aye too, somehow."

"I look forward to seeing you both tomorrow then after lunch, after the eating bell?"

"Aye, great."

"Right. Off you go and have a wee lie down before the bell goes for lunch."

16 Helen

Helen had barely managed to get her two feet through the staff room door before Irene was on her back.

"What did you do with that pathetic excuse for a boy? He didn't return to my class at all after he wandered out to see you. Not that I was missing his scintillating conversation or intellect."

"Oh, sorry, Irene. Did you not get my note? He took unwell and had to go down to the medical room for a lie-down. He was looking ever so poorly," Helen informed Irene.

"No, I didn't get your note. What was going on anyway? That was a hell of a racket his sister was making. My class could hardly concentrate to do their work. Is there something mentally wrong with her?"

"I really don't know what was wrong with the wee soul. All I know is she was terribly upset by something or someone and Connor was a star making her feel better again. Nothing I tried worked."

"God. He actually has some sort of purpose in life? He does next to nothing in my class."

"I'm surprised by what you say, Irene. He was helping me this morning before class and was a great help, so much so I've asked him to come in twice a week at lunch to help me with some filing."

Irene stared at Helen as if she had lost her mind.

"God, are you going for a sainthood or something, spending your own time with a creature like that? Well, seeing you are new to the profession, all that enthusiasm will soon disappear after a few more years in the job."

"Think what you like, Irene, but I would prefer to spend my

lunchtimes in the company of humans with a heart and soul."

With her last remark hanging in the air, Helen decided she wasn't that hungry after all and left the staffroom, leaving the others to listen to Irene's depressing and cold words. At the end of the corridor, she heard the staffroom door open and turned her head; saw Irene emerge, heading off for the lunch hall. *Cow*, Helen muttered under her breath.

17 Connor

"Son, son, it's time for lunch, the bell has just gone."

Connor opened his eyes and saw Mrs Young peering over him and shaking his shoulder. He had just been enjoying a really good sleep and it took him a few seconds to get his bearings. He quickly pushed himself up the bed as he realised her boobs were rubbing against his arm as she tried to wake him. He gave his arm a rub to rid himself of her.

"Aye, right, Miss, I'll get going."

"You feeling better?"

"Aye, fine."

"Don't worry, I won't let anyone know about your snoring." Connor shot Mrs Young a look. "Och, I'm only teasing. Away and get your lunch."

Connor pulled the wooden door open and nearly fell upon the busy throng of tiny kids trying to get their jackets on, arms repeatedly trying to reach armholes that just didn't stay still, others with eyes steadily fixed on hands that made desperate attempts to make zips pull together. Lifting his hands over the tops of the wee people's heads, he made his way to the lunch hall, and used his nose to decipher what delights were for lunch.

If he had got it right, it was spag bol, worse case mince and tatties. *Not bad*, he thought, *hit the spot nicely.*

Nearing the dinner hall, he saw the queue and joined the end next to a group of girls from his class. Towering above them, he could see his teacher getting her lunch upfront. He groaned to himself hoping to have missed her, and suddenly found the floor very interesting. He bent his leg and rested it on the wall, with his back making use of the support too. He heard her coming. The sound of her clicking heels would be one that stayed with him for a while. Being so short, she needed all the help she could get.

Connor heard the goody two-shoes from his class sickeningly saying 'hi' to her and he imagined her giving them her infamous cursory nod as he didn't hear her reply. Waiting for her to pass, he kept his head down, then he saw the shoes stop in front.

"Feeling better?" The sarcasm cascaded off her tongue.

"Aye, a bit."

"Something wrong with your head, too heavy to lift? Look at me when I'm talking to you!"

He didn't need to look at her, he knew the words were snarled out between gritted teeth. Connor could feel everyone's eyes waiting for the drama to unfurl. Weighing up his options and considering the hunger in his belly, he lifted his head slowly, with just a hint of reticence to give the crowds a little bit of drama to bite onto. He glowered at her through his heavy fringe refusing to appease her anymore.

"You will find a pile of work at your desk. I expect it finished by tomorrow morning."

"Fine."

"Fine, what?"

"Miss."

She clicked her heels and tottered off to the staffroom. Connor smirked as he watched her battle with door while balancing her lunch on her tray, watching it lurch from one side to the next, as if it were a boat caught in a rolling sea. He willed it to fall, but alas it never.

"God, she's got it in for you has she no?" asked Hayley as she chummed up to Connor.

"I think she's got something permanently lost up her huge arse, she's so twisted."

Connor gave a wee demonstration to his audience, impersonating Mrs Gallows tottering on her heels, sashaying her sizeable bum from side to side like an elephant walking through the tall grass of the savannah. He was duly applauded with a round of chortles. He even caught Tony having a laugh. The appreciation shown made him glow inside and feel a little more accepted in this new domain and he allowed his scowl to drop momentarily.

"You should have seen her face when you never came back to class. Oh my god, it was a pure picture. I was wetting maself. She did that sucky in thing with her face and shoggled her erse so much I thought I wis going tae get slapped on the face by one of they big erse cheeks."

This time Hayley got the crowd going with the giggles. Connor couldn't help but join in too as his mind conjured up a disturbing mental image. Becoming a bit noisy, the queue attracted the attention of Mrs Barr who was on lunch duty. She floated over in her usual dreamy way to ask if she could join in all the fun. Everyone squirmed, knowing they would be reprimanded for being so disrespectful to their teacher – though most thought she deserved it.

"Just telling jokes, Miss," Jenny piped up to try and deflect from the real subject.

"Oh, really? I love a good joke. Try me."

Everyone looked at one another, desperately trying to think of something suitable to share with their headteacher. Connor eventually spoke up.

"What goes green, red, green, red?"

"Erm, I don't know. What goes green, red, green, red?"

"A frog in a liquidiser."

"Ohh," she groaned. "Right you lot, it looks like Elsa is ready for you, off you go. Oh, and Connor …"

"Yes, Miss?"

"It is nice to see you having fun with your classmates, keep it up!"

"Err, yes, Miss."

"Just as well she does nae know wit we were really talking about," Hayley whispered to him.

"Aye, you're right." Connor smiled back. He lined up behind her waiting for his spag bol. *Brill*, he thought, *my favourite*.

"Want tae sit beside me, Connor?" Hayley enquired.

"Aye, whatever."

Not having had any other offers, he was glad of the invite and moved his tray along the metal rail as if it were a conveyer belt. Grabbing his milk after having a rather large portion of spag bol doled out in his plate, he quickly scanned the hall to see where Hayley had sat. He saw her long blonde hair at the bottom of the hall and made his way over, glad she had chosen to sit away from the others. Not fully sure of his position amongst his peers, he couldn't be bothered having to wrestle it out when there was some serious eating to be done. He plopped himself down onto the tiny circle of a seat, wondering who thought this was a suitable seat for anyone to eat their lunch from. Then he imagined his bitch of a teacher trying to perch on one and began to giggle as he imagined the whole seat being sucked up into her vacuous arse. It was too funny and had to share it with Hayley, who ended up laughing too.

"God, you are wicked, you know that?"

"Aw it's too funny, ma belly aches."

"How's yer sister anyway?"

"She's fine. Well as fine as a nutcase like her can be."

"What? Is she really a nutter?"

"Na, no really, just gets upset sometimes."

"Come here," Hayley instructed Connor.

"I am here," Connor replied, not knowing what she meant.

"No, I mean really here," indicating to Connor to put his ear next to her lips as she whispered quietly to him. Connor's body gave an involuntary shudder as he felt her breath tickle his ears, pricking his inside awake.

"I think I know what happened to your sister, but you need to promise no to say to anyone I told you."

"And who am I going tae speak to? All ma bosom buddies?" Connor joked. "Come on … spill the beans," he urged.

"I think it was Jenny. She told me she was going tae get her cause she got pulled up by Miss Kane."

"Is that right? Silly wee cow better watch her step."

"Don't do anything – she'll kill me."

"Don't worry, Hayley. She'll no have a clue."

"God, *your* nuts, never mind your sister."

"Aw, thanks a lot."

"But I still like you. Come on, let's go – oor turn for the footie."

Grabbing their trays they dumped them on the trolley, then jostled past each other trying to be first outside.

18 Lucy

As soon as she spotted the window of the flat she knew something was different. The window was open slightly and the thin voile that attempted to shield views into the first-floor flat flicked back and forth. She grabbed Connor's hand and shook it, pointing with her other arm to the window. He looked up and they both bolted towards the house. Opening the door, Lucy heard the clink of dishes and the drum of water falling into the sink.

Connor pushed her out the way, so he was first into the living room. Lucy ran behind him squeezing her way next to mum, arms overlapping her brother's as they vied for attention.

"Well, that's a nice hello!" Bubbles from the washing liquid dripped off her hands onto the back of their heads.

Lucy snuggled in further once Connor left, not wanting to be separated. Joined as one her mum guided her towards the sofa lost under discarded clothes and duvets. With one sweep of her arm, her mum cleared space on the sofa for them to sit down. Putting her head next to her chest, Lucy listened to her mum's raspy breath as she panted after the brief exertion. She studied her mum's face worrying until her breathing returned to a more normal repetition.

"I'm fine, hen. Get that look off your face. A good day at school?"

Lucy nodded.

"Oh my god, look at they nits, hen. We'll need tae do something about them. They're everywhere. Minging wee beasties."

Lucy allowed her mum to pick at her hair, relieved she was

doing something about them. She heard them crack as she pinched them between two fingers. Lucy watched as the pile mounted as she pinged them down onto the floor, amazed at how many she'd got.

"Right, that'll need tae do for the now. My arms are killing me."

Lucy nodded, then ran to get her school bag. Emptying the contents out, she rummaged past the broken pencil and crumbs until she found the picture she had drawn earlier. Lucy held it up in front of her mum so she couldn't help but look at it. Lucy pointed at the female character she had drawn with the long hair, eyes that matched her own, holding hands with the boy that towered above. His brown hair was so long only the comical ear to ear grimace could be seen, whilst his stick legs were coloured in blue. Then Lucy pointed at her mum and over at Connor.

"Aye, I can see you've made a picture of us. That is you with the hair in the pony and the red dress on. Well done, hen. Get my fags, hen, will you? They're on top of the shelf."

Lucy handed her mum the drawing and then got the smokes. Sitting back down beside her on the couch as her mum struck a match. The first inhale brought on a bout of coughing. Lucy darted backwards as her mum's hand shook uncontrollably, the glowing tip just missing her hair. Captured between her mum and the sofa, her eyes followed the cigarette, watching its every move. The coughing subsided and Lucy sat while her mum took long draws, her eyes closing every time she inhaled. Her face relaxed with every exhale, savouring every bit of it. Lucy watched the puffs of smoke as they dispersed with the breeze blowing in from the window, whilst the smell loitered in the air creating a new layer of stains.

"Is that all you can do?"

Lucy looked up as she heard her brother throw his angry words. He was standing in the doorway waving his hands in front of his face attempting to rid his space of the cigarette poison.

"We've been starving for days now. There is no food and you're just sitting there smoking those stinking things?"

Lucy grew agitated as she'd seen her brother like this many times before. She didn't like it and looked over at him, wishing and hoping her look could disperse the building tension. Lucy watched as her mum scrunched the fag up in the ashtray until there was no glow left.

Letting out a loud sigh, she looked up at her son and rubbed her hand harshly over her face. Lucy stared at the lines that bunched up under her mum's eyes then touched her own face to feel if she had the same fate starting. Getting no response, Connor huffed his way out of the room into the bedroom.

Lucy relaxed a little, thankful there was not going to be an argument. Jumping out of her seat, Lucy signed 'tea' to her mum and the positive shake of her mum's head led her to fill the kettle. After shoogling the wire a few times, she managed to create a connection and heard the building sound of the water boiling. She picked two mugs off the steel drainer and waved them in the air to get rid of the bubbles hiding inside; brushed them against her skirt to ensure they were bubble-free. Fetching a teabag, she dumped it inside one, got a teaspoon out, then grabbed the milk out the fridge, automatically giving it a whiff. Deciding it had passed the nose test, she set it down and twirled behind the sofa whilst waiting for the kettle. Eventually, it clicked off and she slowly poured the boiling water into the mug; squeezed the tea out of the bag before putting the bag into the empty cup to repeat the process. This time, she gave the bag a bigger squeeze to get the last drops out. The remnants of sugar that lay at the bottom of the bag had clumped together and Lucy scraped what she could between the two cups.

Walking slowly, she carried her mum's cup way out in front, staring at it intently.

"You would think that was a crystal vase you were carrying. Are there no any biscuits?"

Lucy shook her head.

"I should have known better than to ask. Better get tae the shops, I suppose. Aah, watch ma fingers – you're burning them. Sit it doon on the table, ta."

Her mum shook her fingers as Lucy returned for her cuppa. The two sat in silence taking tiny sips in between blowing. From the bedroom, Lucy could hear her brother rhythmically tapping his foot off the metal bed frame. She could imagine him lying on the bed. His top leg would just be reaching the bed end creating the bang-bang as his hands boxed an invisible partner above him, his face set in extreme scowl mode. She knew he loved mum. She had seen the way he fussed over her when she wasn't 'here'; the way he had run and hugged her when they got home. He was just grumpy, she thought, and probably hungry, like she was.

A loud fart reverberated from her mum's bum. Lucy playfully hit her mum and giggled. Her mum joined in, leaning into Lucy, tickling her with her free hand.

"God, that stinks!" Connor had wandered through, hearing the laughter. Wafting his hands in front of his face as he sat down beside them.

"Jesus, what have you been eating?"

"I don't know," his mum laughed in reply.

Lucy rolled off the couch, giggling, holding her stomach and nearly choking she laughed so much. The mood in the flat had lightened and was now a better reflection of the bright, sunny day that had emerged outside.

A knock at the door brought the three to a standstill. Lucy quickly pushed herself off the floor and sat on the couch next to her mum, cowering in behind her arm. Connor had reflexively crouched down behind the sofa. Lucy saw him looking at the door then back at his mum. Mum had put her fingers to her lips signalling to them both to keep quiet. A second knock came. This time with more conviction.

Sat stock still, the three hardly took a breath.

Lucy heard the metal of the letterbox being lifted.

"Hello, anyone at home? It's Fiona Smith, the school nurse here. The school have asked me to come and have a chat. They said they called you and left a message on your phone. Hello? Connor? Lucy? You're not in trouble I just want to speak to mum."

Lucy tugged her mum's arm and pointed to the door. Mum looked at Connor who shrugged his shoulders. Lucy watched as her mum nodded to Connor.

Lucy beat him to it, running past her brother, quickly pulling the door open, smiling at the stranger. Mum stayed on the couch and Lucy heard her coughing resume as another stick was lit.

"Hi, you must be Lucy. We haven't met before, but I'm Fiona, the school nurse. Is this your brother Connor?"

Lucy nodded.

"Hi, Connor. Is mum in?"

"Aye, how?"

"Would you mind if I came in and spoke to her? It's nothing bad, I'm just here to have a chat really."

Lucy stood beside her brother blocking the entrance. Fiona tried to see round them, but they remained where they were, saying nothing.

Another eruption of coughing and spluttering came from within. Connor looked behind him whilst Lucy shifted uneasily from one foot to the other.

"Lucy, go and get mum."

Lucy turned and went through to her mum and pointed at the door. Her mum sighed then, using one hand pushed herself off the sagging couch, she shuffled through to the door and stood behind her two children.

"Hi, you must be Lucy and Connor's mum. I'm Fiona Smith, the school nurse. It's lovely to meet you. I just wanted to have a wee chat about the letter we sent home yesterday."

Waiting for confirmation that she had received the letter, Fiona stopped talking but continued again when no one answered.

"You two remembered to give mum the letter, didn't you?"

Again no response.

"Well, it was about the head lice outbreak we have had at school. It seems quite bad and I just wanted to offer my services to you. I can help get the correct ointment and show you how to comb them out. The school had noticed Lucy had quite a few in her head."

"No, thanks. We're fine."

With that, Lucy was pulled back by her mum as she signalled to her brother to shut the door. Lucy saw Fiona go to say something, but she was too slow as the door was slammed in her face.

Mum and Connor went back into the lounge, but Lucy just stood and stared at the door. Angry with herself for not being able to speak up, she kicked the wall. Not having heard any footsteps retreat down the hallway, she knew Fiona was still outside but was too afraid of the reprimand she might receive if she opened the door. Instead, she slid herself down the wall and sat in the dim light sobbing quietly to herself. She jumped as a piece of paper was pushed through the door. She picked it up, but was unable to read it. Then ripped it in half.

The squeak of trainers on the concrete floor faded as they stepped down towards the door. Lucy buried her head in her hands as her opportunity slipped away.

19 Helen

Two more days to go, Helen thought as she finished what had been a long day. Envisioning a trip to the chippy to fulfil her need for a stodgy dinner made her finish her preparation for the next day a little quicker. A calmness descended over the school once again as the few kids attending netball training finished up and went home. Munching a biscuit, Helen walked down the corridor with fewer bags of work than usual. The light in Linda's room was still on as she passed. She stuck her head round the door, scanning to see where her friend was. She spotted her at the back of the room sifting through piles of artwork trying to somehow arrange them into a unified masterpiece.

"Enjoying yourself?"

Linda lifted her head at the sound of the voice and looked over at Helen.

"Always. I've spent the afternoon trying to teach them about the finer points of pointillism. If you pardon the pun." Holding up some work she showed it to Helen. "Guess what this is?"

Helen turned her head one way, then the next. "Hmmm. Looks like a fine interpretation of the pavement pizza I stepped over last weekend outside the Jock Inn. Am I right?"

"Nearly, but not quite. It is actually a bunch of spring daffodils."

"Oh, wait a minute …" Squinting her eyes shut, she held her hands up making an imaginary frame to peer through. "So it is, silly me."

The two giggled.

"Is that you finished?"

"It sure is. Heading to the chippy as we speak for a haggis

supper with plenty of salt and vinegar."

"You still suffering from last night?"

"Not so much, just got to get some stodge in me before I plonk my arse in front of the box tonight."

"Wow, I meant to say earlier, but nice work with Irene at lunchtime."

"Shhh," Helen closed the door before replying to her friend.

"Shit," Linda quickly put her hand over her mouth, "Is she still here?"

"I think so. I'm sure I heard her claw sharpener working overtime."

Giggling again, Linda agreed with Helen, "God, she is one evil bitch. How she manages to still be in teaching is beyond me. Her face was a picture in the staffroom after you spoke to her. I thought she was going to have an apoplectic fit."

"I fuckin wish she did, excuse, my French. Give that poor wee boy Connor half a chance. Not to mention the rest of the kids in her lair."

"Was Lucy ok? I heard it was her that was crying. Wee lamb."

"Aye, she was. Eventually. I've no idea what was wrong. Strangest ever. Think she is a well fucked up wee thing. Connor didn't really give anything away. Carol has sent a letter and a telephone message for mum to come up and see me. Something not right a child that age not speaking and no one doing anything about it."

"I thought you got in touch with their old primary?"

"Aye, good old Carol hunted them down and Rosie ended up speaking to them. But by the time they had got mum's permission to get the psychologist involved they had moved on. Seems to be a familiar pattern. Everyone struggling to keep up with them. Kids apparently seem ok and social work not on board as result. Beggar's belief if you ask me. That nit situation is abuse for starters in my book."

"Aye, I would agree with you there. The other parents will start complaining if nothing is done about it."

"Think the school nurse was going round today. I'm hoping she has some success. Anyway, nothing more I can do just now. Want me to help you with your masterpieces?"

"No, you're fine. I wouldn't want to put you off your dinner. Away with you to the chippy!"

"No need to tell me twice. Right, see you tomorrow, missus."

"Night. I'll no be long behind you. See you in the morning."

"Aye. Bright and breezy."

Stepping out into the corridor, Helen saw the snake of wire belonging to the cleaner's vacuum and stepped over it. Ahead, she saw Elsa shifting the plants on the window sill, cleaning beneath them.

"Night, Elsa."

"Is that you finished, hen? You're early the night."

"I know. I've got a date with the chippy tonight."

"That sounds braw, better than a date with any man, any day, believe you me."

"You might just be right. You heard anything about wee Mrs Turner?"

"No much. My neighbour was up visiting her the other night. What a mess she says her face is. She says she cannae really remember what happened, but I think that's a load of shite. Her lassies have told the police to get a restraining order on that bastard tae keep him away from the mother, till he goes up tae court. I think she'll be in for another week. Poor wee soul. I might go and visit her tomorrow after work. I need tae catch two buses though so I'll no get home till after ten and that's just a wee bit late. I'll see though."

"Aw, don't be doing that. I'll take you straight after work in my car."

"Aw no, hen, I cannae put you out your way like that."

"Isa, I'm happy to help. It's no bother."

"You're sure, you're sure, hen? I don't want to put you out."

"It's no bother at all. When do you finish here?"

"No till about 5:30."

"Perfect. I'll work till then and take you straight up. I can go for a walk or something while you visit. I've nothing else on, it's fine."

"Aw, you're a wee darlin. Betty is gonnae be pleased to see me I'm sure. Great."

"Right. I'm off for ma chippy."

"Enjoy, hen. See you tomorrow."

Pushing open the door, Helen blinked at the first glimpses of sunlight she had seen all day and walked down the steps. Glad to be out in the open, she gulped in deep breaths of the salty sea air. Out the corner of her eye, she caught sight of Johnny, one of her pupils, sitting high up on the old stone wall. He was busy kicking his legs against the end of the wooden gate post, chipping the standard green paint smothered on every council fence. Flecks gathered in a pile on the ground.

"Hi, Johnny. That you finished all your homework?" Helen asked in good humour.

"Eh, aye, miss."

"Good stuff. See you tomorrow."

"Aye." He jumped off the wall thudding down onto the pavement below and walked up the street; he kicked his football off the ground up into his hands, then bounced it along the road as he walked home, alerting his mum of his arrival home.

Helen walked over the old railway bridge and glimpsed over the edge at the tangle of brambles and discarded couches that lay below. It always amazed her that people went to the lengths of dragging their unwanted belongings down a steep embankment and over fences, rather than phoning for the council to uplift them. She cut through the narrow opening that led to a shortcut behind the chippy.

Wondering whether dodging all the crap and possible vermin that lay amongst it was worth the risk, Helen hurried as much as her wee legs allowed her. Getting to the end of the alley, she swung her legs over the barrier and was glad she had worn trousers.

The familiar smell of fish and chips with the hint of vinegar hitting her nose made her mouth water. Pushing open the door, she saw Frank behind the counter, busily dipping large pieces of fish into a pail of milk batter before laying it delicately with his two fingers into the bubbling fryer. The sound of sizzling oil was always comforting.

Standing in the short queue, Helen had already decided it was a night for two pickled onions and she wished the old biddy in front would hurry up and make her mind up. Frank gave her a wink and Helen nodded back, the signal for her usual supper. *Not good*, Helen thought *when the local fryer knows your order without a single word being uttered.* She watched as Frank lowered the fat haggis finger into the oil. Helen tried not to concern herself with the calorific content of her dinner. Eventually, it was her turn.

"How you tonight, Helen? Not often we see you in here mid-week."

"I know. I caught a waft of your chips cooking and couldn't keep away. Don't be shy with the vinegar now, Frank."

"No bother. How is work? That boy of mine working hard?"

"Aw, he is. He's such a good boy. Bit of a character like his dad though."

"As long as he is no giving you any cheek. Right there you go £5:60."

"You better put a can of Bru in there as well, Frank."

"There you go an extra eighty pence for the Bru, hen."

Helen fished around in her purse and managed to scrape the exact amount from the dross at the bottom of her purse.

"Cheers, Frank."

The warmth of her dinner seeped through the paper it was wrapped in. The smell swept past her nose. Unable to wait until home, she poked a hole in the corner and managed to sneak a rogue chip out. It burnt her fingers, but she persevered and put it in her mouth. It then proceeded to burn her mouth. She quickly chewed down on the chip, whilst trying to open her mouth to let the hotness out and some cool air in. Chiding herself for being unable to wait, she put the rest of her dinner in the bag and walked briskly home.

Settling down on her couch, Helen had decided that dinner on a tray in front of the telly was just what she needed. She squeezed a good dollop of ketchup on her plate as she watched a travel programme about Italy, her fingers helping her munch her supper. Burping loudly after taking a gulp of her Bru, Helen rubbed her greasy fingers over her trousers, unable to find the energy to get kitchen roll. Her evening involved more TV and not a lot else. Feeling disgusted at herself for being so lazy and fat, she heaved herself off the couch and went to bed, deciding that tomorrow would most definitely be the start of the new healthy Helen.

20 Connor

Enjoying the extra space in bed as his sister slept with mum, Connor stretched out his legs. He rested his hands behind his head and contemplated his day ahead. His itchy scalp distracted him from his thoughts. His mum had tried to get rid of the beasties from their heads by dousing them in the green washing up liquid, the closest cleaning product they had. It had just left his scalp burning though and instead of itching from the beasties, it was now itchy from the soap.

The visit from the school nurse had terrified his mum, he could tell. After, she had gone about the flat shutting the curtains; double-checking the door was properly locked. Not speaking, she had taken them both into the bathroom and scrubbed then combed their heads till they were red raw, despite their protests. Everyone was by then starving. But she refused to let him go and buy anything. Instead, she found a tin of beans and shared it out between the two of them, going without herself. Connor had been raging and kicked off, giving her a hard time. Just as quickly he stopped when he saw her tears start to fall and Lucy retreating into a corner. The last thing he needed was the two of them acting like basket cases.

This reminded him that he still had to pay Jenny a visit. He wondered when the best time to do this would be. The last thing he needed was to get caught by his bitch teacher. Deciding he would wait till after school, he hatched a plan. *Give the little cow a taste of her own medicine*, he thought.

He sniffed his oaxters and decided he better go and have a wash. His lunchtime was going to be spent with Miss Kane and he didn't want to be stinking of 'b.o'. This put a spring in his step.

He couldn't remember the last time he felt so excited about going to school. Having to spend the morning with Mrs Gallows first didn't even dampen his spirits.

Jumping out of bed, he went through to the tiny bathroom, carefully treading on the wooden floorboards. They weren't quite like the lovingly restored ones seen on those restoration programmes. Ensuring he didn't stand round the edges where the odd carpet staple still protruded, he began to fill the bath. A trickle of hot water came out. It barely covered the bottom of the bath, but it looked like all he was getting. Adding some cold to fill it up, he braced himself before lowering in. God, it was a farce to be calling it a bath. He'd seen more liquid at the bottom of a finished pint glass. He wasn't sure whether his dick tried to shrink back into his body due to the embarrassment or the cold. Glad it was summer, he quickly soaped himself then lapped the water over his body. Grabbing the towel and did his best to dry himself. The dampness was still evident from the hair washing escapade the night before.

Putting on his clothes, he poked his head into the living room. Lucy was clinging onto mum, whilst she had an arm around her to stop her from falling off the side of the couch. They were both still out for the count. He put the kettle on figuring the noise would eventually wake them. Sorting out mugs, teabags and a scraping of sugar, he made their morning cuppa. His mum stirred, first lifting her head up to see over the back of the couch to where he stood.

"Morning, son. You're up early, are you no?"

"Aye, I suppose. School this morning."

"Aw, son, I meant to speak to you aboot that. How's aboot a wee day off. Ah know you don't like the school and I need a wee bit help tae get ma money and some shopping."

He felt himself freeze as his mum spoke. His heart began to sink, and rage took its place. Pacing up and down the short length of lino, he clenched and unclenched his fist, unable to speak. His thoughts fumed at what his mother had in store for him. In the past, he had begged for days off school, but never had he been to a school like this. Never had he actually wanted to go to school. The movement woke Lucy. He saw her out the corner of his eye as she pushed herself up and stared at him, trying to work out what was going on. Those big eyes of hers penetrated him. He knew then he wouldn't be going to school that day.

He stormed off into his room and threw himself down onto his bed, biting the duvet between his teeth, swearing. His legs flailed up and down behind him.

He felt a small hand on his back and was unsure of how long he'd been by himself. He turned round and she was watching him again, those eyes piercing into him, trying to speak to him. She bent forward and swept away the salty remnants from the corners of his eyes.

"Of all the days … of all the fuckin' days she wants us no to go tae school, Lucy. Why did it have to be today?"

Gently touching his arm, she hung her head.

"Did you know Miss Kane wanted you and me to go and help her at lunch? I've never in my whole life been asked to do anything like that before. Have you?"

Lucy shook her head and Connor saw her tears brim. He hugged her and the two sat on the crumpled bed as their tears dripped down their faces.

Pulling himself together and wiping his nose with his sleeve, Connor spoke, "Don't worry. I bet Miss Kane will understand. She is something else, is she no? We will go in tomorrow and explain. Suppose we better go and get ready to go down the street. At least we'll have some food the night. Think she's just been spooked out by that nurse coming round. Don't want her going off on one again. Come on."

He pushed her off the bed by kicking her bum. Lucy turned

round and walloped him back before running into the living room where Mum was lighting up.

"What were you two up to? You been greeting, son? Your eyes are red. Thought you'd be happy at a day aff the school?"

"I'm fine, Mum. Just wanted to go and see ma pals. Can you stop going on?"

"You can see them the night. We'll get my money from the postie then we'll go and buy something nice for tea. What dae you fancy? Ma mouth is shaped for a mince round, peas and mashed tattie. What dae you think?"

"I think we better go now. I'm starving," Connor grumbled.

"Aye, right. Give me a wee minute till I get organised. Hen, go and get ma jacket, would you?"

Connor stuffed his feet into his trainers using his finger to release the heel that had got stamped down. Standing up ready to go, he sat back down as he realised they were not nearly ready.

Pulling open the curtains he let the sunlight flood the room.

"Don't do that, son. I don't want folk peering in here seeing what we're up to."

"Mum, it's a lovely day and we're no up to anything. And folk around here don't have giraffe necks."

"Connor, you just don't know who is out there watching us and what we're doing."

"Mum, don't start all this again. Come on … there is nothing out there, just folk going tae school or work like we should be doing."

"Connor, son, please listen tae me."

Connor heard the shrill of desperation creeping into her voice and knew he was pushing it too far. He stopped and slowly huffed and puffed as he pulled the curtains shut. Annoyed at his mum's pathetic paranoia, he had made up his mind that today was going to be a shit day and fixed his face accordingly. He slouched down onto the couch and folded his arms just to make sure his mum realised how pissed off he was. He watched her slowly faff around, drinking her tea, lighting another fag.

She eventually put her arms into her black jacket, signalling she was nearly ready. Lucy bent across her mum helping her put it round towards the other arm. *God, it's like care in the community with this pair,* he grimaced to himself. Suitably attired, his mum got to her feet and looked at him.

"Right, come on, son, we've no got all day. Get that miserable look off your face and help yer mum doon the street."

Muttering obscenities under his breath, Connor stood and went out the door before them. Standing at the close entrance, arms folded, he hawked spit to thud on the ground, waiting till his mum and sister were in the vicinity before launching it.

"You dirty wee bastard. Did you have to do that? You nearly gobbed all over ma shoes."

Ignoring his mum, he let them walk past then he trailed behind them. Glancing up the road to the left, he caught a glimpse of the school and felt a pang of regret surge through him.

21 Helen

Every time a straggler came into the classroom Helen lifted her head hoping she would see the smile that belonged to Lucy. As it neared ten o'clock, she knew it was unlikely she would see her wee waif and stray that day. Frustrated that she hadn't turned up on the day she had everything planned for her, Helen grumpily sent Jason along to Mrs Gallows with a note to ask if Connor was at school, thinking perhaps Lucy really wasn't well and her mum was taking good care of her at home. When Jason returned he didn't have the answer she wanted to hear.

"Damn," she said in a quiet voice.

The news didn't sit well with her. Not being able to concentrate, she asked Chloe to go down to the office with a note requesting a call to the mother as soon as possible. Not that this was likely to yield anything.

Putting her grumpiness to one side, Helen set about teaching her class the ins and outs of the three times table. Taking them to the gym hall to use hoops and bean bags to demonstrate, she began to think of how much Lucy would have enjoyed this. As predicted the whole class had a great time sorting the bean bags into lots of three, totally engrossed with their task. Glad her lesson had gone well, Helen lined them up and challenged them to walk as quietly as they could down the corridor. Following behind them, she slowed as she neared Irene's room and took a sly glance through the slit of glass in the door. *Good old-fashioned learning going on for a change*, she thought. *Bums on seats, textbooks opened. Some things just never change.* Irene turned just at that moment, catching Helen having a good old gawk.

Helen smiled and waved, giving her a thumbs-up before sniggering to herself as she caught up with her class. Just as she was turning the corner to go into her class she heard someone shout her name. Turning, she saw Carol busying up the corridor towards her.

"Hi, just to let you know I phoned the Jackson's number, but guess what? No reply as usual. Fiona Smith was in earlier though."

"Was she? Hold on a wee second, Carol, until I sort this lot out." She poked her head round the door of the classroom, instructing the class to behave and get on with the activities set out at their desks.

"Sorry about that. So how did Fiona get on?"

"Not great. Kids answered the door just as she was about to go away. They took ages to answer, she said. She had to ask Lucy to go and get her mum, who then stood at the door smoking a fag. After Fiona had explained why she was there, mum told Connor to shut the door and that was the end of that."

"Really? Oh my god. I can't believe she shut the door on your face! I mean who does that? I really want to meet this woman now. Oh god, and now the two are off school. You don't think she will have moved them on again, do you?"

"Surely not after three days? I spoke to Rosie. She said to just note down everything and keep an eye on it. Maybe they've both got that bug that is going round."

Helen rolled her eyes. "Aye right. I better go or these kids will end up fighting or something and I'll get shot."

"Ok, see you later."

Desperate for a cuppa, Helen made sure her class were ready for the bell, sending them out before the Primary Sevens came hurtling round the corner, jamming up the door.

She gave herself a double scoop of caffeine and a double sugar hit and was halfway through her chocolate bar when she remembered she was meant to be doing 'healthy' today.

"Shit!" she said.

"Shit, what?" Ted asked as he plonked his corded derrière down next to her.

"Shit, I'm meant to be eating healthily today and I've just finished this chocolate bar and put two sugars in my coffee."

"Well, you must have needed them, then. How is your little class behaving today?" he kindly enquired.

"They are really good actually. Had a great lesson on multiplication in the gym hall. But my little Lucy isn't at school and neither is her brother. Just worried something is up."

"Oh, I'm sure they are fine," Ted answered.

"I'm just glad I've got peace and quiet to get some proper teaching done without that impudent boy hanging around," Irene piped up.

"Irene, you are funny. We know you really love all the little scoundrels you get," Ted remarked.

"No, I think you are now being the one who is funny, Ted. Why should the teaching resources of the school get wasted on children like Connor Jackson? … who, as we all know, will probably end up in prison or the very least producing more children that are a waste of time and a drain on our resources," Irene said.

"For precisely that reason, Irene, so we can make a difference. To stop the same thing happening, to give kids like Connor and Lucy and all the others a chance that they are clearly not getting at home," Helen retorted.

"Helen, we are a school, not a babysitting service for parents who don't want to bring up their children."

"Perhaps if we spent time with the kids and the parents, we would get the whole picture of what is going on and not just some warped one that seems to emit from your mind."

"Another biscuit, Helen?" Ted shook the communal biscuit

tin in front of her.

"Ever the peacemaker, Ted, aren't you? Thanks … think I'll just inhale the rest."

The rest of the staff break was non-eventful with the coming weekend's events discussed and coffees hastily slurped before the bell went again.

Linda walked Helen down the corridor dodging kids as they came in from the lines.

"She needs to retire from teaching. I don't think she has one empathetic bone in her body," Linda whispered to Helen.

"God, I know. I'm not normally a violent person, but sometimes I would like to stick the heid in her. How old do you think she is?"

"Dunno. Fifty-something?"

"Is that all? Think of all those poor weans she is going to destroy between now and when she retires. It's actually criminal."

The two teachers parted company. Each went off to share some more pearls of wisdom with their little cherubs.

Forgetting it was her non-class contact time, Helen got a surprise when she went into her class and found Claire in the midst of getting her class organised for their music lesson.

Helen sidled up next to her and murmured, "God I must be losing the plot. I totally forgot what day it was. Let me grab a few things and I'll be out your way."

Claire flashed a smile back. "No problem, take your time."

22 Lucy

Sitting watching the TV with a full belly, snuggling with her mum put a smile on Lucy's face. Stretching her legs out, she put them on top of the coffee table to make herself a little more comfortable. Truly, she was looking forward to spending time with Mrs Kane, but being with her mum, when mum was feeling good, was hard to beat. She just wished her brother could chill out a bit. He was still miserable and didn't know what to do with himself. He had sat and watched a bit of TV after eating his tea, then he had got up and gone into the bedroom. Now he was back in the living room perched on the edge of his seat as if he was about to take flight.

Lucy got up to go to the bathroom, which was to the rear of the building that housed their flat. The window looked out to the courtyard below. Mid-pee Lucy heard the shouts and laughter of kids playing outside. She stopped her pee so she could listen more clearly, sure it was her friend Jane from school. Turning her head, she went to look out the window forgetting it was that funny marbled glass that you couldn't see out of. Resuming her pee as quickly as she could, she wiped her bum, skooshed her hands under the cold tap and ran into the bedroom.

Jumping across the bed, she saw she had guessed correctly. Below was Jane and her wee sister playing with the washing lines, Jane shouting out instructions that were being carefully followed by the younger sibling. Lucy banged the window with her fist and waved, but being so far away, Jane didn't hear her. But Connor did and he came through to see what was going on.

"What you doing? You trying to escape?"

Lucy pointed down to the ground and Connor hopped on the

bed next to her to get a better look. "Is that the lassie from your class?"

Nodding, Lucy continued to wave and bang.

"Wait a wee minute." Connor bent down and tried to open the window, pulling the two handles at the bottom in an upwards motion. Lucy could see his scrawny muscles bulge with the force he exerted, but the window didn't budge. Confused, Connor tried again, but nothing.

"Wait a minute," he said, reaching up and pulling out bits of newspaper that were wedged in to stop the window from rattling. After releasing the paper, the window shot up, giving both of them a fright.

"Hey, you!" Connor hollered out the window.

Jane stopped abruptly and turned her head all ways trying to see where the noise had come from. Then she squinted and put her hand up to shield her eyes from the sun.

"Cannae see who you are because of the sun. Who is it?"

"It's Lucy. Well, it's no Lucy – it's her brother, shouting for Lucy," Connor tried to explain.

Jane took a step back. "Aw, I see you now. You coming oot?"

Lucy looked at Connor, her eyebrows raised in hope.

"Well, you'll need tae go and ask her. I'll come with you."

The pair raced through the short hall to the living room, trying to burst through the door at the same time. Lucy, beating her brother, rushed up onto her mum's knee and began motioning with her hands towards the back room.

"What's going on? I don't know what you want, hen. Is something the matter? Do you know what she wants, son?"

Connor had sat on the table watching his sister trying to tell their mum her desires. Her efforts were comical and, when Lucy turned to him for help, she saw him smirking, and raced over to punch his arm in annoyance.

"Aye, I do, Mum. Her wee pal from the school is down the

stairs playing in the backcourt and she wants tae go doon and play with her."

"I didn't know you had a wee pal, hen, but I'm no sure about you going out there by yourself."

"Mum she'll be fine. Ye can see her from the window."

"But, son, you just cannae tell who's about watching."

"Mum, we were fine for all the days you were lying on the couch out of it. We could have been anywhere and you would have been none the wiser."

"Connor, you know I cannae help that and I know that when I'm like that you're watching her."

Lucy put her puppy dog eyes on and stared at her mum, fingers crossed behind her back, bouncing up and down on her mum's knee.

"Well, I suppose I could go doon the back with her," Connor suggested.

"I'm still no sure, hen."

"For god's sake, Mum. Are you just tryin' to stop us havin' any fun? She's going down the back tae play, she's no going on the train by herself tae Glasgow."

"Right, ok. You better keep an eye on her and you don't leave the back, do you hear me?"

Not waiting for her to change her mind, Lucy kissed her mum, knocking her backwards, grabbed her brother and dragged him down the stairs and out the back. Before they'd even reached Jane, she'd begun chatting to them.

"You took your time, did you no? Feeling better the two of youse?" Jane inquired.

"Aye, we are," Connor informed her.

Not that interested in the reply, Jane shouted at her wee friend. "Come on. We're playing at houses. This is ma house. Your house can be here."

Jane indicated to a patch of ground next to hers. Stones were piled up in various spots as a makeshift kitchen. Spoons and other utensils were made out of sticks and other bits of rubbish. The old milk crate had been a lucky find. Lucy found a dandelion and pulled the leaves off to make food for them all. Jane kindly shared her things with her friend much to the annoyance of her wee sister.

Ignoring her complaints, Jane continued: "Katie can be your wee sister and Connor can be ma hubby."

"What? I'm no playing at houses with you. I'm just out to see who's about. Think am playing with youse? No chance. I would'nae be seen dead with youse. I'm away tae see ma pals. Lucy, remember, no tae go out of the back and Jane you're in charge of her. Don't let her leave the back or your dead meat, ok?"

Lucy looked back and forth between her friend and her brother, finally pushing her brother away when he started threatening her pal.

"Don't worry, Connor. She'll be fine. Who you away tae see anyway? And what will I tell your mum if she comes doon the stairs?"

"None of your business where I'm goin' and I'll no be long. I'm sure you will think of something tae say and cover for me, won't you?"

"Aye, I suppose so. Come on, Lucy, let's play."

Not batting an eyelid as her brother sloped off, Lucy busied herself in her wee 'house', making the most of this time with her friend. Jane took centre stage as usual telling her and Katie what was happening. Lucy was only too happy to play along, enjoying the chance to be a wee girl for a change.

23 Connor

Connor felt a little bit guilty leaving his sister after promising his mum he would stay and watch her. He thought about it again and decided that his actions were actually well and truly justified. Imagine his fellow classmates caught him playing at houses with Lucy and her pals? The response was not worth thinking about. Not sure what to do, he wandered round to the front of the flats to the busy main road.

He plonked himself down on the low wall there, far enough away from the girls not to be associated with them, but close enough if his mum took a wobbly. He picked a handful of gravel up from the flower bed behind him and let the small gritty pieces run through his hands. He rolled the stones between his hands, digging them into his palms, making tiny indentations in his skin. The dirt made his hands dry and dirty. A lorry loaded with logs rumbled past, sending a cloud of dust his way, making him blink furiously with little effect. He dropped the gravel and rubbed them as the tiny particles stung his eyes. His eyes began to water and he had to use the bottom of his t-shirt to wipe them. When he could see again he looked down the street and saw Hayley walking up towards him. She still had her school clothes on – a short grey skirt that inched up past her knees. Her long blonde hair fell forwards, bouncing off her wee chest as she walked. Connor felt his heart skip a beat and his insides go all funny.

Not wanting to appear too eager, he pretended to be enthralled with the moss growing in between the bricks on the wall, bursting the wee green buds off with thrusts of his fingers.

"You feeling better then?" he heard her shout over at him as she neared.

"Aw, hi. I never saw you there. Aye, I'm feeling better, ta."

"What you up tae?"

"Nothing much. Just hanging about. You?"

"Aye, the same. You missed yourself the day at school."

"How come?"

"Tony let off a stink bomb in the class and Miss Gallows went bush. It wis dead funny."

"Aye?"

"Aye! That bun on top of her head wis doing some waggling about as she tried to work out what was going on. Then her lip was doing that funny trembling thing. We were aw boaking with the smell, it was totally stinking, gads. Here, smell ma shirt ... you can still smell it."

Hayley thrust her arm under Connor's nose. All he could smell was the fresh clean smell of washing powder, which was like roses to his nose. Especially on Hayley. She plonked herself next to him, her thighs touching his. She seemed totally at ease and totally unaware of the effect she had on him. She cocked her head to the side so that her hair fell to one side and she stayed like this inspecting him. He could feel his cheeks burning up.

"You alright? You're going a funny colour."

"Me? I'm fine," he replied trying to play it cool. Desperate to keep her for a while longer, he racked his brains for something to say, not just something, but something cool and interesting so she would want to hang around. He hated being put under pressure and came up with nothing.

Luckily, Hayley was not burdened with the same problem and she chatted away, totally unaware of the mental battle going on inside his head.

"So do you live round here?"

"Aye, in those flats. What about you?"

"I live doon near the harbour next to the Swan Hotel."

"What? In one of they giant hooses!" Connor exclaimed.

"Aye, well sort of."

"Explain ..."

"Well, ma pappi owns the big house, but it's split into wee flats, bit like yours. I stay in one with ma pappi and two brothers. Tiny really. I've got to share with ma two brothers it's a nightmare."

"I know how you feel I share with ma sister. Where does yer mum stay?"

Hayley turned her head away and stared out onto the road. "She's away the now."

"Away? How long for?"

"I don't know. Ma pappi says she is away working, but I don't believe him. I mean who goes away tae work in the middle of the night when the polis come tae yer door?"

"Maybe they had a special job for her?"

"Aye, right. Ma pappi thinks I'm five and won't tell me the truth. She's been away since last October. No seen or heard from her."

"I'm sorry."

"Aw, don't be sorry, 'cause when she wis here she wis aye drunk and talking rubbish. At least with ma pappi he always has our tea made and I know what's happening, even if he likes the whiskey a bit too much. Do you stay with your mum and dad?"

"Naw, just ma mum, and ma sister of course."

"Do you no know who your dad is either?"

"No, I know him alright, just don't see him."

"How no? Does he stay away?"

"I don't know where he stays."

"Why don't you find out? Maybe he'll come in visit you and take you out somewhere nice?"

Connor had been pleased to chat with Hayley at first, but now she was verging into clandestine territory. He didn't know what to say. Fearful he would upset her by not answering and she would leave, he squirmed uncomfortably. Hayley seemed oblivious to his discomfort and chatted on. Maybe, Connor thought this was what normal girls were like and he was kind of glad his sister didn't talk.

Hayley just didn't seem to stop.

"If I knew my dad I would be trying tae get in touch with him so he would take me out, maybe tae McDonald's or that big fancy restaurant at the marina. Sometimes I imagine he comes tae my door and he's driving some big fancy car. One with those blacked-out windows that's got a driver and it's about a mile long, wearing designer jeans and one of those smart polo shirts. Then I remind myself dreams don't come true."

Hayley let out a sigh. Then turned her head back to face Connor. "You know you're a good listener. Ma two brothers would have told me tae shut it by now."

Connor smiled back at her and stole a glimpse into her green eyes, making him blush again.

"I need tae go in a minute. You comin' tae school tomorrow?"

"Aye, definitely."

"Great. I'll see you there. Friday tomorrow. Want tae catch up after school?"

"Aye."

"Right you are then. See you tomorrow."

"Bye."

With that, she jumped down off the wall and sauntered back down the street. Connor gazed after her, lost in his own wee reverie. That was until he heard Jane screaming his name.

"Shit!" he said, totally unaware of how long he'd been chatting for. He looked at the sky and saw it was getting dimmer; he ran in the direction of the hollering and nearly ran into Jane as he rounded the corner to the backcourt. Jane was puffing and panting and couldn't talk. There was just her and Katie. Connor's stomach flipped, stopping him in his tracks.

Grabbing Jane's shoulders, he shouted, "Where's Lucy? Where is she? I left you for five minutes and you lose her. Fuck!" He burled his head around looking for her.

"Calm doon, will you," Jane said between breaths. "She's up the stairs with your mum. I did what I said I would and covered for you. Said you were away for a pee round the side. You better go up because your mum looked a bit mad."

"Thank fuck."

Connor ran off leaving the two girls standing. He bolted up the back stairs two at a time. She must have heard him coming as she was standing waiting for him at the door, her face like fizz, one hand on her hip, the other waggling.

"I told you tae look after your sister, no tae go and leave her. Anything could have happened. I near died when I looked out the window and she wis there playing herself."

"Mum, I wis bursting for a pee. Wis I tae pee ma pants? And Jane wis with her. I wis away for five minutes tops."

Connor shot his sister a glare. She was standing behind them watching the two of them argue. This was when he was most glad his sister couldn't speak.

"I thought I could trust you."

"You can, Mum. Ask her, I wis away for only a few minutes. I could practically see them where I wis peeing. Isn't that right, Lucy?"

She nodded back.

"Well how come when I came doon the stairs tae get Lucy you did'nae see me and shout where you were. That wee pal of Lucy's had tae go and get you?"

Connor didn't expect that. His mum never left the house alone unless it was major.

"I must've been concentrating on ma pee so I did'nae get it on ma shoes."

"You know why I'm angry. You ken how important it is you do as I say. I need to make sure you're both safe. Do you no remember what he's like?"

Connor hated when she got like this, bringing up the past. It had been two years now. And he had worked hard at forgetting about it. But when she spoke like this he could feel it poking up from his depths and he didn't like it. He felt his mood turn to anger. Before he knew it his hand was raised, his mum ducking down brought him to his senses.

Giving his head a shake, he turned and slammed the door shut that had been open all this time, making his way to his room, hurling that door too, leaving her standing with her wee shadow behind her. Why could she not just move on? Let them live their lives like normal people. As far as Connor was aware he hadn't been in touch since, but mum behaved like he was just round the corner ready to pounce.

He lay on the bed and stared at the darkening sky outside, blocking out the high pitch of his mother going on and on about what might have happened to Lucy. He let his mind wander back to earlier and his chat with Hayley. He tried to remember everything about it. The way she looked. What she said. The wee smile she gave him. And that smell. He could smell that forever. He could feel himself go all funny again, tingling all over. He did his best to hold onto those happy feelings.

24 Helen

Elsa stuck her head round Helen's door. "You still ok for tonight, hen?"

Looking up from her desk, Helen replied, "Of course. See you at the front door five-thirty?"

"Aye, smashing, hen. Better get ma work done super-fast the night. See you later."

"No worries, Isa."

Helen finished marking the writing jotters, a laborious task, but it had to be done. She was still anxious about the Jackson kids and wished she could get an answer to their non-attendance that day. Thinking ahead to the following day, she got the kids' work organised. Friday was one of her favourite days and not just because it was the weekend. Her 'special child of the week' was picked, involving lots of fun and hilarity for the kids. The kids just seemed to love it, as did she when she saw their wee smiles. The lucky child then got to invite a family member to class the following week to play games and have juice and biscuits. A simple idea, but they all loved it. Helen had already decided that Lucy was going to be the special person, hoping this would entice the mother into the school. All she needed was for Lucy to attend school the next day. The kids were none the wiser to the fact that she rigged the special person every week, depending on who needed a little boost. *Teacher's prerogative*, she decided.

Needing the toilet, she left her class and went up the corridor. As she neared Irene's room the fart stench still pervaded the area causing her to cover her nose with her hand. Helen had missed all the chat about it at lunch as she'd been busy in her class and decided to go and search for someone who could fill her in on the details after.

As she came out of the toilet, she heard chatter coming from Ted's room and went for a nose. She opened the door and the huddling of Ted, Linda and Carol came to an abrupt stop. They turned and looked to see who it was.

"Aw, it's just you. Come in and join the party," Ted said, patting a seat on the table.

"What's the gossip then?" she asked.

"Just talking about the stink bomb fiasco. Did you hear about it?"

"Can't say I have, but I've certainly smelled about it. Do tell all ..."

"No one has owned up to it, but Rosie is sure it was Tony. Just as well your boy was off today or Irene would have been gunning for him, that's for sure," Carol said.

"Oh, you're missing out the best bit, Carol," Linda said.

"Tell me! Tell me!"

"Ok, ok. Well, wee Sarah came running down to my room saying that Mrs Gallows was having a fit. I wouldn't normally have bothered if it had been any of the others, but Sarah's a good wee thing. I asked her what she meant and she said her head was shaking and her lips kept moving and no sound was coming out like one of those birds you see on the telly at Christmas."

"A turkey," Ted explained to a bemused Helen.

"Really, and I missed that? Damn?"

"Well, I sent a runner up to get Rosie and she went in. Rosie said that Irene was just absolutely raging and Rosie had to send her to the staff room to calm down while she tried to get to the bottom of it. The whole class is in detention at break time until she gets an answer as to who the culprit is. They are all being very loyal."

"Probably Tony got them all shit scared," Linda added.

"And Irene?" Helen asked.

"She went back in after lunch. Think she went home early though. I couldn't help laughing though when Sarah described her as a turkey, got her to a T," Carol laughed.

"Linda and I were trying to work out when she would be putting the chalk down. Is she in her fifties?"

"No, she's only mid-forties."

"No way, Ted. She must be at the very least late forties?" Helen said.

"No. She's just a few years younger than me."

"Jeezo, all those poor kids she is going to be teaching."

Just at that, the squeak of the door opening stopped them once again and Rosie walked in.

"There you all are. Carol, could you come and help me with that damn computer of mine. I can't get it to print?"

"Sure, I was just catching up with this lot."

"Oh, I don't need you right away, just when you're ready. I'm sure it won't take long. Anyway, one more day to go troops and not long until the summer holidays! Right, I'm off to get some caffeine."

At that the three staff dispersed to their own rooms, leaving Ted in his. Helen chuckled to herself, imagining Irene as a turkey. At five-thirty, she made her way to the front door to meet Isa. The school always seemed a happier place the closer it got to Friday and as she reached the door she saw Isa standing with her blue cleaners overall draped over her arm, a smile planted wide on her face.

"Hi, hen, it's good tae get finished, isn't it?"

"Definitely is, especially when there is only one more day to go. Right, let's go. Will you sign me out, Isa? My hands are full?"

"Done it already. I really appreciate you doing this, hen. I would have been on the bus for at least two hours, not tae mention all the waiting about."

"No trouble at all. I've brought my laptop. I'll just sit and get some work done in the cafeteria."

"You teachers are all the same: you never stop."

The pair chatted back and forth as they walked out to the car. Helen's car sat alone in the carpark awaiting the return of its owner. The tarmac was loose and broken beneath their feet and pieces flew as their shoes sent them skitting across the ground. A breeze blowing in off the sea sent white clouds into a frenzied dance in the sky above them. Grit flew into their face and made them both blink. Helen tried to pull her cardigan shut with her one free hand, whilst wrestling with car keys to get the door opened.

"God, it's a bit blowy out here," Isa remarked.

"I'll get the heater on, it'll no be long in heating up."

"Bloody summer and you still need the heater on. What is this place like?"

The wee car's heater blew out gusts of air that got hotter as the car started to move. Helen drove the wrong way out of the car park, nobody about to complain and it made her feel just a wee bit rebellious. She had forgotten how much of a gossip Isa was, but was soon reacquainted with her ways and spent the entire journey being informed of all the happenings in her neighbourhood. Not getting the opportunity to say very much, Helen zoned out, giving a few 'uhus' along the way. Gazing out at the green fields, watching the cows as they stood munching the abundance of food around them, she thought how easy it would be to have the life of a cow: no dramas, no meddling, just eating and milking; *though there is the standing around in the cold, and the rain pelting off you most of the year and then your baby calf being taken off you ... maybe not so nice after all*, she thought.

"Helen? Helen, are you listening tae a thing I'm saying?'

"What, eh, aye, Isa, I totally agree."

"You looked like you were a million miles away!"

"No, just a few things going through my mind."

"Aw, you know you can share with me, hen. I'll no say a word. Is it men problems? I know you don't have a man the now, but sometimes they are more hassle than they are worth. The right one will come along when you're least expecting it, I tell you."

Isa continued to prattle on, which was just fine and Helen tried to keep an ear on what she was saying rather than getting lost in cow thought.

As she turned off the dual carriageway, the monstrosity of grey loomed before them. *Quite possibly the ugliest hospital*, Helen thought. Pulling into the car park, she found a spot not too far from the entrance.

"Aye, hen, that's a good spot, save ma wee legs. I better go and buy her a wee bag of sweeties. Cannae go up empty-handed. You sure you don't want tae come up for a wee blether? Get the story straight from the horse's mouth?"

"No, I've got too much work to do." The lie slipped out easily. In reality, Helen hated hospitals and ill people. They made her feel queasy. Plus, she was looking forward to giving her ears a wee break.

"But please pass my good wishes onto her."

"I will do, hen. Right, how dae I get this door open?"

"Just pull the lever, Isa. Aye, that's it."

The pair walked up to the doors and passed the small throng of people huddled round the doorway puffing on their cigarettes, adorned in their fluffy dressing gowns and slippers.

"Just doesn't seem right that, does it?"

"What? Those folk smoking at a hospital, I know. We should nae be treating folk that cannae stop smokin, waste of money if you ask me. Right, hen, I'll get you back here in about an hour. That ok?"

"Aye, fine. I'll just be in the cafe, no rush."

"Ok, hen."

Helen watched as Isa shuffled off towards the lifts, being

overtaken by a hoard of others who were in a much bigger hurry than she was. Joining the end of the queue at the cafe, Helen perused the menu up on the board whilst trying not to breathe too deeply. The smell that pervaded every hospital Helen had ever been to was not one she particularly cared for and was another reason she hated hospitals. Choosing a large cappuccino and a small scone, she inched her tray along the metal rail waiting her turn. *Just like school,* Helen thought, *only worse.*

The lady behind the counter must have been about eighty, Helen decided, her tight-knit perm sitting in perfect curls upon her head, dyed a rather fetching violet colour. Moving with the speed of a snail just awakened from a particularly long hibernation, Helen was glad she had plenty of time to kill. She spied her seat whilst waiting in the queue, one of the few comfy chairs hidden in the corner, *just perfect.* Turning to get her order, she hoped the guy in front didn't take her seat.

Becoming anxious and territorial over 'her' seat, she skipped past the guy in front as he stopped to inspect the tiny portions of plastic milk containers. Thrusting too much money to the wee wifey, she instructed her to keep the change and claimed her seat.

Kicking off her shoes, she curled her feet underneath herself and tried to get comfy. It was then she realised how tired she was. She hadn't stopped all day. She was aware of the faint aroma of sweaty cheese emanating from her well-trodden feet but didn't really have the energy to care. Fiddling with the corner of her jam portion, Helen became exasperated as she couldn't get it open and resorted to trying to tear it with her teeth. When that didn't work, she began to stab it with her useless plastic knife, which bent in half in the process, before becoming aware of someone in her vicinity.

"Need a hand there? I could go and get one of my scalpels?"

Helen looked up and immediately felt her face turn beetroot. It was the guy she'd been chatting to the previous weekend, who just happened to be drop-dead gorgeous and, as it turned out, a surgeon? Or at the very least a doctor?

Caught totally off guard, Helen scrambled for something witty to say.

"Well, actually that might not be a bad idea. This is well and truly welded on. I didn't know you worked here?"

"Well, you wouldn't. You left in such a hurry last week I didn't get a chance to tell you much or for that matter find out anything about you."

"Aw, yeah. I'm really sorry about that. My friend wasn't well and I had to take her home pronto."

"That is a relief. I thought I had scared you off."

"No, not at all."

Helen positively squirmed now as she remembered her smelly feet and was sure he could smell them too. Shifting on her seat, she tried to sit on top of them to prevent the smell from escaping, only this made her look totally uncouth and she could feel a cramp developing in her calf muscle. *Damn, what's his name?* Helen desperately tried to recall but failed.

He stood watching her and she struggled to maintain eye contact, he was just too good looking.

"So are you not well?" he asked.

"Who me? No. Why do I look unwell? I'm just tired as I've just finished work. And I've got a cramp in my leg, but other than that I'm fine."

Helen started to fuss with her hair in an attempt to make herself look more presentable and then stretched her foot out in front of her, before quickly recoiling it as her foot went stupidly near drop-dead gorgeous doctor man.

"No, I just mean because you're at the hospital. Do you work here then? I've not seen you around here before. What department do you work in?"

"Oh no. I definitely don't work here. I would be fainting every two seconds. I was just doing a friend a favour by giving her a lift to visit someone. So are you a doctor or something?"

"You got me. Did the white coat give it away or was it the stethoscope?"

Helen cringed and then blushed some more. Trying to deflect from the red glow emanating from her face, she picked up her coffee and began to take a sip, burning her mouth in the process.

Then his beeper went off. "Damn, not again. Just getting to know you and now I get called away. Do you fancy going for a drink sometime, Helen?"

So surprised he knew her name, she almost spat her coffee over his pristine white coat. "Eh, yeah, that would be ok."

"Great. Meet you Friday night at the Mitch if you're free, say 8 pm?"

"Yeah, great."

"Gotta go, duty calls. See you Friday."

With that, he hurried off, leaving Helen sitting dumbstruck, unable to move, awed by all that had happened. She suddenly realised she still didn't know his name and, in her hurry to catch him up, she nearly fell off her chair. Scrambling to her feet, she raced after him down the corridor, keeping his white coat and languid strides in sight, her shoe-less feet slapping the plastic hospital floors.

"Hey!" she shouted, but he kept walking. Helen exerted her body to the max and got a little closer before trying again. "Hey, excuse me."

He did a half-turn over his shoulder and then, realising it was him that was being summoned, stopped and turned and smiled at her.

"Hey yourself ... missing me already?"

"No, well, erm, I just realised that I've ... um ... forgotten your name, sorry."

"I made such an impression on you the first time I see that

you couldn't even remember my name?" he said in jest. "It's Ed, Helen." With that, he gave her a smile then jogged off down the corridor looking at his bleeper as he did.

Helen stood watching, inadvertently touching her arm where his hand had touched her then he vanished behind the automatic doors.

"Holy fuck!" she said to no one as she sauntered back up the corridor, not caring that she had left her keys and bag on the chair for all to pilfer.

The journey home zipped past and, despite Isa giving her a blow by blow account of her visit to Mrs Turner, Helen could recall none of it. Instead, she was totally preoccupied with her doctor encounter.

After dropping Isa off, she couldn't wait to get upstairs and phone Wendy.

"Hello, it's me. Guess who I bumped into at the hospital tonight?" Helen rushed out in one breath to Wendy.

"The hospital? Why were you there? Are you not well?"

"No, I'm fine. Just guess who I bumped into?"

"No clues? I've no idea. Tell me."

"Remember that guy I was talking to last Friday night at the Mitch?"

"You seriously think I remember what happened last Friday night? I was so wined up I could barely remember my name. But do tell all, you sound as though you're going to burst."

"Well, before I had to take you home I was talking to this totally gorgeous guy. I was sitting tonight in the hospital cafeteria trying to get into my jam when he appeared in front of me in his doctor's uniform. He totally remembered me, my name and wants to meet me tomorrow night. Can you believe it?"

"Oh, my god. Why didn't you tell me about him before? Was he totally lush? What was his name? Check you going out with a doctor. What are you going to wear?" Wendy blabbed.

"I know. I can't believe it. Fuck, I actually didn't remember his name and had to ask … total cringe! It's Ed. He is wheetwoo hot though. Dark hair, dark eyes and one of those dodgy beards that guys seem to think are all the rage, but still hot. Never in a million years did I think I would see him again. You'll need to come round tomorrow and help me choose something to wear."

"Want me to come to the Mitch too?"

"Nooooo way. I'll be totally awkward. Oh my god, I'm so excited."

"So you should be. Look I need to go. See you tomorrow at about 5."

"Fab, you're a star."

"Sweet dreams."

"Ha, ha thanks."

25 Lucy

A mob of kids hovered obediently at the kerb, eyes on the luminous yellow figure as it stopped in the middle of the road, signalling to the motorists with an oversized lollypop to stop. Once they got the nod, they bolted across, making it safely to the other side. Motorists cautiously moved off once the roadway cleared, gathering speed to make up for the time lost. Lucy walked amongst the straggling line of kids making their way to school, absorbing their chatter as she went. Some still rubbed sleep out of their eyes or yawned their heads off. She was sure a wee boy, Alli, that she and Jane had played with the day before, still had his jammies on. She could just see the checked collar of a pj top peeking out beneath his wee jumper. Bags were slung over shoulders or dragged along the ground.

Lucy tugged hers to make sure it was secure over her shoulder and checked that the zip at the side was fully closed so her crisps for break didn't fall out, delighted her mum had given her a snack. It was surely a sign that today was going to be a good day. Her tummy felt full of the toast she'd enjoyed earlier, washed down with her sugary cup of tea. She noticed Stephanie from primary six enjoying her 'on the go' breakfast, although Lucy preferred cheese and onion. A school jotter went flying over Lucy's head and a shout of 'heids' went with it, followed by laughter. The jotter landed face down and open on the dirty pavement.

The owner of the jotter pushed past Lucy and stopped to pick it up, mumbling about the trouble he would get into from his teacher. More laughter followed. Lucy gave a wee smile at the carry on. A more subdued group walked on the other side of the street, chaperoned by mums, who tutted at the shenanigans, and shepherded their precious wee ones away from the rabble. Lucy decided she was glad she was on this side enjoying the rough and tumble.

Nearing the school gates, she saw the girls from her class playing at the wall and she sidled up to them, waiting for them to notice her. This didn't take long.

"Hi, Lucy. You feeling better?" Harley shouted. A puzzled look crossed Lucy's face.

"You were off yesterday. Do you no remember?" Harley clarified, backing her booming voice up with hand gestures just in case there was any confusion with what she meant. Lucy, understanding, nodded and wondered why everyone spoke so loudly to her.

"You want to play with us?" This time it was Robyn who spoke, slowly enunciating each word and dramatically emphasising with her hands.

Lucy nodded again. Oblivious as to why the girls were regarding her like this, she flung her bag down on top of the pile against the wall, bent down and picked up a stone and tried her best to get it near the bull's eye. A stroke of luck meant she got it right on target, receiving a few gasps and 'well dones'. Hearing the bell ring the girls stopped playing and shot off to the lines, trailing their bags behind them.

Lucy felt a funny feeling inside her tummy, not bad just funny, which went crazy when she heard Miss Kane's voice welcoming the kids into her class. Feeling shy all of a sudden, Lucy stopped dead outside the class door, her feet refusing to walk any further. Gary pushed past, nudging her shoulder, not understanding what she was doing.

"Eh, ye need to go through the door."

Lucy remained stock still and Gary tutted and went in and announced to Miss Kane that the "New lassie was standing in the way at the door."

Lucy's head ducked down and began carpet gazing and this time it was a bad feeling in her stomach.

"Ok, Gary, in you come, nice to see you. You mean Lucy is at the door? I'll go and see to her."

Lucy could hear Miss Kane walking towards the door, her heels clipping over the linoleum. She felt the warmth of Miss Kane's hand slide over her shoulder; could smell the sweetness of her perfume and feel her hair tickle her nose as it strayed past her face. Next, Miss Kane's eyes were down trying to meet her gaze, which was no easy feat. Lucy slowly lifted her head until her eyes met her teacher's.

"How lovely to see you back. Looking well too. Are you feeling better?"

Lucy nodded and put her hand inside her teacher's when she put it out in front of her. Securely attached, she walked into the class when asked and went over to her seat. The class was alive with chatter and Lucy could feel the excitement bubbling up from the other kids. From the corner of her eye, she became aware of something colourful bobbing in the air. Turning her head fully, she saw a large bunch of balloons being held hostage, their desperate attempts to escape hampered by the thin straggly lines of string.

"I'm so glad you're here the day, Lucy, cause it is lucky Friday, the day."

Lucy tilted her head to the side and scrunched her face. "Lucky Friday?" Jane reiterated "Do you no know what that is? Have you no done it in your other school?"

Lucy shook her head. Jane began to tell Lucy all about the ins and outs of 'lucky Friday' but was stopped mid-flow by their teacher.

"Ok, everyone, I think there is just a little too much chattering going on in here this morning. Let's settle down."

"Miss, when are you going to see who the lucky person is?"

Gary asked.

"Soon, Gary, soon. Now, not everyone will know what lucky Friday is. Lucy, have you heard of it before?"

Lucy shook her head again and Miss Kane continued. "Ok, let me see ... Nicole, can you explain to Lucy what happens?"

"Aye, miss. Well, each Friday a balloon is popped and inside is someone's name. If it's your name then you are the special person the whole of the next week and you get to bring your mum and dad up tae the class for juice and biscuits and play games and have lots of fun and I really hope it's me this week."

"Thank you, Nicole. That was well explained. Ok, I'm going to put you all out of your misery and pop the balloons now. This week we are going to pop two. Rachael, you pop one and I'm going to pop one."

The kids sat in total silence waiting to see whose name was inside. Rachael carefully chose a red balloon and took the pin from Miss Kane. Despite knowing the balloon was going to be popped, a few individuals still yelped and jumped as they heard the bang. The scrolled-up piece of paper was fired under a table and a swarm developed as everyone dived for it. George triumphantly waved it in the air and the class was calmed so he could be heard reading out the name.

"It is Alan!" George turned to his friend sitting behind him and gave him the thumbs up. Alan punched the air with his fist shouting: "Yes, I'm going tae bring ma gran, miss."

"That is fine, Alan. It will be lovely to see her. Ok, let's see who the next lucky person is. Oh, I wonder which one I will pick."

Making a show out of which balloon to choose the kids got noisier and noisier. Clutching a purple balloon in her hand, Miss Kane shot a quick glance over at Lucy. Lucy was transfixed by the goings-on and the fun everyone was having. She watched as Miss Kane pierced the balloon and swiftly bent down to grab the paper. Unfurling the scroll, she shot a look around everyone before resting her eyes on Lucy. "It is you, Lucy. You are my second lucky person. Well done. You can ask mum to school on Monday. Ok?"

Lucy enthusiastically nodded and a smile spread across her lips from the inside out.

26 Connor

Hayley nudged him under the table and Connor looked just in time to see her puffing her cheeks out and shaking her head, mimicking the teacher. A silent snigger crumpled Connor's face as he did his best to go undetected by the 'Gallows'. He just wished she would do one for the day and leave him in peace. Everything was going quite smoothly, and if his teacher would just disappear things would be perfect. Sitting next to Hayley, he struggled to keep his mind on anything else. Every time she shuffled in her chair he just hoped her arm, in fact, any part of her anatomy, would touch him. He kept his body leaning to one side of his chair to make this more likely. She was amazing. Nothing seemed to phase her.

He had been on a downer, as he'd walked past her house twice that morning before deciding that he must have missed her. He had gone through the shortcut at the back of the school, over the rocky path strewn with a plethora of unsavoury used items. But it turned out that his downer was for nothing.

He couldn't believe his luck when his scouring eyes found her unmistakable blonde hair up ahead of him as he neared the school. His stomach had flipped and swirled like the avalanche of pennies cascading down at the penny falls at an arcade.

Once he had spotted her, he ached to go and be beside her. His legs just wouldn't take him. Staring at the back of her head, he willed her turn round and notice him. Stupidly, he took a 'reddy' when she did and instead of saying something smart as he had rehearsed in his head, he just gawked awkwardly until she shouted him over. He could hardly speak, worrying he would say something wrong, but it didn't matter as Hayley chatted effortlessly, making him glow as they walked to school.

A knock at the classroom door shattered his daydream as a male teacher walked in.

"Yesss!" Hayley whispered not too quietly under her breath, causing the 'Gallows' to cast her a glare.

"What is it?" Connor whispered, delighted to have something to say to Hayley that sounded semi-normal.

"Mr Hay … means he is taking us for the rest of the day so 'Gallows' does her teaching stuff. Happens every Friday, I totally forgot."

Connor's body slid down his chair as a feeling of total relaxation spread over him. It didn't matter that he had no idea what this teacher was like, he just knew he couldn't be as bad as his present one.

"You look happy," Hayley beamed at him.

"Aye, I am."

Mrs Gallows gathered a box of books and jotters and made her way over to the door, stopping at Connor's table. In a feeble attempt at asserting her authority, Mrs Gallows said, "Mr Hay, I don't know if you have had the pleasure of meeting our new pupil, Connor?"

"No, I don't believe I have."

"Well you're in for a real treat is all I can say. Enjoy."

Laughing as she left the room, Connor managed to stifle the 'fuck off' that was about to fly off his lips and smack her on the face.

"Connor, I'm Mr Hay. It is lovely to meet you. Did Mrs Gallows tell you I cover her class every Friday?"

"Eh, no."

"Well I do. We do lots of hard maths and language, don't we everyone?" Mr Hay looked round the class for some confirmation and was met instead with smiling, laughing faces. "Listen, as long as you try your best, you and I will get along fine, ok?"

"Eh, aye."

"Great. Ok, kids, let's get the computers out, maths games out and get some of this hard work done."

Connor sat unsure what to do and watched the others happily move about getting their equipment sorted. Mrs Gallows hardly let him move his bum cheek to fart, never mind get out of his seat.

"Come on, you. Are you just going tae sit there all day? Come and get a laptop and we'll play this cool game."

"Aye ok."

Following Hayley, he kept sending sly glances over to Mr Hay to ensure he wasn't going to get roared at. But he was halfway across the class and all he'd had back from him was a smile. *Amazing*, Connor thought. The next half hour was possibly the best half-hour Connor had ever had in school. Sitting right next to Hayley *and* playing a game. Hayley gave him a total slagging for the shite score he got, but he could hardly concentrate being so close to her. His heart skipped a beat every time she squeezed his hand when he got a question right. The bell went for break and there was a stampede to be first outside.

Hayley grabbed his hand. "Come on, let's get tae the play park first."

Running after her, he sprinted round to the side of the school and jumped over the metal railing just missing the spikes at the top. Grabbing the edge of the slide, he pulled himself up it and waited for Hayley to go through the gate.

"You're lucky you never punctured your arse on that fence, you tube." She grinned. "Here do you want a crisp?"

Connor shoved his hand inside the crisp packet. "I'll race you up tae the top!" Connor shouted.

"Right, you're on."

The two climbed up the interconnected wire ropes, Connor

bouncing on each wire making the whole thing shake. Younger kids lower down began to scream as they wobbled, clinging on for dear life. Connor rapidly reached the top and punched the sky triumphantly. Hayley staggered up behind, clutching her open bag of crisps.

"Aye, well done," she puffed out. "Let's go and sit on the bench."

"Watch out, youse!"

Connor leapt off from the midway point, landing in the squelchy bark below, putting two wet, dirty circles on his knees. Securing a place on the bench he waited for Hayley to join him.

"You're a nutter, jumping off that."

"How? It's a soft landing?" He grinned back at her.

"Check it out. If it's no the two love birds? What you doing hanging around with him, Hayley?"

So engrossed in being with Hayley, Connor didn't notice Jenny and her wee possy making their way over. He immediately felt his hackles go up and his face flushing red in response.

"What is it tae you anyway?' Hayley asked. "You just cannae keep yer neb out other folk's business, can you?"

"You're hanging around with nitty boy? Thought you would have better sense, gads."

Connor stood up but was quickly pulled back down by Hayley.

"Just ignore her. She's no worth it. Think she forgets that she's had a nitty head or two herself."

"No, I haven't?" Jenny screeched back. "So I've no?" She turned for backup from her two supporters who just looked. "Anyway, at least I've no got a retard as a sister."

Connor's buttons were well and truly pressed by this point and he leapt up and stood right in Jenny's face, causing her to scream in alarm. His chest had puffed out like a chicken's after a good preening and Jenny had to reaffirm her connection with the ground, by putting her foot back.

"You better fucking watch yourself on your way home the night, 'cause you're going tae be dead meat."

Finding some bravado in the safety of the playground, she retorted, "Aye, right, we'll see. I'm going tell ma cousin, he's in the academy."

"Good. See you after school. Oh, and by the way my sister is'nae a retard."

Connor let his shoulder thump against hers as he walked past, sending her sideways into her pal. The group of onlookers parted the circle they had created round the show and let him walk off, his eyes glaring at anyone that looked. Hayley tottered behind, trying to keep up just as the bell went.

"Get into line, Hayley!" shouted the classroom assistant.

Hayley opened her mouth, her hand pointing in the direction Connor had just travelled but, thinking better of it, shut it quickly and made her way to the back of the queue. Passing Jenny, she let her eyes do the talking.

Connor stood in the boy's toilet, his fist throbbing from where he'd smashed it against the brick wall on the way in. He sneered into the scratched and faded mirror and sabotaged himself with a hefty mental beating: *'you're ugly/you've got nits/nae body likes you/you cannae read/your mum cannae be bothered with you/your sisters a retard ...'* The barrage of insults kept flying and he could feel himself sinking deeper and deeper. Hanging onto the edge of the sink, he battered the pipes with his feet, the self-inflicted pain not even registering. Kids noisily filed in from outside, chattering and laughing as they pushed and shoved past the toilet door. Every so often, the door would push open slightly as someone fell against it on the way past. Connor didn't hear Hayley shout through after him and he only came to his senses when she stuck her head round the door.

"What are you doing? Are you losing it? Come on, don't let her bother you."

She cocked her head towards the door, and he slowly, without thinking, released his grip on the sink and followed her faithfully back to the classroom.

Mr Hay approached him as he entered the class. "Can I have a wee word outside Connor? Nothing to worry about."

Shrugging his shoulders, Connor retraced his steps back out the door and stood with his back to the wall and eyes on the floor.

"Are you ok? I heard a few whispers that a certain somebody was winding you up."

Connor made no attempt at replying, his head so full of self-loathing and turmoil that he couldn't produce anything sensible to say. Sensing his pain, the teacher put his arm on his shoulder. Connor froze awkwardly, hardly daring to breathe. The teacher continued talking.

"Listen, why don't you go into the class get a laptop and play a game. Once you've sorted yourself out, you know where I am if you want to talk, ok?"

Connor managed a nod and reluctantly trailed his feet into the classroom, feeling all twenty-seven pairs of eyes boring into him as he went to the laptop trolley and removed one from its shelf. Managing to not engage with anyone, he sat himself down at his desk and tried to switch himself off from his peers and the mess inside his head.

So caught up in his own affairs, he hadn't noticed Jane from his sister's class coming in with a note for his teacher. "Earth to Connor, earth to Connor?" Mr Hay jokingly said, receiving giggles from the class.

After a nudge to the ribs from Kyle, Connor slowly realised he was being spoken to.

"A note here from Miss Kane, Connor. You have to go and see her at lunchtime, ok?'

"Eh, aye."

Connor could feel his cheeks flushing red for at least the

second time that day. Not enjoying being the centre of attention, he ducked his head back down and busied himself with his laptop, wondering what she might want. Scouring his mind, he couldn't think of anything he'd done wrong that might involve her, and if it was Lucy he would have heard her if it was anything major. The bell went for lunch and his thoughts moved onto what he might get for eating.

As he headed for the door, Mr Hay shouted him back. Not wanting to be delayed in filling his belly, he skipped out with a group of boys, pretending not to hear his name being called. As he reached the corridor, Mrs Barr shouted the primary seven class to go first for lunch and Connor raced up the corridor, deftly moving ahead of the other boys, his stomach commanding to be fed and fast. First in the queue, he picked up a tray and requested the ubiquitous Friday fish and chips followed by apple crumble. *Not bad for a school dinner*, he thought.

Plonking himself at the end of the long line of tables, he hoped to be left alone, but wee Alec bounced up beside him. "Friday fish and chips, ma favourite," Alec said to Connor.

Connor jerked his head by way of agreeance.

"What've you to go to see Miss Kane about?"

Connor, in no mood for chatting, shrugged his shoulders, gulped what was left of his lunch then cleared his tray off the table and made his way to Miss Kane's class. Reaching her door he peered through the glass panel and noticed Lucy was there before him. He reticently chapped the door and, when he heard Miss Kane answering, pushed it open.

"Well, if it isn't our very own Connor. How are you?" Miss Kane enquired.

"Fine, miss."

"I'm so glad you could join us. I missed your help yesterday."

Not knowing how to answer, he made a grunting noise with his throat. Wondering if he was going to get into bother for not being at school the previous day, he hovered, unsure of what he should be doing.

"Well never mind, I'm just glad you are both here and are both feeling better. Now could you help me put these paintings into the art folder like Lucy is doing?"

"Aye."

Relieved he was only there to help, Connor set to work, helping his sister match up the names on the paintings with the names on the art folders. Miss Kane busied herself about the class tidying and chatting away to them. Connor visibly relaxed and soon forgot the incident at playtime. Lucy all of a sudden jumped up from her chair, giving Connor a start.

"What are you doing?" he exclaimed.

Lucy ran over to Miss Kane and began pointing at the balloons, the excitement evident from every crevice of her body.

"Oh, that's right, Lucy. Will we tell Connor and he can ask mum? What a good idea."

"What?" Connor enquired. He had noticed the balloons bobbing in the corner of the room when he'd first entered but hadn't bothered to give them much thought. Miss Kane explained it all to him.

"So do you think mum will come up on Monday?"

Connor noticed how excited even Miss Kane was, her eyes shining brightly as she spoke, hands waving in the air explaining how exciting it would be for Lucy if mum came up. He looked at Lucy, knowing she knew in her heart there wasn't a chance in hell of mum making her way up here by herself. Lucy looked back at him, imploring him with those deep dark wells, desperate for him to say what she wanted to hear.

"Aye, maybe.' The lack of conviction in his voice seemingly went unnoticed by Lucy as she managed a grin. But his heart ached with the uselessness of it all. He continued doing his job, but with a gnawing in his stomach as he remembered the crappiness of his life. He just didn't understand why his mum thought the way she did. Maybe Jenny was right after all; he was living with retards, not just his sister, but his mum as well. It had been ages since they had seen or heard from him, but mum was still convinced he was round every corner, behind every closed door, at the end of every phone call waiting to get them.

His mind enjoyed taking him on a wee jaunt to happier times – it was usually the Friday night trip that he recalled. Dad would come home from work smelling of oil, black stains smeared down the front of his overalls that he was made to peel off standing gingerly on the bristly, jaggy doormat, hopping from one foot to the next as he released his foot from each leg. Connor would run to his dad and he would ruffle his hair and call him a 'wee champ', the rough calluses scraping across his forehead. Dad would then bend down gather his grubby overalls and stuff them into the machine and mum would load up the drawer with the clean smell of washing powder as his dad kissed her on the back of the head before going to the sink and using the 'green slime', as Connor called it, to get the rest of the grime away from his hands. Dad then went through and picked his wee sister up out of her bouncy chair and twirled her in the air, his eyes locked on hers as her giggles escaped with excitement. Connor would have by this point been desperate to get in on the action and would attempt to crawl up his dad's legs, wanting a shot of his attention.

His happy trip was cut short as Miss Kane brought him back into the room as she patted his shoulders.

Just as well, Connor thought, as he knew how the story ended and it wasn't no fairy-tale.

27 Helen

Helen looked back at Connor and wondered if his nonchalance about the special day for his sister was because he felt a little left out and jealous. She had been so sure this would delight not just Lucy, but also Connor. It now seemed like Connor's mood was rubbing off on Lucy as she sat next to her brother, the excitement slowly ebbing from her. How Helen wished she could do something more to help this poor wee family. The pain emitting from the two was tangible.

Walking past him, she patted his bony shoulders, feeling the tension wrapped beneath them. He sat stock-still, unsure of how to react.

"Is everything ok Connor?" she asked.

"Aye," he replied predictably.

"You know if I can help with anything I will? Is mum ok?"

Helen caught Lucy flick her eyes up towards her brother. He sat motionless in his chair.

"Aye."

"Goo ..." The end of her reply was drowned by the shrill of the bell. Dropping his job, Connor pushed his chair back, scraping it noisily along the linoleum. He stood as if waiting for an instruction.

"Thanks for your help, Connor. Will you remember and say to mum? I've put a wee note in Lucy's bag too."

Nodding, he turned and made his way to the door. Helen watched his wee, thin child's body full of adult problems make its way to the door. His feet almost scuffed along the ground. *Poor wee guy*, she thought.

As he opened the door, she heard Mrs Barr's calm voice instructing the kids to make their way along the corridor quietly, the noise dropping as the kids spotted their 'head' watching their entrance. Deciding to seize the moment, Helen made her way to her class door and caught Mrs Barr's attention, and asked her for a quick word.

"What are they like? A herd of elephants would be quieter. Still, it's our favourite day of the week. How can I help, Helen?"

"Just my usual headache, Rosie. Lucy and probably more so, Connor. He in particular just looks miserable. I've never seen a child look so ... despondent and depressed ... is the word I would use. Have you had any luck with social services?"

"I'm afraid not. They seem to have no record of them, which does seem strange. How is the head situation?" Rosie whispered so as not to embarrass Lucy who was busy tidying the art trolley.

"Better, but not cured. Any luck getting a hold of mum?"

"Again, no I'm afraid. Carol has tried several times."

"I had rigged my special balloon day so Lucy won, but judging by Connor's response to the request of telling his mum about it, I don't think we should hold our breath."

The door of the classroom swung open, announcing the arrival of primary four. A group of boys fell in the door laughing and carrying on, full of the Friday afternoon spirit, totally oblivious to the guest in their room. Helen and Rosie watched them fooling around and then, one by one as they realised they had more of an audience than they had bargained for, regained their composure and found their seats with a ruddy glow emanating from their cheeks.

Smirking privately to Helen, Rosie then turned to address the class: "Well I'm glad to see some of us have lots of energy left for all the work Miss Kane has planned for you." After raising her eyebrows at the three boys in question, she turned and left the class, leaving the boys decidedly uncomfortable in their seats.

Helen, wanting to have a quick and easy afternoon in preparation for her exciting evening, had planned a fun-filled afternoon to minimise her stress. She could feel the butterflies in her stomach beginning to dance as she anticipated her evening ahead. Her outfit had just about been finalised. She had tried it on in her head and was going for the shabby chic look in a bid to look cool, calm and collected – not that she felt anywhere near that, more like shit scared and skitterish.

So obsessed with her evening she was oblivious to the noise levels and general carrying on of her children and they all had a great afternoon. The 3 pm bell couldn't come quick enough and once the last of her little class were out of the room, Helen grabbed her things and made a beeline for the door. Tonight, was going to be a quick sharp exit.

"Good luck for tonight. Don't do anything I wouldn't do ..." Linda joked as Helen zipped past.

"Ha, thanks. See you Monday."

"I'm expecting an update before then, missy!"

"Will do!"

Running down the front stairs, she gently moved some stragglers to the side so she could get on her way. Nearing the bottom step, she was aware of some raised voices over by the gates, a group of children and adults were congregated under the branches of the towering oak tree. Not wanting to get involved, she ducked her head down, trying to feign total unawareness to the goings-on. That was until she heard her name being hollered.

"Haw, Miss Kane, Miss Kane!"

Swearing quietly, Helen looked up, putting on a good show of wondering where the shout was coming from, then a little more drama as she put on a concerned face and voice. "Ms Carter, I didn't see you there. Everything ok?" thinking *of course it isn't ok* – 'Ms Carter', as she liked to be known, was one of the biggest shit stirrers around and things were rarely ok if she was involved.

"Naw, it's no ok. Me and all they other mothers are sick fed up with our weans getting nits. And ma Sophie told me it wis that wee minger over there that wis the cause."

Following her finger, Helen looked over and saw Lucy standing with her back to the group of kids and mums, surrounded and shaking like a leaf.

"Oh my god." Helen ran over to Lucy, pushing the kids and mums out the way. "Right everyone I think you should all go home. I don't know what you've done, but you've certainly terrified this child enough today."

Searching for an ally, she spotted the janitor and told him to go and get Mrs Barr.

"What do you mean? I think you should ban her from the school, infecting ma poor wee Sophie. This is no the first time you know."

"Ms Carter, this is not the way to deal with any issue. This is bullying."

"What? Are you calling me a bully?"

Sensing Ms Carter's hackles rising, Helen got Lucy and began making her way towards the door, but Ms Carter, now enraged, followed. Mrs Barr's voluptuous figure filled the door and, sensing the problem immediately, showed the antithesis of her usual quiet voice, shocking everyone in the process.

"Ladies, I'm not quite sure what is going on here, but I see a very distressed child and that is my priority. And to say that I am enraged by what I have seen is an understatement. Please make a line at the door if you wish to speak to me, once I have dealt with the needs of this little one. And I can assure you if I don't speak to you today, I will be speaking to you all soon." Her booming voice stopped the group of kids and most of their parents in their tracks, bringing them to their senses. Not Ms Carter, however.

"Ah think you'll find that all this is her fault, or at least her mother's."

"Ms Carter, if you wish to speak to me, please wait at the door and I will get to you as soon as I can."

Being put in her place didn't sit well with Ms Carter. She turned to her supporters to find them all making their way towards the gate and their cars on the road. Having lost her back up, Ms Carter called her beloved Sophie over to her, ranted a wee bit more before promising it wasn't the last they'd heard of her.

"Nor is this the last you've heard from me, Ms Carter. Rest assured I will be in touch," Mrs Barr retorted.

Rosie put a protective arm around Lucy and Helen and ushered them inside.

"What on earth was that all about? You poor thing, Lucy. Come and we will get you sorted out."

Lucy's whole body shook and the wee thing was clearly in shock.

"Helen, I'm sorry, but I'm going to have to keep you for a wee while so you can write a report of what happened, just in case this goes further. That damn woman. Where is Connor?"

"I'm not sure. He usually walks Lucy home."

Lucy was in no fit state to comprehend what was going on she was so utterly terrified. She sat on the sofa in the head teacher's office, staring blankly into the carpet in front of her. She hugged herself and rocked ever so slightly backwards and forwards.

"Do you think we should try calling mum?" Helen asked.

"We will try, but I'm not sure that we will get anywhere. To tell you the truth, I'm not quite sure what I should do. Let's try a wee drink and biscuit for Lucy. Ask Carol to try and get a hold of mum. I am so angry. Ms Carter has well and truly crossed the line. I am not letting Ms damn Carter get away with this. Harassing a poor child."

Mrs Barr began rummaging in her biscuit tin to find something sweet to tempt Lucy out of her shock. Helen set to the tasks she had been delegated.

Fingers flying across the keyboard in the front office, Helen typed as quickly as she could so her memories of the incident did not allude to her, and to speed her exit from school. She was aware of Carol making several attempts to get a hold of Ms Jackson, with no success. Helen jumped as the office door unexpectedly flew open and a very flustered Connor landed in the office, panting heavily from running.

"Where is she?"

"Connor, I'm so pleased to see you. Lucy is fine. She is with Mrs Barr getting a wee drink. How did you know she was here?"

"Kyle telt me she was battered by Sophie's maw? I'm going tae get her," he exhaled.

He punched the door with his hand, his face scrunched with the anger emanating from his skinny body.

"Connor, nothing like that happened. One of the parents acted in a very wrong way, but Mrs Barr is dealing with it. Come through and we'll see Lucy."

Helen chapped the door and stuck her head round, advising of Connor's arrival.

"Excellent, bring him in."

Connor went straight over to his sister and bent in front of her. Holding her head, he made her look into his eyes. The bond between them was evident and made both the women's eyes fill. A very different Connor crouched in front of them, one much older than his years, playing a role that just shouldn't have been his.

Lucy slowly focused on his face. The rocking stopped and after a couple of seconds the realisation of who it was seemed to sink in. Throwing her arms round his neck, they embraced, before Connor pulled away, suddenly aware of his audience. Patting her back he pulled her up by the hand, and made his way to the door.

Rosie spoke first. "Connor, I need to ask Lucy a few questions and I would really like to speak to mum. I've been trying to get her on the phone. Is she working or something?"

He awkwardly stopped in the middle of the room, looking from Lucy to Mrs Barr. Lucy looked back at her brother, waiting for his lead. Standing up from her desk, Mrs Barr ushered them back to the sofa.

"She is at home. She's no feeling well."

"Ok, we will deal with that in a minute. Lucy I'm going to ask you some questions and I need you to answer them as best as you can."

"Just nod or shake your head Lucy as we do in class," Helen advised.

Lucy nodded.

"Ok, Lucy. What happened out there should never have happened and I am going to do my very best to sort it out, ok? Tell me, did anyone touch you when you were in the playground?"

Lucy shook her head.

"Did they come over to you?"

Lucy nodded.

"Did they shout at you?"

Lucy nodded again.

"Ok, Lucy, thank you. I promise, I'm going to do my very best to sort this out, ok? Now I think I will drive you pair home, so I can speak to mum. She needs to know what happened."

"I'll tell her miss, it's ok. I'm going tae walk hame with Lucy. She'll be fine, honestly."

"Connor, I would rather take you home. Lucy has been given a fright and I need to let mum know."

"I'll tell her. Come on, Lucy," Connor said grabbing his sister's arm.

"Connor, please don't worry. Everything will be fine. I'm just going to give you a lift home, nothing to worry about. I'll have a quick word with mum at the door, ok? Come on, let's go."

"Write a letter, I'll give her it."

"No, Connor. Please listen to Mrs Barr. You don't need to worry; we just want you to be safe."

Connor reluctantly agreed and followed Mrs Barr to the door, Lucy holding his hand. Helen's phone began to ring. Fetching her bag, she rummaged in the bottom of it until she eventually found it, by which point the call had stopped. Clearing the locked screen, she saw she had a missed call from Wendy and it was then she saw the time.

"Damn!" she muttered. Grabbing her things, she ran to the door. The car park had long been deserted by now and her wee red car sat alone, neatly between the two allocated white lines. Making the short journey home in record time, she abandoned her car on the street below her flat, luckily finding a place close to the entry door. She spied Wendy's car and saw her friend sitting in the driver's seat, head down busy on her phone. As Helen neared the car, her friend looked up, giving her a smile whilst pointing to the imaginary watch on her wrist.

Helen went straight for her closed door and heard the squeak of her friend's car door as she flung it open to follow her upstairs.

"You're cutting it a bit fine, are you no? Hard day at the office?"

"Something like that. God, I am so not going to be ready on time. I've not even washed my hair. Fuck!" Helen said as she gave her watch another glance.

"Your hair looks fine to me," Wendy said after picking up the ends and examining them as Helen made her way up the stairs.

"You have got to be joking me! Second-day hair going on here. I'd rather call it off than be seen with it like this."

Helen scrabbled with her keys and eventually got her door open. Flinging down her bag on the couch, she began to strip off as she made her way to the bathroom.

"Listen, you've got plenty of time. It's good to be fashionably late. I'll pour you a glass of wine while you're in the shower," Wendy told her, pulling out a couple of wine glasses.

"Aw, you're a star!"

Helen reappeared in the doorway, her hair cocooned in a towel balanced on top of her head. Picking up her wine glass, she gulped a large mouthful.

Helen's face scrunched as the wine hit her taste buds.

"Sorry, I'm skint. I had to grab the cheapest shit on the shelf, but it's 14%, it'll do the trick."

Gulping it down, Helen felt the alcohol hit her empty stomach and went for a swift, second gulp.

"It's got the aroma and taste of a well-aged basket of potpourri with the after-hit of fuckin paint stripper."

"Who do you think you are, some French wine geezer? Get it doon your neck and yer patter'll be like watter," Wendy replied.

"Aye, it is doing the trick, but fuck I think ma guts are being burnt alive. Right, I'm going to get changed, please be honest. Actually, scrap that, if you don't like it, don't tell me as I've spent all afternoon working it out and I really have nothing else to wear."

"Aye, right, you've more clothes than Imelda Marcos has shoes. Anyway, you would look fab in a bin bag. Get another swig down you and chill."

Following Wendy's instructions, she stole another quick drink and went to get a quick shower and towel off, in between grabbing gulps of wine. Breathing in, she fought to get the top button closed on her jeans and was grateful she'd decided to wear a long top that covered all her jelly bits. Getting out her favourite boots she pulled them on and inspected herself in the mirror and smiled at what she saw.

"Right, what do ya think?"

"Perfect, not too over the top, just perfect. Right, come and I'll tame those locks for you and put some slap on you."

The pair shouted at each other as they competed with the noise of the hairdryer, filling each other in on their day's news. Blemishes covered and colour slapped on in record time, Helen was done.

"Right go and have a gander and tell me what you think," Wendy told her.

"Aw, I love it. You are a genius with a set of brushes. God, ma heart is pounding."

"Be yourself and you'll be fine. I want plenty of sneaky under the table text updates."

"Here goes nothing. Stay and finish your wine."

Helen air-kissed her friend then tottered out the door, laughing as her friend wolf-whistled at her.

Reaching the door of the pub, Helen snuck a look at her reflection in the glass door, then pushed the door open. Scanning the room, she couldn't see him and her heart sank. Taking a walk further in and still not seeing him, she began to retreat, feeling like a total fool and imagining every set of eyes following her. *The dumb ass without a date.* Reaching up to pull the door open, she could feel her face flushing red. By her watch, it was quite a bit later than the planned meeting time and cursed Ms Carter for ruining her chances of ever finding a date. Stumbling down the stairs at the front of the pub, she pulled out her phone, then decided she wasn't ready for telling Wendy about her epic fail.

A car horn tooted beside her, but being lost in her own misery she never even lifted her head. A car door slammed and a voice shouted her name.

Turning her head, she tried to work out where the voice came from then turned fully as footsteps sounded behind her. And there he was, panting out of breath from trying to catch her, but looking rather suave in a pair of scruffy jeans and a t-shirt.

"Helen, shit I'm sooo sorry. An emergency at work. Will you please forgive me and come for a drink?"

Like I even need to think about that, Helen thought. Giving one of her best smiles, she tilted her head to the side and said, "Maybe."

He grabbed her hand and they made their way back up the steps to the pub and headed straight for the bar.

28 Lucy

Squirming on the makeshift bed with her hand between her legs, Lucy prodded her mum, trying to wake her. She was too afraid to go to the toilet alone, daylight having not yet replaced the darkness. Shadows created by the orange hue of the street lamps outside merged and moved when she dared take a peek. Whimpering quietly to herself, she eventually felt the hot stream seep down between her legs, helpless in being able to stop it once it started. Somewhat relieved, she felt around the floor beside the couch and found a jumper that she quickly pulled up under the duvet, arranging it over the worst of the wetness. Mum lay undisturbed, oblivious to her daughter's distress. Huddling in next to mum, she closed her eyes and willed herself back to sleep.

When she next awoke, it was proper morning, the shafts of light filtering through the makeshift curtains in a haphazard fashion alerting her of its arrival. Shivering from lying in her own dampness all night, Lucy pushed herself off the couch and pulled her wet knickers off, letting them lie where they dropped. Next was her t-shirt. Prickled with goosebumps, she went in search of some clothes and, finding a bag, rustled through it until she found what she needed. The flat felt quieter than usual that morning, mum lying out for the count on the couch. The only clue of her still being alive was when she put her ear up close and heard the faint sound of her breath exhaling from her nostrils. Her still body was like a heron she'd once seen down at the river. She remembered watching him for ages as he stood motionless waiting for a fish to pass by standing resolutely, on his long, twig-like legs. She'd been completely transfixed by his stillness.

The bedroom door remained firmly shut and as quiet as it had been from the night before. Moving silently across the floor, Lucy pushed the door to the bedroom open. Her brother was curled up in the middle of the big bed, covers crumpled all around him. Willing him to open his eyes, she stood and stared, but when that gained no response she left as quietly as she'd entered, managing to squeeze the door shut without a creak. Her rumbling stomach sent her in search of something to eat.

Opening the cupboard door, she found an open packet of custard creams. The first few had been eaten and the packet twisted shut again to try and keep their freshness. Pulling out three, she sat cross-legged on the floor and set about eating them. First, she nibbled round the outside. Then she prised the two halves apart and ate the side without the filling first. Then leaving the best until last, she licked the cream off the remaining part. She ran what was left of the biscuit over her bottom teeth, leaving teeth marks in the thin, hard layer of cream. The next two were devoured in the same manner.

Hunger briefly sated, she wondered what to do next.

Her heart pounding at the decision she had made, she stealthily stood up and edged her way to the main door, stupidly waiting for her mum or brother to stop her. When that didn't happen, she gingerly lowered the handle of the door and pulled, jarring it against the lock. The noise it made gave her a fright and she froze, holding the handle halfway down before slowly releasing it back to its usual state. Turning the key, she released the lock and swiftly opened the door, closing it behind her before she skipped quickly down the steps, without looking back. As she went out the back door, she saw the spot she and Jane had been playing in the previous day and was delighted to see her wee house still intact. Racing over, she busied herself sorting out the leaves and the stones into the correct order in her kitchen and made breakfast for her two 'friends', who were as quiet as she was.

Lucy hadn't noticed how quiet it was out in the street. She hadn't noticed how few cars there were about or how few houses had their curtains open. Content in her own wee world she was oblivious too to the man in the car quietly watching her.

Before long the street began to waken from its slumber ready to face the world for another day. Bin lids were slammed shut as rubbish was turfed, the rattling bottles alerting the world of the goings on the night before. Doors closed as workers set off for their unfortunate Saturday shift. A girl in a short dress tottered past where Lucy played, just heading home from her night out. Makeup that had been painstakingly troweled on, now askew across her face, streaks of black surrounding her eyes. Hearing the clatter of high heels, Lucy looked up and for the first time took note of her surroundings. Her gaze followed the girl until she rounded the corner.

Lucy then felt spurred to move from her play spot. Standing up, she glanced back up at her flat window and, seeing nothing, began to walk down towards the pier. Jumping down onto the rocks, she scrabbled along, clambering over the rocks in search of smaller stones to throw in the water, all the while moving further away from the pier and her street. A dog ran along the beach just in front of her and she stopped and watched it. It ran first one way then without warning turned and ran the other. Then it stopped and took a bite of the dark sand, sending grains flying everywhere as it tossed its head back.

Lucy smiled as she watched it having so much fun. Jumping down off the rocks, she followed the paw prints left by the dog that led her to the sea. Kicking off her shoes, she paddled in the water. The icy cold sea made her feet tingle, she was definitely awake now. She waded in further and jumped the waves, quickly attempting to pull her leggings up before she became completely drenched. It didn't take long for the cold sea to seep into her wee thin bones, causing her whole body to shake. Retreating from the waves, she made her way back along the beach towards the rocks then realised she was much further along than she had thought. Freezing and feeling overwhelmed at the distance she had to walk back, she sank her shivering body down onto the rocks, wrapped her arms around her drawn-up legs, and tucked her head down to retract some warmth from her chilled body.

Out the corner of her eye, she saw a man approaching her. She watched as he awkwardly clambered over the rocks, unsure if he was coming towards her or if the unevenness of the rocks were sending him on a wild goose chase to get to his destination. His hood was up and she couldn't make out his face.

She saw him look over his shoulder and then back round. Then the smell hit her – almost as if the wind had sent it her way as a warning. It slapped her senses awake; spun her back in time to a memory she had firmly lodged into the depths of her being - a memory that was now hazy and maybe not even real. But despite this, it engulfed her with a feeling that made her want to bolt as far away from this approaching figure as possible.

Tripping and falling as she moved, she tried to scream, but no sound came out. She heard him speak, but was so lost in her own world, she couldn't hear what he was saying. Being nimble, she quickly made it over the rocks and hauled herself up the wall and through the metal railings, not even acknowledging the bump her head received from the cold metal. Her shivering body was now forgotten. On reaching the promenade, Lucy ran all the way along it, not looking back, the bareness of her feet not even registering as they hit the hard pavement below.

Unable to keep up with Lucy, the man instead had to watch as she raced off. He turned and saw two dog walkers who were watching the goings-on. He shrugged; held his hands up in denial.

Hammering up the close stairs, Lucy flew through the door and slammed it shut, shaking as she tried to lock it.

29 Connor

The slamming door finally roused Connor from his bed, quicker than he anticipated as he fearfully thought of who could be shutting the door like that when it was just the three of them here. Seeing Lucy and the state she was in, he ran to her.

"What the fuck is it now?" He had his hand round her shoulders as she sat on the floor, her back against the door, tears streaming down her face.

"Were you outside?"

He watched as Lucy nodded. Looking down, he saw that her red leggings were soaking wet and her feet were bare. Sand clung to the tops of her feet, whilst the rest had escaped onto the floor below.

"Were you at the beach?" Lucy nodded again, and Connor shook his head in disbelief. "What has got intae you? Gonnae no do that. Did you get in bother with someone?"

Lucy shrugged her shoulders.

"What does that mean? You're greeting like a baby, but you don't know why?" Lucy pushed his arm off her shoulder and went through to the living room and sought solace from the body of her mother. Connor watched as she hid her head under the blanket and curled herself into her wee ball.

"Fucking nut jobs, the two of you. Her last night, now you. I'm out of here," Connor shouted, not that either of them reacted to what he had said. "Bloody hell, Lucy, it's stinkin of piss in here. You pished yourself again? For fuck's sake, I'm defo out of here."

He pulled on the jeans and hoody he'd had on the day before and made for the door, stopping to take what he could find from his mum's purse. Taking one last look at his mum and sister, he shook his head and exited the flat.

Glancing up and down the street, he wondered which direction he should take. Something in his feet made his mind up for him and he found himself walking down past the bookies and its groupies all huddled outside smoking their fags, scouring newspapers for their dream ride. He headed towards the alley at the back of the old church. The brambles had grown furiously in the recent spate of fair weather and he pulled his sleeve down over his hand to stop himself from getting scratched as he brushed them to the side. At the end of the alley, he met a sandstone dead-end that towered above him and heaved himself up, stubbing his feet off the face of it as it helped him on his way. Resting at the top, he gazed out to sea and saw the tide was out and in front lay miles of dark sand dotted with rocks, seaweed, *and the odd dog shit*, he presumed. There was no sign of life at Hayley's door, but having nothing else to do he carried on.

Taking a quick breath in and counting to ten, he chapped the door with more gusto than he had expected. When this brought no reaction, he looked around, thinking about what he should do. Then he saw the doorbell and pressed it. Not the ding-dong variety, but a shrill buzzer that did the job as, through the frosted glass, he saw the outline of someone approaching. Realising it wasn't Hayley, he slunk away from the door.

As the door opened, Connor suddenly felt the urge to bolt and was turning on his heel as the old man spoke:

"What can I do you for? You looking for John?"

"Eh, naw. Hayley."

"Hayley? Haud on a minute." The old man shuffled round in his slippers holding onto the edge of the door, then let out a roar that made Connor jump.

"What?" came the reply from a room off into the back of the house.

"Get your arse over here. There's someone at the door tae see you."

After that, the man left Connor standing at the door as he retreated back into the room on the left, letting the door slam behind him.

Watching and waiting he couldn't see or hear Hayley and, just as he was about to ring the bell again, he saw a door open and Hayley's body emerge.

"Aw, it's yourself. Come on in."

Hayley disappeared again and Connor just stood awkwardly at the door not sure whether this was a good idea or not. Slowly looking about him, he crept as quietly as he could into the house. He gently closed the door behind him, keeping his eyes on the door he had seen Hayley's foot disappear behind. He chapped, hoping that it was the right thing to do.

"For god's sake, come in. Did you get lost?"

Pushing the door open, he was met with some resistance and had to put his shoulder against it. A pile of clothes was acting like a draught excluder bunching up underneath it. A dog began barking and he stayed with his body hidden behind the door for protection. Skelping the dog on its rump, Hayley quickly quietened it.

"He does'nae bite. Come on in."

Moving into the room, he saw Hayley lying on the bed, her legs bent, and her hand round the dog's neck giving it a hug. Despite its deafening bark, it was relatively small and when it saw Connor, wagged its tail enthusiastically.

"See ... he likes you. What you up to?" Hayley asked.

Connor shrugged and hung about unsure where or what he should do.

"Sit doon, will you. You're making the place look untidy." Hayley nodded with her eyes towards the bed and Connor crouched on the edge furthest from her. "You're up early are you no? I wis still sleeping till ma pappi shouted me. You had your brekkie? I'm starving."

Not able to get a word in, Connor watched as she bounced off the bed with the dog in tow and went to the door. Connor sat stock still. "Come on, let's get some brekkie. Ma stomach thinks ma throat's been cut."

The dog ran in front, barking as it negotiated its way down a narrow passageway littered with shoes and toys that had fallen air to the dog, all in various states of distress. Hayley ran after it and Connor did his best to keep up. The end opened out into a kitchen crammed full of all sorts. Connor cast his eyes on the vast array of stuff that had been accumulated. In one quick glance round the room, he couldn't see one free surface. There were used mugs next to spanners and hammers, piles of clothes next to bundles of newspapers. Hayley had pulled herself up onto a counter, using her feet to make a space, then clinging onto the top of a cupboard she maneuvered her body expertly back to allow it to open. Once the contents of the cupboard were accessible, her head disappeared as she rummaged. The dog bounced off the floor, its four legs leaving the sticky linoleum every time it leapt up. A cacophony of barks and a tail that wagged quicker than a metronome set on prestissimo accompanied each jump. Every so often Hayley threw something down at the dog and it would dive to get it, barking, jumping and wagging forgotten.

"Right, what about one of these?" Hayley asked, holding two chocolate biscuits wrapped in gold foil in her hand.

"Fine."

She threw the biscuit at Connor and he missed. The dog pounced forward in double quick time and picked it up, shaking it from side to side, slevers flying across the room. Hayley roared. "Nooo Dfur, that's no yours."

Jumping down, she ran towards the dog, but wise to her, he

scarpered off out the kitchen back up the way he had come. He scoffed the biscuit as he went, wrapper and all.

"You need to be quick when he's about. He's a total wido! Here." Hayley opened her wrapper then snapped her biscuit in half. "There's no much else to eat. I could make you toast?"

Connor shrugged again, and Hayley took this as yes and slid the metal door of the bread bin up so that it slid into the top concealing its existence. Pulling two slices of bread out, she put them in the toaster, then pushed the slider down until the pale bread sunk down into the white machine.

"Butter and jam?"

"Aye, please."

Connor watched her opening cupboard doors then slamming them shut until she found what she was looking for. Unscrewing the lid, she pulled a spoon out the drawer and foraged around inside the jar scraping what she could off the sides, just about filling the teaspoon she held. The toaster pinged and the bread popped up golden and brown, filling the room with a familiar smell.

"No much left. Can you go and get the butter out the fridge?"

Connor yanked the fridge door open and saw that it housed slightly more items than his at home and found the butter easily on the middle shelf. He took it over to her as she crouched on the worktop, yielding a knife in one hand as she awaited the arrival of the butter. She flashed him a smile as he handed her the butter and she set to work clicking the butter lid off the tub by prising her fingers under the stiff lid. Standing close to her for the first time that day, he smelt her smell and his tummy went all funny. He then felt something warm and furry against his leg and looked down to see that Dfur had joined them, looking up hopeful for another morsel or two.

"Right you, beat it. This is for Connor, no you. Come on, let's go back intae ma room and we'll shut the door."

Hayley carried the plate of toast above her head away from the salivating mouth of Dfur. He dutifully followed her, his eyes never leaving the plate. She was like the pied piper with the two of them following behind.

"Right, you go in first, I'll hold Dfur, then you take the plate and I'll come in."

"Ok," Connor replied unsure of how it was all going to work out. Pushing the door open a crack, he slid inside then took the plate. Dfur, seeing the transfer being made, made a lunge for it. Hayley, used to his antics, grabbed his tail, stopping him in his tracks. He snapped his head back to see what was stopping him, allowing Connor to get the toast safely inside. Using her body, she battled the determined Dfur out the way and managed to squeeze in the narrow gap.

"What was that like?"

She laughed. "All for a bit of toast. I'm starving. Come on, get up on the bed so we can munch it down."

Clambering one-handed onto the bed, he plonked down next to Hayley, offering her the toast first. She grabbed the outsider and took huge bites until it was gone. Connor watched her. He was amazed that someone so wee could eat something so quickly.

"I thought you were hungry?" Hayley said, eyeing up the toast.

"I am." He picked up the toast and enjoyed the taste of the sweet strawberry jam as it slid down into his empty stomach. After, he licked his sticky fingers and wished there was more.

"I heard there wis a fight last night at the school with your Lucy?"

"No exactly. I'm actually no sure what happened. Chrissy told me Lucy wis greeting and I had better go and get her. She wis in the heidy's room with Miss Kane. I had tae get a lift home with Mrs Barr. I wis mortified."

"OMG. Did she take you all the way home? OMG!"

"Worse. She walked me intae the close as she wanted tae talk tae ma mum."

"What? Did your mum go bush?"

"No exactly. She had'nae been very well and wis a bit sleepy. It took me ages tae get her tae the door and once there she never said much."

"What did Barr do?"

"Nothing. Just asked if we were ok, then left. Well she never actually left. As I heard her ootside the door phoning someone. Eventually, she left."

"Jeeso. Where's the chatterbox the day?"

"In the house wi' ma mum."

"I'm bored, want tae go out?"

"Aye, ok."

Hayley shoved her feet into her trainers and grabbed her zippy. She grabbed a hairband from the top of her chest of drawers, Connor watching as she twisted it up onto the top of her head, accentuating her delicate features. The pair left the house with a dejected Dfur staring out the window after them.

It was cloudy but dry and they made their way to the top of the old hill, running towards the swings once they were in sight, to claim the best one. Hayley had won and she worked her legs in and out, gaining height and momentum. Connor ran over to the monkey bars instead and climbed to his usual spot. Jumping off the swing, Hayley ran over to join him.

"Help me up then," she commanded with her hands outstretched towards him. Connor bent forwards, securing his weight with his legs bent beneath the bar and heaved her up onto the first step then stopped. Then he managed to pull her the rest of the way up.

"You can see for miles up here."

"I know," he replied. "It's no ma favourite bit though. Want me tae take you to ma wee den?"

"Aye, defo. Is it far?"

"No really, come on."

Connor leapt off, landing with a thud on the grass below while Hayley sat, unsure of the best way to dismount. Connor went over and offered her a hand that she took and swung down, smashing into his side.

"Sorry, pal."

"It's alright." Connor was thrilled that she had landed on top of him, any excuse to get close to Hayley was fine by him, even if it involved a little pain.

"Where is it then?""

"Down by the pier. I found it the first day I moved here. I escaped from the flat for a while and it was the first place I found. It's great. Nobody knows you're there. Come on and I'll show you."

Connor ran ahead allowing the steepness of the hill to carry him. He could feel his feet race ahead of him and allowed himself to be carried forward by the momentum. He felt free when he was with Hayley. Free from his crap at home. His crap at school. A smile crept over his face as he enjoyed this unusual sensation. As he reached the bottom, he had to use the end of the terrace wall to stop himself. His beaming face, turned and waited for Hayley who was using a more sedate pace.

The street was full of Saturday morning shoppers, bustling to get their bits and bobs in, ready for their weekend. Cheery voices exchanged pleasantries and arrangements for the night ahead. Most conversations revolved around drink, and deciding whether it would be in the pub or a carry-out. The street would be dead this time tomorrow as people dealt with their drouths and hangovers.

Reaching down, Connor eased his hand into his jean pocket and fingered the coins he had lifted earlier. Pulling them out, he saw he had quite a stash. Hayley stood by his side, bent double, clutching her side, puffing heavily.

"I'm knackered. What's that you've got?" she asked, peering into his outstretched palm.

"Dosh. Want tae go and spend it?"

"Aye. I'm still starvin. I could eat a scabby heided wean wi shite fleeing fae it?"

"What?" Connor spluttered through giggles.

Laughing, Hayley explained, "Ma pappi says that all the time when he's hungry. Where do you want tae go?"

"The wee corner shop. We'll get some supplies then head doon tae ma den."

Making their way into the shop, they made a beeline to the sweetie aisle, picking up one sweet then another, trying to make a decision. Meanwhile, the shop owner behind the counter kept his eyes firmly on the pair, waiting to pounce on any false move. Hayley chose a chocolate bar and Connor picked a packet of jammy biscuits up.

"You got enough?" Hayley asked.

"Aye, hunners."

Placing the merchandise up on the counter, Connor dug deep into his jeans to get his money. Bleeping the sweets under the scanner the total flashed up on the till screen and Connor counted out the money exactly. Not believing it was right, the shop owner stood and counted every penny before letting the pair have their booty. As they exited the shop, Hayley dunted Connor in the ribs causing him to let out a cry of pain.

"What did ye do that for?"

Hayley ignored him. She was watching something further down the street. Following her gaze, he saw that it was someone, not something. Quickening his pace, Hayley grabbed his jumper to try and keep up with him, which slowed him down slightly. His determination propelled him forward. Connor gave his stride an extra push as the subject disappeared off the street round the corner towards the seafront, losing Hayley in the process. The thump of his trainers as they slapped the ground was all he could hear. Rounding the corner, he homed in and just as he was on her, she turned round.

"Ahh, fuck, Connor, don't touch me. Ma cousin is just up at ma hoose and he'll kill you," Jenny spluttered as she edged backwards trying to keep her distance.

Encroaching into her space, he could see the fear dancing in her eyes and felt the power exude from his being. The uneven thud of trainers and panting alerted him of Hayley's presence, egging him on to put on a good show.

"I don't care if Muhammad Ali is up at your house, nae body interferes with me or ma family, right?" He gave Jenny a wee push to the shoulder to drive home the message as he swaggered up to her face, gritting his teeth.

"I don't know what you're talking about."

"Naw? A wee birdie told me it wis you that made ma Lucy greet. I'm no sure what you did, but see this fist? You're going tae get tae know it really well if you ever so much as look at me or ma sister the wrong way. Do you know what I'm saying?"

White and visibly shaking, Jenny could only nod her head and before anything else happened, she turned on her heel and fled up the street.

"God, you are one mean machine when you get going. She was shitting herself. Were you really going tae thump her?"

Connor stood, his teeth still gritted, his fists clenched, pumped up. Not answering Hayley, he moved over to the bridge at the pier and threw his fists into the supporting pillars, barely registering the solid wood beneath each punch.

"Jeesus, you are fucking nuts. Come on, where is this den of yours? I'm starving?"

Connor stopped and cast a look back at Hayley, then swung his body round the metal railing, landing heavily on top of the pebbles, knocking them together. He stooped and picked a handful and flung them forcefully one by one into the sea.

"Right, come on you, give us a hand."

Connor crunched back over the stones and put his hand up, helping Hayley across the gap between the open topside and the secluded underside. She followed him up to the back of the bridge that was dark and private, and shared their feast, eating hungrily. The pair, comfortable in each other's company, whiled their time away listening to the voices and footsteps of those that trotted above, enjoying the ever-popular child's pastime of stones and water.

30 Helen

Snuggled beneath her duvet, Helen refused to fully awaken; she was too busy alternating between the replays of last night's date and enjoying her made-up dreams of how the next date should play out. Totally struck down with the light headiness of love, she had no appetite, her thoughts only of her beau and the permanent smile upon her coupon. Eventually, she reached for her phone in case there were any messages she had missed. *None since that one the night before* – the one that she had read at least four times. The one she had traced her fingers over the screen to try and connect more fully with. The one she had held against her chest. She read it again and the smile on her face grew wider.

Sighing, she rolled out of bed and wandered aimlessly about her flat, first into the kitchen, where her heels lay where they had been flung off the night before, like a burglar deterrent, spike side up in the middle of the floor. Her jacket was half draped over the kitchen chair, sleeve dragging on the floor. The contents of her bag were upended on the kitchen table. Helen remembered she'd been looking for her mobile, which always seemed to get lost no matter what size of bag she had it in. Next, she moved into the lounge. The two wine glasses she and Wendy had been drinking from still sat on the coffee table. Drawn to the large bay window, she moved across and perched on a chair, pulled her knees up and gazed down at the street below. She watched as cars stopped at the lights to let pedestrians cross. Her eyes then followed a couple walking hand in hand down the street, looking at each other as they walked, setting her off on another daydream, involving her and Ed.

The buzzer for her door went, shaking her from her sickness. So, preoccupied with herself, she hadn't noticed anyone she knew walking up the street. Thinking it might be Ed, she dashed into her room and pulled on her dressing gown and tried to tame her hair into something human-like. The buzzer went again.

Worried that he might go away, she skipped through and pressed the button. "Hello."

Wendy's voice replied and Helen's heart sank a little. "Only me!"

Helen buzzed her up and stood waiting at the door for her, glad she could share her love bug with someone else rather than just having it on repeat in her own head. Before she had even reached the top of the stairs, Wendy had started drilling Helen on her date.

"So, I'm hoping you now know a bit more than his name?"

"Ha, I know way more," Helen smiled.

"Well, get the kettle on. I want to hear it all. Oh my god! Look at you, you are so loved up. Check the smile on your face."

Hugging her friend, the pair retreated to the kitchen to make tea and chat.

"So, do tell all. What's his name again?"

"Ed."

"Dr Ed … I like it. Still as good looking?"

"Hmmm mmm. He even made his beard look hot. He was soooo nice. Kind, caring, thoughtful. Even though he was late and I nearly went home alone."

"What?"

"He got held up at work with an emergency. I had left the Mitch totally destroyed when he wasn't there and was walking home. He arrived just as I was walking up the street and was so sweet and apologetic, so I had to forgive him."

"So, did you just stay in the Mitch?"

"Yeah, we did. We got a booth and sat and non-stopped

chatted until throw out time. He is so easygoing."

Wendy raised her eyebrows, signalling for more information. Helen spent the next hour telling Wendy all that she had learned about Ed; that he was a junior doctor at the hospital, had been single for too long, liked travelling and lived in one of the Victorian conversions down the seafront.

"God, I've not seen you like this in ages, all gushy and glowy. When are you next seeing him?"

"I'm not sure. He works loads of shitty shifts. He said he would phone," Helen informed her friend.

"So, did you get a good night winch?"

Helen rose from the table and went to tidy away their mugs in a bid to evade her friend.

"Maybe!"

"No way, I want more than that ..."

"Ok, he never came upstairs, but we did have a long, very, very long snog on the stairs and it was steamy hot. I can't wait for some more. I didn't even mind his itchy beard, though my face was a bit red after."

The two ladies laughed and Wendy watched as her friend floated around the kitchen tidying up. Smitten.

"So, what are you up to now? Fancy going a drive to the centre? Keep you from checking your phone every second and you can go and choose yourself some saucy underwear for your second date?"

"Aye, why no. Give me half an hour to get a shower and I'll be right with you."

Helen turned the shower on and waited for the hot water to come through. Once it was piping hot she threw her dressing gown over the hook on the back of the door, tied her hair up into a loose bun and stepped under the water. Still, her thoughts wandered back to the night before and how delicious Ed had been. Trying to shake him from her mind and focus, she quickly finished washing and dried herself before pulling on her jeans and her favourite t-shirt.

"It suits you, you know?"

"What my trusty old favourite?"

"No, you being in love. You look radiant and skinnier than you did last night. Think I need to find myself a new man and lose some weight overnight," Wendy said.

"Aw, there is nothing wrong with the way you look and Jack is a gem of a guy. You don't want to go trading him in for nobody!"

"Hmmm, most of the time he is ok! Right, is that you ready? Let's go."

Helen grabbed her bag and followed her friend downstairs and into her wee car. After a tour of the car park, they found a space and Helen abandoned it as best she could between the white lines. Grabbing a trolley designed for single people, they walked through the automatic doors of the supermarket, battling to make the trolley go in the desired direction. Saturday lunchtime was the wrong time to go for a quiet shop. The place was full of shoppers of every age. The worst Helen decided were the hoity-toity middle-aged women who thought they were the only ones that should be in the supermarket. They frowned and tutted when you stopped to look at an item, as apparently, you were getting in their way. It was worst for families with young kids. Helen observed some killer looks being drawn by the old dragons as kids, (god forbid) accompanied their family to do the weekly shop.

As they neared the frozen foods aisle, Helen suddenly stopped and ducked down beneath the side of one of the middle aisle freezers. Wendy had been busy looking at the pizzas and when she turned round couldn't work out where her friend had gone. After a second, she realised where she was.

"What are you doing? Are you feeling sick?"

"Shhhh," Helen hushed Wendy and indicated to her friend to

come next to her as she kept her eyes on the mismatched pair. The female was tall enough to reach the top shelf in the supermarket whilst he could hardly see over the top of the freezer.

"What the fuck has got into you?"

"Gonnae shush. I think that is fat bitch's husband over there."

"Who?"

"Fat bitch from school."

"Where?" Wendy asked, standing up to get a better view.

Helen yanked at her cardigan pocket, pulling her back down. "The old, short-arsed, fat, baldy geezer, squeezing that blondes' arse? Gads I'm going tae boak. God, she looks young enough to be his daughter. Oh, Jesus fuck, you don't think …"

"What?" asked Helen as she popped up so she could verify what her friend had just claimed. "Oh my god, I'm going tae puke now. No, it can't be! But it must be his bit of stuff. Right, we need to leave now before I heave right on top of the frozen prawns."

"He must be fed up getting squashed. She is nothing like you're pal. Three of her still would'nae be the same size as her."

"She is *so* not ma pal. Don't ever say that again. Just come on and keep incognito … he might remember us from the last staff night out."

"Aw, I remember him now. He was the letchy guy that was drooling all over me. I'm so glad you've found yourself a man so I don't need to be your partner anymore and go to your school nights out."

"Thanks a bunch, and he isn't exactly my man… well yet," Helen said dragging her friend as she half crawled along the aisle trying to hide. As they turned the corner, they resumed a normal stance. Helen then heard laughter and the clack of high heels on the polished, cement floor.

"Fuck, they're coming, quick." Helen looked up just in time

to see them rounding the top of the aisle smooching, his hands so inappropriately placed. "Aw no, I really am going to be sick."

A quick, sharp, empty-handed exit was made and the two jogged back to the car.

"What does she see in him? He is disgusting. Is he rich?" Wendy inquired.

"No idea, but there must be something for her to be happily groped in full daylight by him. He's like a little mole with those glasses and tiny eyes, his hands had to stretch up to put them up her skirt."

"*Stop Now*, Helen! My eyes and brain have had enough abuse for one day."

"God, I know. Think we need to go to Mac Donald's to console our souls. What do ye think?"

"Aye, let's hit it."

31 Connor

Darkness crept slowly upon them, the long summer nights making a mockery of the real hour. Neither was desperate to go back to their existences in their so-called homes. Overhead, sounds made the change from day to night apparent. Friendly, chatty voices and the quick light feet of children were swapped for slurred words and staggering stops and starts of those who'd had one too many at the local. The tempting, wafting smells of chips and candy floss changed to sickening smoke and alcohol. Shivering now as the cold set in, Hayley edged nearer to Connor, trying to steal some warmth.

"I'm freezing."

"Me too," Connor chattered back as his teeth clattered off one another.

"Suppose we better go. Dfur will need tae get fed. What you going tae do?"

Shrugging, Connor replied, "Dunno."

"Want tae come back tae mine?"

"Aye, ok."

The duo climbed up from beneath the bridge and made their way toward the lights and bizz of the town. Tired and cold, their steps were slow and awkward and they bumped into one another as they moved. Music blared from the pub and a crowd of smokers hung around outside, puffing and chatting. The unusual presence of two so young out and about at such a late hour brought them some unwanted attention.

"Aw, look at those two weans, Jackie. They cannae be much older than your Jenny? What are you two doing out so late?"

"Is that you, Hayley?" one smoker asked, trying to improve her drunken vision by half shutting her eyes. She stumbled forward to get a closer look. Hayley grabbed hold of Connor and they quickened their step as others began to take notice of them.

"Come over here and your Uncle Charlie will look after you, hen," a lecherous individual sleazed at her.

"Shut the fuck up, Charlie. You fucking sick paedo?" another fired back.

Their hearts racing, they ran across to the quieter side of the street to escape any further unwanted interactions. Gone from the view of the pub-goers, their passing presence was soon forgotten; the drinking and smoking resumed. Casting a glance back, Connor relaxed as he saw they were well out of harm's way. Continuing to make their way to Hayley's house, they kept walking, heads down, their chat exhausted for the moment as they put their efforts into getting home. It felt strange being out so late at night. *Exciting,* Connor thought, especially as Hayley was with him. His thoughts flitted briefly to his mum and Lucy, but he knew they would be both where he had left them. Nothing would happen if he wasn't there to direct them.

Today had been amazing. The whole day spent with Hayley. How he had shown Jenny not to mess. And now going back to Hayley's.

The glare of a car's headlights startled the two as they neared the end of the street. Momentarily blinded, they did not see that the lights belonged to a police car. Their hands flew up to shield their eyes. The car door opened and slammed shut twice. Heavy shoes clumping on the pavement alerted the stunned pair to the proximity of the feet.

Eyes still adjusting to the lights that had been left on, the two stood side by side, rendered to the spot. Shit scared, they hadn't a clue who it was or what was going on.

A brief flash of something Jenny had said flashed into

Connor's mind and he could feel his body tensing, ready to react. Only when the officer spoke did they realise it was just the police.

"Well, well look who we have here, Officer Cochrane, Miss Hayley Craig, am I right?"

"Aye, how do you know?" Hayley impudently asked, not realising the reason they were there.

"How do we know? Because we've spent the last three hours searching the whole of the town looking for you after your pappi phoned to say you hadn't been seen all day and you were missing."

"Oh," Hayley replied as she suddenly realised the trouble she was going to be in. Shifting uneasily from one foot to another, she kept her head to the ground. Feeling brave, she stole a look at Connor who was furiously studying the street behind them.

"So, are you going to introduce us to your friend, Hayley?" the other officer asked.

"Eh. This is Connor."

"Connor? Well, Connor, I think you better get in the car along with Hayley. A young man like you shouldn't be out at this hour."

"In the car? I just live round the corner, I'll just walk," Connor exclaimed.

"I don't think so, son." The officer walked over to the car and held the car door open for the two of them. Hayley dutifully followed, realising doing anything else was pointless. Connor had other ideas, however, and once the officers had their backs turned he darted off, heading in the direction he'd just come.

"What the …" Officer Cochrane exhaled.

The other activated his radio control and alerted other patrols in the area of the situation. Hayley smiled to herself as she watched Connor speed off down the street, weaving in and out the throng of drunks causing a few expletives to be thrown his way.

"So where does yer wee pal live?"

"I don't know," Hayley replied.

"Aye, right. You've spent the last ten hours or so with him and you don't know where he lives?"

"I don't. I've never been to his house. It's over there somewhere." She pointed to the flats in the opposite direction.

"Well, I'm sure we'll find him sooner or later and deliver him back to his house. Now it's time for you to go and see your poor pappi who has been worrying all night about you. The door locks are on, so don't even think about making a run for it after your wee pal."

Rolling her eyes at the last remark, Hayley looked out the window as the police car drove through the town back to her house, desperate for a glimpse of Connor. She chuckled to herself at the balls he had and the story she'd have for Monday.

Connor crouched down behind the huge hunk of metal that served as the bin for the Chinese carryout shop next to his block of flats. It was pitch black. Working street lights were obviously not a priority for his neighbourhood. His heart had calmed to a quick beat instead of the rapid one that he'd worked up. He tried not to think about what might have happened if they had taken him home and his mum had been out on one.

Poking his head out, he could see no one and the only noise he could hear was the clang of metal as the wok was worked in the kitchen. He salivated as the smell of Chinese food drifted towards him. Pulling the insides of his pocket out he found nothing. Deciding that his hunger was more important than going home, he slid silently from his hidey-hole and through a narrow lane to the front of the street. Edging carefully along staying in the shadows he made his way back to the pub, knowing from past experience that drunken punters could be a source of income if he played his cards right. If not, there could be a whole lot of trouble, but he was a chancer.

As he neared he saw his victim, a wee lady standing with her drink getting some fresh air, the glow of her fag waving haphazardly in front of her. Approaching slowly watching out for his two uniformed friends and any other undesirables he may have to deal with.

"Haw miss, I've lost ma keys and cannae get intae ma hoose. Can ye lend me some money tae phone ma mum?"

"Wit son? I cannae hear ye."

Connor moved closer and repeated his request, adding a bit of sniffle this time.

"Aw son, haud on a wee minute."

She rummaged in her bag, sending hankies flying and brought out her purse. The potent smell of whiskey could have made him drunk if he'd had to hang around much longer. Pulling out a note she squinted her eyes trying to see what she'd found. Beckoning Connor to come closer, he inched forward and she thrust the note into his hand, putting her hand over his.

"Off ye go son."

Connor didn't need to be told twice. Clutching the money, he stealthily made his way back up the street, stopping outside the foggy glassed window of the takeaway.

Crossing his fingers that the police hadn't decided to go for a late-night snack, he pushed the door open and made his way in. He was in luck. The only other customer was a wee man on the way home from the pub, sitting on the lonely plastic chair, eyes closed, head down, mouth open, drool dripping. Connor made his way to the counter and stood waiting for the Chinese man to take his eyes off the game show he was watching and serve him. After clearing his throat a few times, Connor was eventually acknowledged by the thrust of a head.

"What you want?"

"How much is fried rice?"

"£2:45. You want fried rice?"

Connor checked his finances and then nodded. Holding up

two fingers. The man shouted Connor's order through to the kitchen in a language Connor could make no sense of. Feeling conspicuous, he tried to hug the wall in the hope it would hug him back. Nervously waiting, he tried to peer out the glass door, but between the window fog and the plethora of menus, he could see little. A bell pinged from the kitchen and a white bag was handed to Connor containing the two little foil tubs of hot, deliciousness.

Darting back through the narrow lane, he was consumed by the safety of darkness once again. He found the back stairway to his flat and jumped up the stairs two at a time. Pushing the door open, he paused before entering, trying to work out the lay of the land. He heard nothing and took this as a good sign. The flat was in total darkness. He could just make out the shape of his mum and sister huddled on the couch. The stench of pee hit him straight in the face, causing him to gag. One of the shapes on the couch rustled and he guessed it was Lucy.

32 Lucy

Hearing the noise at the front door, Lucy froze to the spot. Hoping it was Connor, she listened carefully and when she saw his outline coming through the door she began to push herself up. Her body shape was sculpted into the couch, she had lain there so long. Relieved to see her brother after so long alone, she rushed over to him and ignored his boaking and slagging as he referred to the stench of pee that permeated the air.

Seeing the white bag in his hand reminded her of her hunger and she didn't need to be asked twice if she wanted some. She followed him into the bedroom and scampered up next to him, waiting for him to open the plastic bag.

The first few bites were slow to go down, her belly so empty they were almost painful. She soon got used to the warm rice melting, adding more than just calories to her emptiness.

Having spent most of the day curled up next to her mum on the couch, she was glad to stretch her body out. Nobody had spoken to her since Connor had left that morning and, although Connor was busy eating and not speaking much, she was glad of his animated presence. Even when mum had been awake to smoke her fags and go to the toilet, she hadn't really been awake. Despite Lucy trying to gain her attention, she had stared straight through her and had made no sound other than the one her racking cough produced from deep within her lungs.

Lucy had tried clinging onto her mum, gripping her arm fiercely to get a reaction, but that only resulted in her being shaken off with a force that threw her to the ground. Feeling utterly dejected, Lucy had resumed her place on the couch with her battering thoughts for company.

Having someone to annoy, she let her pent-up energy loose. The pair were like a couple of kittens rolling around after a ball of wool, batting each other. Giggling and laughing, they soon aroused the attention of their grumpy upstairs neighbour, who unceremoniously thumped the floor above, alerting them to her displeasure. Panting for breath from the exertion, Lucy sat still on the bed and waited to see what Connor's reaction would be. She smiled as he referred to their neighbour as a grumpy old bat.

Announcing that it was really late and time for bed, he tossed the empty containers and forks from the bed onto the floor. Pulling off his jeans, he slipped under the duvet and told Lucy to put the light off. Lucy dutifully followed her brother's instructions and put the room into darkness.

Being wide awake, she was unsure what to do with herself. Gently, she sat down on the edge of the bed, so as not to alert Connor to her presence. She was all too well aware he was not keen on sharing a bed, but longed for his company. Once she heard Connor's gentle snores, she shifted her body cautiously up the bed, trying to crawl into spaces that had no arms or legs hiding beneath the duvet. Despite her valiant efforts, this proved quite difficult without a guiding light and twice she put her weight on top of him. Each time she froze, holding her breath, waiting for his protestation, but none came and she continued until she reached the top of the bed. Laying down next to him, she tried to relax and send herself to sleep, but it just wouldn't come.

Listening to Connor's calming breath, she tried to synchronise her breathing with his, but ended up getting light-headed, his pattern was so different from hers. Bored and still wide awake, she flipped over onto her belly, this time hopeful that her movement would arouse him. Nothing. He continued his steady breathing.

Once on her tummy, she realised she could gaze out the

window. There wasn't much happening out there. She gazed at the slither of moon that appeared then disappeared as the clouds floated across it, mesmerised by the steady stream of cover the wind blew across the sky. A noise in the street below caught her attention and, gazing down, she captured the outline of two bodies walking across the street towards the long line of garages. One staggered a little, missing the pavement, and shouted out a garbled yell. The other continued on the path, not even registering the noise.

Tingling sensations tickled Lucy's nose and she quickly pinched her nose, fearful that her sneeze would alert the two wandering bodies below of her voyeurism. Grunting as the sneeze hit, she quickly looked up, worried the sound had transported below. The two remained oblivious. Having both progressed to sitting on the curb, Lucy wondered what they would do next. She kept her eyes just level with the top of the bed to stay concealed; kept her gaze fixed on them. Her belly felt tight, her breathing short and shallow as she expectantly waited. The pair below, unaware of their new career as entertainers, failed to fulfil their duty and promptly fell asleep.

Bored once more, but feeling a little sleepier, Lucy snuggled in next to her brother and quietly fell over. Every so often throughout the night, her hand reached up to scratch at her head as her itching intensified once again.

33 Helen

Busy preparing lessons for the following day, Helen had to repeatedly tear herself away from the screen of her phone. Having heard nothing from Ed since her last text on Friday, she began to feel her gnawing paranoia creep up. Maybe he was just being polite when he'd said all those nice things. Maybe what she felt when they kissed was just one-sided. Her thoughts went round in never-ending circles and slowly as the day wore on she began to slip into a morose mood, making her task of preparing work even harder than usual. The perkier side of her nature tried to reassure her, reminding her it was him that had asked her out and that he had made all the moves. Searching deep within she could still feel the gentle flutterings inside her tummy and desperately held onto the hope they gave her.

Slouching in her joggys, she gave up with her prep work and put the kettle on, deciding that an afternoon movie was just what she needed on a wet, miserable day like today. Sighing, she reached for her emergency chocolate stash, deciding that soothing a disturbed heart was very much an emergency.

The click of the kettle going off was drowned out by the alarm of the entry buzzer. Thinking it was Wendy, Helen pressed the button to allow entry into the stairway and left her front door ajar. Grabbing two mugs from the cupboard, she began the automatic process of tea-making, putting her thoughts into how she was going to mask her disappointment to her friend.

The sound of a male voice caught her completely off guard, rooting her to the spot as the realisation of who it belonged to smacked her in the face, at about the same time as her heart dropped to the floor and her breathing took a hiatus.

"Eh, hello? Helen?" Ed tentatively shouted, hoping he'd got the right flat.

Fuck, fuck, fuck! Helen quietly berated herself, wondering how she was going to look fabulous in point two of a second with hands for a hairbrush and chocolate as makeup.

"Hello, erm I'm looking for Helen, I'm not sure if I've got the right flat?"

Pushing herself through the door, she was enthralled once more by his good looks and only managed to mutter an incoherent response. "How ya doing?"

"Hey, Helen, I was worried I had the wrong place. I hope you don't mind me stopping by unannounced?" His words languidly oozed from his mouth, making it all the easier for Helen to study his face as each syllable formed, re-familiarising herself with every detail – how his beard had gently scratched her face, how his dark eyes had locked her in his. Definitely a cuteness about him with his glinting eyes and cheeky wee smile, but it was his calmness that captivated her. Not believing her luck in securing a return visit from him, she soaked in every detail. Unfortunately, her attention to this meant her brain was overloaded and she forgot to reply to his question.

"Helen, do you mind?"

"Mind what?"

"Me being here."

"Sorry, no, no not at all. It's lovely to see you. Though a bit of warning would have helped me look a little better than a skanky raj, ready to go and spit some gob down the high street."

"Ha, to be honest I hadn't noticed, but now you come to mention it, maybe I should have worn my shell suit and we could have been a dynamic gobbing duo."

"Ha! So, do you fancy a cuppa? I thought you were Wendy and was in the middle of making one for us."

"Aw, are you expecting her? Do you want me to go?"

"No and no. Grab a pew and I will get on it. What do you take?"

"Just milk, thanks."

Doing a little dance as she went into the kitchen, Helen's mood soared and her happy feelings came rushing back. Piling a plate with her emergency chocolate, she suddenly had a thought that being a doctor he would disapprove and she shook the chocolate off the plate back into the tin.

"So, am I not getting a bit of chocolate? Keeping it all for yourself?" he asked, sticking his head round the door and watching her.

"Have you any idea how precious chocolate is to a girl? Seeing as it's you ... I suppose I could share a teeny, tiny bit with you. Don't want you to pick up all my bad habits seeing as you're a doctor."

"From that comment, you have obviously no idea how us doctors survive. Get the chocolate piled on, I'm famished."

"Think I like you a whole lot more now that you've just said that."

Ed flashed one of his smiles at her, picked up the plate of chocolate biscuits and carried them through to the lounge, and there was nothing Helen could do, but follow him completely enraptured.

34 Connor

Rain rolled down the window in repeated streams while the grey clouds prevented the day from believing it was really morning. A Hoover in the flat above noisily rolled backwards and forwards sooking the life out the carpet it was haranguing; it woke Connor from his slumber. Stretching, he felt the lump of his sister curled at the end of the bed, and groaning, he tentatively felt for a wet patch. Finding none, he relaxed and allowed his body to continue with its morning rituals – a loud, reverberating emission ensued. Obviously not being fully asleep, Lucy dealt him a mean blow that landed right on his buttock, unimpressed by the unexpected smelly gust. Giggling, he forced out another and awaited his sister's retaliation, which she dutifully delivered by launching her pillow at him with all the strength of a wet paper bag. It failed to hit anywhere near its intended target and thumped to the floor not far from its starting position.

"You're a shite throw, Lucy." Connor now hammered his sister playfully with his pillow as she shrieked and tried to escape by crawling off the bed backwards. This resulted in an epic thud as her body landed on the floor. A moment of silence followed as Lucy assessed herself for damage. Connor hovered on the bed waiting for her cry, thankfully it was more noise than pain and Lucy rose triumphantly to take her brother by surprise battering him with her fists.

"You wee shite!" Connor shrieked as he fell backwards, his fall ever so slightly cushioned by the 80's grey, red and black striped duvet that may well have last seen the inside of a washing machine round about that decade too. Lucy, realising she was for it now, ran through to the other room to seek protection from her mum. Shrieking with falsely anticipated fear, she jumped onto the couch where her mother sat, fag in hand, eyes looking at god knew what, and tried to delve under her free arm to gain immunity. Connor raced closely behind her, jumping over the back of the couch, tipping it ever so slightly in the process, but he was too slow. Lucy had reached safety. The pair sounded like a herd of cows puffing and panting on a cold morning.

"You're lucky this time. Next time will be a different story," Connor joked. "What you doing the day, Mum?"

Mum failed to register his question as she sat staring into her place in space. The robotic movement of hand to lips was one of the few indications there was life in the body.

"Mum … Mum," Connor prevailed, using a little more than just his voice to gain her attention. She whipped her head round, but her eyes were still lost, engulfed in a deadness that registered nothing. The last draw of the cigarette made, her hand crushed the remaining life out of it before she swung her legs round on the couch and closed her eyes once more.

"For god's sake, Mum. Can you no get off your arse for once and do something? You cannae still be tired. You've been sleeping for days now. Mum. MUM!" Connor hit the base of the couch with his feet, then slapped his Mum's leg as he stood up. Connor saw Lucy watching and noticed that even she wasn't jumping on the bandwagon to protect their mum. Yanking the cupboard door open, Connor raked through what was there out of habit more than anything else. Having done the same yesterday, he knew there was nothing worth eating, but his hunger gnawed away at him and drove him to take action. He pulled on his mum's big, baggy jumper and his trousers with the pockets, then announced to Lucy, "Right I'm away tae get food. I'm starving."

Lucy moved off the couch, her signal that she was going with him. Rushing, she went to the bedroom to pull some clothes on, desperate for him not to leave without her. He sighed as she seemed to take forever to get ready and he wanted to let her think she was a right pain in the arse for going with him, though he was secretly happy of the company.

Pulling the door shut behind them, they bounced down the stairs, released for the day. He had no idea where he was going to get food, but knew his mum's baggy jumper had helped him out before. They made their way down the street. It was deserted, either because it was raining incessantly or because it was earlier than they thought on a Sunday morning. The greyness above draped down over their shoulders ensuring the rain never missed them as they squelched through the streets that had been turned into a meeting place for a few inches of rain. The goal of food spurred them on and before they knew it they found themselves at the doors to the big supermarket. Delighted, they ran the last few feet as the sliding doors pulled apart, offering a dry haven. A pool formed around them as they stood on the polished concrete floor and rain flew off Connor's hair as he flicked his head side to side.

"Would you look at the two of youse?" the friendly lady welcomed them. "You're like a pair of drowned rats. What are you looking for? Can I help?"

Flustered, as if he'd been caught even before he'd done anything, Connor rummaged in his head for something plausible to say.

"Eh, just getting a few messages for ma mum."

"Aw, what a good pair you are, saving your mum from going out in a day like this. If I can help gives us a shout."

"Eh, aye, it's ok I know what I need."

"Ok, son."

Pushing Lucy in front of him, he went up the first aisle they found, which happened to be the feminine care aisle. Lucy turned and looked at him as if to say: 'What are you doing?'

Connor's face turned scarlet and he kept pushing her forward. Risking a quick glance behind once they got to the end of the aisle, he checked that no one followed them. Stopping at the top, he looked at the jars of coffee advertised on special, trying to hatch a wee plan out in his scrambled head, but Lucy made it twice as hard as she kept looking at him with those eyes. Speaking in his quietest voice, he told her what was going to happen.

"Right, you know what you've tae do?"

Lucy nodded, and he fished in his pockets and gave her the small change he had left before pushing her in front of him as he went off to do the real business. Sliding down the next aisle, he found the biscuits. After taking a furtive look around, he slipped his hands on a packet of chocolate digestives that disappeared up his jumper. Next was a packet of caramel wafers. Glancing up, he saw a trolley round the corner and quickly stepped away from the shelf before a third packet went missing; he walked down the aisle as nonchalantly as possible with the two packets safely out of sight. Feeling brave, he dived down the crisp aisle. Having seen Lucy at the checkout, he knew his plan was going well. Seeing the tube of crisps he loved, he went for it, not thinking about practicalities until after he had lifted them. As he maneuvered the tube down his trousers, he heard the voice signalling that it had been a step too far.

"Right, pal, think you'd better put that back."

Not even looking up to see who the female voice belonged to, he sprinted down the aisle towards the door and hoped and prayed that Lucy was outside at their rendezvous point. Behind, he heard the cacophony of voices as the usually quiet store was disturbed by his behaviour. Fortunately, the inexperienced staff were no match for his sleekit ways. On reaching the bridge, he allowed himself to look back but saw no one. He jumped down and at first couldn't see her. Slowly his eyes accustomed to the dim light that broke through the broken planks above. The crunching noise directed him to her figure sitting at the back munching through the packet of mints.

"Hungry?" he asked as he released the pilfered packets from his body, smiling.

35 Lucy

The greyness still loomed, but the rain had stopped as Lucy and Connor chittered, the wet having eventually sunk into their bones driving them home. Struggling with the cold that had found her, Lucy lagged further behind her brother than usual, the dampness stripping him of the little patience he had. Her feet sloshed around inside her borrowed trainers as her toes gripped to keep them from falling off. She imagined her lost trainers being washed out to sea, bobbing over the waves to the isle. Her glistening cheeks and the intermittent wipe of her nose with her sleeve, were the only indication of her distress.

Glancing up, she saw Connor striding on without her. This momentarily halted her progress, and the need to curl up and savour any warmth left was overwhelming. Feeling the scrunchy bag in which her remaining share of the biscuits were secured gave her the wee boost to propel her forward again.

Her mind went racing up the stairs and onto the couch. She imagined her mum's warm arms tightly around her, her soft kisses on top of her head and her smile that made everything all right again. Legs going like pistons with brakes on didn't deter her from her intention and she persevered. The entry door didn't budge at her first attempt but, with her back pushing against it, it gave way and she slipped her body through the smallest of gaps, too tired to even try and stop it hitting against her. Her hands crossed over themselves as she used the bannister to hoist herself up the stairs. Once inside, she rushed over to the couch, threw herself down next to her mum's still body. Rocking her mum's body back and forth emitted no response. Lucy got the biscuits and crinkled the packet noisily next to her ear and was batted away like a pesky fly. Settling for the warmth from her body, she bent her wee shape into the contours of her mum and drifted off into a haze only to be crunched between her mum's knees and chest as one of her bouts took hold. Alarmed by the ferociousness of the cough, Lucy escaped from the coughing body trap and got a glass of water. She watched with wide eyes as her mum's face turned red and her breath got swallowed then spat out in a fast fury causing her eyes to water.

"What have you done tae her?" Connor inquired, the noise bringing him through to the room. Lucy gave him a look and pointed to the water.

"Mum, are you alright?" he asked, hardly being heard over the bellowing coughs and sharp breaths being sought. Scared, Lucy moved to stand behind her brother and could hardly bear to look at her mum. Slowly the coughing subsided, leaving her exhausted and panting for breath.

"Jesus, Mum, you had me worried," Connor said in relief, "If nothing else it's woke you up."

"You, cheeky, wee shite. God, I thought I wis never going tae catch ma breath again," Mum gasped, between breaths reaching for the glass of water and sipping carefully from the rim. Lucy watched as she picked up her cigarette packet, her stained fingers fumbling fervently inside for a new stick. Upending the packet, she gave it a shake, allowing the few last strands of tobacco to float gracefully, feather-like, onto the table below. The box was demolished in one single movement and slammed carelessly away. Remembering the biscuits, Lucy picked up the packet and clambered round the table excitedly. She pulled a digestive out of the creased casing, held it in front of her mum's face.

"For god's sake, Lucy, it's a fag I need, no a biscuit," her mum recoiled, her eyes flipping to mean mode, her lips snapping into a snarl. Lucy froze, the biscuit dangling feebly from her fingers as if it were a shield protecting her from the erupting anger.

Rocking backwards to gain some momentum, but failing, her mum had to make use of the table to get out of the couch. Not making any effort to move out the way in time, Lucy found herself knocked by her mum's knees, causing her mum to lose balance and topple back onto the couch.

"Will you get out ma face, for god's sake, Lucy? You're standin there like an eejit."

Pulling her knees up onto the couch, Lucy began to shrink, hiding herself beneath her arms. She couldn't really hear the banging of doors and cupboards as her mum searched for money or a lucky fag, nor could she make out the words being shouted between Connor and her mum. She climbed into her tiny place and locked out the world.

36 Helen

Helen still hated requests to go to the head teacher's office, particularly first thing on a Monday morning. Racking her brains, she tried to think if there was anything she had done or more likely not done. Nothing obvious jumped into her head. Making her way along the corridor, she felt her heart beat a little faster as she began stressing about what the problem might be. As she turned the corner, she saw Irene's sizeable behind making its way through the head teacher's door in front of her. Helen's heart groaned as she realised whatever it was must involve her. Chapping the door before sticking her head round, she saw Rosie and Irene exchanging pleasantries about their weekend. Remembering her spying escapade on Saturday, Helen hoped she had been as incognito as she had thought she was.

"In you come, Helen. Come and grab a pew. Do you want a wee coffee?" Rosie asked.

"No, I'm good thanks."

Neither Helen nor Irene made any pretense at pleasantries; they averted their eyes from each other's gaze and looked at Rosie. Wittering away to no one in particular with her bangles clanging against each other, Helen followed her Head's movements as she went in and out of drawers searching for something. The sleeves of her long floral tunic waved around like a butterfly ballet. Eventually, she shimmied her body between the coffee table and chair and plonked herself down with the grace of an elephant at a tea party.

"Sorry to drag you away from your preparations on a Monday morning, ladies, but I wanted to update you on the Jackson children after my visit there on Friday night," Rosie explained.

"Let me guess, was that imp of a boy causing bother for Jack Hay after school on Friday? Doesn't surprise me at all. He is nothing but trouble with a capital T, if you ask me. I take it he was expelled?" Irene careered off on a tangent and, even though she tried, Rosie had been unable to stop her.

"Irene, if you let me explain, you will see you are on quite the wrong tracks." Rosie couldn't hide her annoyance at Irene's total lack of tact. The thunder on Rosie's face made it clear even to the usually thick-skinned Irene that she had well and truly pissed her off. Helen looked on bemused and wished there was more than her here to see Irene being brought down a peg or two. Helen, now hoping to catch Irene's eye, had no chance as Irene reverently studied the palms of her hands as she realised her mess up.

"Ladies, I want you to listen to me carefully, in particular you Irene as you clearly know none of what happened on Friday." Helen nodded affirmatively back at her boss and out the corner of her eye saw Irene do the same.

"Well, one of our esteemed parents took it upon herself to start bullying young Lucy on Friday after school on account of her hair. I'll let you guess who that was Irene?"

Irene nodded back to Rosie, having more than a fair idea of who it could have been.

"A pupil alerted Connor and he returned back to school to get Lucy but was adamant that he did not need me to take him home after we failed to contact mum by phone, so obviously I insisted on taking them both home. They live in the flats at the bottom of Knox Street, so not the best area, but by no means the worst. I had to persist with the pair for them to get mum. She did eventually come to the door and what a wee soul she was. I'm surprised that Carol didn't say more about her. She has clearly been the butt of someone else's fierce hand I would say ... huge scar on her face and her leg trailed behind her when she walked."

"Was she under the influence?" Helen asked keenly.

"If she was, it wasn't drink. Definitely a smoker: fog that would have put auld reekie to shame, but I want to say no. The kids said she had been sleeping and was tired, which I would agree with. She didn't have that jakey, if you excuse the expression, look about her. She stood and listened to me as I spoke and both Lucy and Connor stood perfectly, cuddling into her. She was just a wee soul and I think she … well all of them … need our help. I offered her support, but she refused. Not surprising, I know, so I put a wee call into social work. Unfortunately, as there is no obvious physical abuse, head lice don't count, and with nothing else to go on, they can't afford to give one of their social workers over to investigate. They are, as usual, so under pressure with more high-risk cases. They have asked us to keep an eye on things and if anything else comes up to alert them. They have nothing on the family … well, nothing they have found."

"It's just so frustrating when you can't get the back-up and you know something isn't right," Helen said, exasperated by the familiar situation.

"I totally agree with you, Helen, but unfortunately hunches aren't enough for social work to act on. The mother looked at her wit's end …"

"No wonder with that boy as her son!" Irene butted in.

"Actually, Irene, I was just about to say that I didn't think it had anything to do with the kids. They did exactly as she said, perfectly well-mannered to me in the car on the way to the house."

"Well, I'm afraid we'll have to agree to disagree on that one. In class, that boy is impudent, rude and nothing, but trouble. Behaviour like that doesn't stop when he goes out of the class. Oh, and are you forgetting the fight he started up at the park?

Poor Tony had an awful black eye as a result of Connor's handy right hook," Irene said with a sour face.

"Irene, I realise Connor has been finding it hard to settle in class, but I think there has been a lot of unrest or something going on at home causing him to behave out of sorts in the class," Rosie said very diplomatically.

"Can I also just add," Helen began, "that the fight up at the park only happened as a result of a lot of provocation by Tony and a few others, where his sister was bullied. From what I gathered he was actually defending his sister."

"Well, you believe what you like, Helen, we all know you take the softly, softly approach. That boy shows no respect and should be dealt with accordingly," Irene snapped back.

"Ladies, ladies, please. I didn't bring you in here to argue. I just wanted you to both be aware of the difficult situation the Jackson kids are in at home and for you to be considerate to their situation."

"Rosie, with all due respect there are other children in my class who have far greater needs than that boy, but don't behave the way he does."

"Irene, we are all different and we all deal with things differently. I am asking you to be mindful of his home situation. I, of course, do not expect you to let him get away with behaviour that is not accepted in our school. I would like you, however, to support him as much as possible in class and be aware of what may be going on at home. I know you are already doing this, Irene, and I know he has been difficult. Perhaps you could brainstorm with a colleague to see if you could change anything in your class to help support you when working with him?" Rosie suggested.

"What do you mean? Do you think I can't cope with him?" Irene asked indignantly.

"Absolutely not. We both know that working with a colleague

can generate new ideas that we may have overlooked. Helen, I'm sure you wouldn't mind working with Irene, would you?"

"Whaaat? Errr no, that's fine," Helen stuttered in shock at being put in that position.

"Great. Well, I'll leave it to you both to sort a time out that suits. Now, Irene, you can go back to your class, but Helen there is something else I need to talk to you about," Rosie said.

"Eh, just before I go," Irene began, "… what is being done about the head lice situation. I for one do not think I should be subjected to working conditions where I may be at risk of catching the little critters. Also, my other pupils are being put at risk."

"Irene, head lice are unfortunately part and parcel of working in a school. There have been kids in the school, in your class, with similar problems. Also, I think head lice are the least of the Jackson kids' problems at the moment."

"But, Rosie, never to the same extent. That sister of Connor's, well I've never seen anything like it."

"Yes, I agree it is a severe case, but as I said at the staff meeting the other day, there is nothing we can do except inform the parents and we have done that. We can't deny the child their education as a result of head lice."

"Well mark my words, there is going to be an outcry from all the other parents if they see the state of her head."

"Thank you, Irene, for your insightfulness. We will be doing all we can to rectify the problem. I'm just asking for you to be mindful, in the meantime, of the fact it is not the children's fault they are in the situation they are in and we need to support them."

"You know this job never used to be like this. We are more like parents than the parents are. If only they would do the job they were meant to do then I could actually do my job and teach," Irene moaned.

"The job is a difficult job, I agree, Irene, but I have every faith you will do the right thing. If you wouldn't mind closing the door behind you so I can talk to Helen I would be very grateful," Rosie asked.

Helen sat utterly mortified at the attitude and the total balls of the woman speaking to her headteacher like that. Her face must have told the story as Rosie picked up on it once Irene had moved to the other side of the door.

"Ok, you can see that I fear Irene is having some difficulty with all of this. I'm thinking that I may try and find some excuse for Connor to spend more time in your class for the next wee while until we get to the bottom of what is happening."

"I don't have a problem with that, Rosie. I just want to help the wee souls."

"I was hoping … no, I knew that would be your attitude. Lucy is not going to give us much information about anything, but Connor might. Did you not already get him to divulge some information?"

"Yes, but only about his previous school, not home."

"Yes, but I think if you continued building a relationship then this would come. He clearly feels comfortable in your company. We just need to think of something plausible to tell Irene so she doesn't feel we are undermining her professionalism. She is a great teacher as long as the kids she is teaching conform to her ways. Let me have a think and I will get back to you," Rosie added.

Helen rose as their conversation ended when an idea came to mind. "I've just remembered it is Lucy's special week this week and her mum has been invited to school. Maybe mum will come? Or maybe I can involve Connor in some way?"

"Good thinking. I'll leave it with you. Any problems just let me know. Also, I would be really grateful if you could find the time to help Irene reflect on her practice. It would benefit you too, looking at all the good systems she has in place for her more able pupils."

"Of course," Helen said as she went out the door, waiting until the door was shut before she made the face that expressed her true feelings about the suggestion.

Carol raised her eyebrow at Helen as she walked past and Helen smiled, then mouthed 'I'll fill you in later,' delivering it with a wink.

Helen sighed with relief that Rosie was on the same page as her; she knew her gut instincts about the two kids had been telling her something and hopefully now with more of a focus on them something would come to light so the kids could get the support they deserved. Still in shock at the way Irene had gone on, Helen shook her head in disbelief.

Walking past Linda's class she stuck her head round the door. "Morning, Missus."

"Morning, Helen. You just in? I was looking for you earlier."

"Was in a meeting with Rosie and ..." Helen put her two arms out to the side, stuck her bum out and waddled further into the class, imitating who the other person was.

"Aw god, bet that was fun. What've the pair of you been up to to get dragged into the heidy's first thing on a Monday morning?"

"Not us, but the Jackson kids. That Irene is something else. Need to go ... will fill you in later when I've got a spare hour."

"Really? Doesn't sound good. Catch up later. Have a good morning."

"You too."

37 Connor

Connor's knees rattled off the bottom of his tray beneath his desk, the pains in his stomach so immense he was doing anything to keep his mind off them. With his mind so far away, he was totally unaware of the persistent noise he made, but was the only one oblivious to it. His fellow classmates spent their time glancing over at him, in awe of his brazen actions, waiting for their teacher to take the bait and get hooked into a battle of wills. Despite the noise going on for the last couple of minutes or so and her voice increasing in volume twice to be heard over the disturbance, the 'Gallows' had, by and large, ignored Connor, except for a few mean glances shot his way.

Connor's gaze stared at the outside world, at the football pitch outside his classroom window. School had been a must this morning for several reasons, though at the moment he was struggling severely from a lack of food. He was aware of the drone of his teacher as he zoned in and out of the class lesson, her voice like the engine of an old fighter plane flying back and forth.

Trying hard to be 'supportive', the Gallows had ignored his rattling, but as it continued she felt it were a complete act of insubordination directed at her and could stand it no longer. She stopped, penetrated her gaze solely on Connor, the class hardly breathing as they nervously awaited the eruption. Still immune to the goings-on, the rumble beneath Connor's desk persisted. Hayley at the other side of the class desperately tried to gain Connor's attention, but her feat only put her in danger. Like an eagle on predation, The Gallows' eyes locked on target, ready to swoop.

A knock at the door shattered the growing tension in the class.

Not moving her eyes from her prey, the Gallows bellowed, "Enter."

The door edged open, pushed open by the small frame of Chloe from Lucy's class. Sensing something was going on, Chloe looked like a rabbit caught in headlights. Staring around the class, she tried to work out what she should do. The Gallows, forgetting her warm, welcoming manner, stood fixated on what lay in front of her; she did not cast her gaze in her direction once.

"Yes?"

"Eh, eh … can Miss Kane see Connor?" Chloe stuttered, almost forgetting why she was there.

Silence filled the room like the first deep fall of snow quietens the earth. At the mention of his name, Connor finally controlled his wayward knees and he also became blanketed with quiet. Chloe looked about her as if planning an escape. Then a thunder of noise bellowed from the Gallows. The audible, sharp intake of breath from a few on the front row was the only sound made by the kids.

"Connor? Connor … …? Hmmmm, well, well, well you seem to have been saved by the hands of the fair maiden once again, Mr Jackson."

Not quite sure if this meant he should go, Connor remained seated.

"Did you not hear, Connor? Those ears still playing up? Miss Kane wants to see you." Her voice sounded mockingly sweet.

Pushing his chair back slowly, he made his way over to the door, Chloe rushing behind him. The door had barely closed when Chloe expressed her relief.

"Oh my god, is she scary or what? The next time I'm no going tae put ma hand up to go on a message."

Connor peered down at the younger child, not quite sure what she was going on about. He was still battling with the lion roaring in his empty stomach demanding to be fed. Suddenly feeling pulling on his arm, Connor moved to shrug her off then he noticed Chloe's other arm pointing up the corridor.

"Look … the police!" Chloe pulled him down, whisper shouting in his ear as if she hiding from them.

Connor's heart stopped and his palms grew sweaty. His reflexes pounced into action, clutching his buttocks just in time, saving him from a smelly, embarrassing accident. Pushing Chloe ahead, he kept his arm on her shoulder while his eyes stayed steady on his other enemy. Connor watched as Mrs Barr greeted them, jovially shaking hands, laughing at one of their comments, then directing them to her office. Oh, how he wished he were a fly on the wall.

Reaching Miss Kane's door, the pair made their way in and were welcomed like long lost family, a stark contrast to Chloe's earlier encounter.

"Aw, Connor, how are you? It is lovely to see you. I'm so glad you could be excused. Did you get lost, Chloe?"

"Eh, no, the Gallows, I mean Mrs Gallows, was erm, busy." Chloe's face had grown the colour of a ripe tomato at her faux pas, whilst her classmates failed to hide their sniggers. Even Miss Kane had a smile touching the corner of her lips. Connor remained still, his mind in a million other places, but mostly on his recent sighting of the two black-clad figures at the school entrance.

Noticing his detachment, Miss Kane directed Chloe and the rest of the class to complete the task she had set, then she engaged with Connor. "I'm sorry for dragging you away from your class, Connor. I just wanted to have a chat about Lucy's special day. Do you remember me telling you about it on Friday?"

So much had happened since then that Connor had completely forgotten about it. His blank face told Miss Kane all she needed to know.

"Remember your mum was invited to school this afternoon to have a special treat with Lucy? Did Lucy give mum the special invite?"

Connor tried to think back, but all he could see were the cops at the school entrance and the cops from Saturday night. He scoured his mind, trying to figure out if they were the same ones. He just couldn't remember. The faces from Saturday night were fuzzy from a combination of the darkness and being blinded by the headlights. Perhaps if he heard them speak he would be able to work it out better. Maybe he could get Hayley to go up for a nosey – she would know.

"Connor? Connor? Are you ok? Connor?"

Blinking, he focused his gaze on Miss Kane and tried to give her his attention. "Eh, I'm fine, miss."

"Something on your mind?" she asked in a quiet voice that only he could hear. "Connor I'm here to help if there is a problem?"

He looked at her and wished he could share his burdens with her, but he knew better than to do that. Realising he was letting his 'face' slip, he gave himself a shake to try and kick his brain into gear.

"No, I'm fine. Lucy's special day Friday, yeah?"

"Yes. Is your mum coming? You know it would mean the world to Lucy, and to me if she could make it. I asked the secretary to phone, but she didn't get a reply. Is mum out today or not well again? I was thinking maybe I could pop down to your house at break and see if she was ok?"

Connor received this information like a cattle prod up his arse and he switched himself fully on.

"She is fine, Miss Kane … probably forgot to charge her mobile. Now that I think of it, I remember Lucy giving her the invite. I need to help her tae the school at lunchtime as she's got a gammy leg. That ok?"

This was definitely the answer Miss Kane wanted to hear and she replied with an 'absolutely fine', nodding and smiling at him.

"I will speak to Mrs Barr and let her know you might be a wee bit late getting back. You must promise me you will get your lunch first?"

"No fear with that one, miss."

Miss Kane turned and spoke out, loud enough for Lucy to hear, "I'm so delighted your mum is coming this afternoon – what a kind big brother you have. You should have told me when I asked you, Lucy, and then poor Connor wouldn't have needed to be dragged out of his class."

Lucy looked over at her brother totally bewildered by what she was hearing. Little did she know this was exactly how Connor felt. How he was going to pull off what he had just voiced was a total mystery to him too.

38 Lucy

After the way her mum had been at the weekend she couldn't understand why Miss Kane thought her mum would be coming up to see her at school. Not once, but twice her mum had shouted at her and hit her. She fathomed this meant that her mum really hated her. *No wonder*, she supposed. *Who would like someone who didn't speak and peed the bed?* She wasn't like Connor who helped her with getting stuff. He was at least good to have around, whereas she just sent her mum to sleep or caused her to get so angry she got hit. Lucy had noticed that her mum was sleeping more and more. Maybe it was because she was bored of Lucy saying nothing. Maybe that was why her mum didn't give her food. Maybe she didn't deserve it. At the mere thought of food, Lucy's stomach responded with a growl that was heard by everyone at her table. They all let out a giggle.

When Lucy had tried to show her mum the special invitation, her mum had barely opened her eyes and mumbled something unintelligible in response. Lucy had left it lying beside her on the couch so that when she did wake she would see it. Lucy had found the invite again last night. Now, however, it was crumpled behind her mum's cushion and almost unreadable. This had speared another hole in Lucy's heart. She wondered what lies her brother had told her beloved teacher as there was just no way her mum would walk to school. Despite this, her heart held onto the tiny shard of hope that kept her going through all of her dark times.

39 Helen

Noticing that Helen was still in her class even though the bell for break had gone, Carol chapped and went in for a natter.

"How's your morning been so far?"

"Ok, I suppose. You?"

"Busy, but nothing new there. How was Lucy today?"

Realising she was fishing for the gossip from earlier, Helen gladly divulged, happy to share her news with trustworthy ears.

"To be frank and brutally honest she stinks like a sewer, has clothes on that wouldn't look amiss in a refugee camp and oh my god, that hair. I've spent the morning scratching my head in what I hope is sympathy."

"God, that sounds awful, the two are wee souls."

"Yup, but on the plus side, Connor said that he is going to get his mum at lunchtime to help her up to school. Which reminds me, could you say to Rosie that he might be late getting back to school, and pass a note to Irene too. If I tell her, she will just slag me off for being too soft."

"Too soft. What do you mean?"

"Och, in our meeting this morning, she took great delight in telling Rosie that I took a softly, softly approach to kids."

"For fuck's sake, if she wasn't such a bitch she might get the sort of results you do."

Helen shrugged in response.

"The police were up earlier," Carol shared.

"What for?"

"Two things. Firstly, to tell us that two school-age kids, boy of about eleven and a girl of about seven were involved with shoplifting from the big supermarket. They both got away and the supermarket isn't pressing charges as it was just a packet of crisps, they just wanted the school to do a wee reminder about appropriate behaviour, blah, blah, blah."

"Aw, gawd, sounds like my two wee waifs and strays."

Carol nodded in agreement then continued, "Rosie then said the police had informed her that Hayley's pappi had phoned 999 in a frantic and slightly intoxicated state, saying he thought Hayley had been kidnapped as she'd been missing all day. He had reported that a young boy with dark hair had come for her in the morning and she hadn't been seen since. He demanded that they look for her. 'The emergency' was passed onto the local police boys and they found her at about eleven at night walking up the Main Street."

"Hayley? That is *so* not like her. Who was the boy? Aw, wait, you don't need to tell me, do you?"

"Nope. It was Connor."

"Fuck. It's no wonder he was away with the fairies this morning. It seems like he's been a busy boy at the weekend. I just wonder what the mother was doing while her kids were running wild. Clearly not bathing them, that's for sure. I'm really looking forward to seeing her this afternoon. Think we'll have a lot of our questions answered. So, what happened did they get lifted or just given a warning?"

"Well, the story goes that due to the time they decided to give them a lift, but Connor did a runner and neither of the police saw where he went apparently."

"Really? They were outsmarted by a twelve-year-old. Dear god, that says a lot for our local constabulary."

"I think it was probably more outran. The two police obviously enjoy lunches from the chippy on a regular basis." Carol joked.

"I get you. Was Hayley allowed to go home to a drunken

pappi? Bet she got an earful from that cantankerous old git."

"He'd apparently sobered up a bit. He's no really that bad. Just an old man tired of looking after wayward weans. There's always something going down at this school. Anyway, did you have a good weekend?

"Ah, that I did!"

A smile settled on Helen's lips.

"You're no saying anything more with that smile on your face? Come on … spill the beans," Carol said settling herself down on the table, waiting for the juicy gossip.

"Bit of a long story really."

"I take it, it involves a man? If I'm right I'm going to get the janny to hold the bell. I've waited too long to hear a story about you and a man, especially one that puts a smile like that on you!"

Helen didn't even try to hide the smile that erupted on her face.

"Ha! I know it's been too long. Well basically I met a guy last week when I was at the Mitch; we chatted then I had to exit without even a name as Wendy was pissed as a fart. I was sitting in the hospital Thursday night as I took Isa to see wee Betty and who rocked up, but …"

"The guy from the pub?' Carol butted in excitedly. Helen's grin made another appearance, confirming the guess. "Oh, my gawd! Helen that is so meant to be. What's he like?"

"He has a big hairy beard … *the* most beautiful eyes and this calmness that completely beguiles me and he is … wait for it … a doctor!"

"Really? Helen, I'm so pleased for you. It's time you had someone in your life. You're such a bonny lassie. So, did the two of youse catch up?"

"Yup. Friday night, though that was nearly a disaster as he was late. Then yesterday he arrived at my door unannounced and we spent the whole day together. We went to his house – one of the huge flats down the shore with the big bay windows – took his dog for a walk then he cooked me dinner. It was so nice: he was just so considerate, not like all those other ass holes."

"Cooks as well as having a good job? Aw, he is a keeper!"

"I really like him. I just hope I can keep him for a wee while."

"Well, if he's any sense he won't let you go. God, is that the time already? Suppose I better be on my way. I'm really pleased for you Helen. You should invite him to our next night out …"

"Ha, you are way too funny, not a fucking chance!"

"Right, I'm away, enough gabbing for one break. Make sure you get a coffee."

"I'm just going now."

Helen followed Carol out of the class and made her way to the staffroom. Before she even opened the door, she could hear Irene's moaning at full hilt and there was no need to guess who was getting slated.

"… I couldn't believe the gall of that boy today. A full ten minutes of brazen, insolent behaviour that disrupted my whole lesson and I've to be supportive towards him? Meanwhile, Carly in my class has lots of issues, but gets her head down and gets on with the work. If he so much as looks at me the wrong way he won't know what's hit him."

Helen watched as the grey bun, the colour of dirty snow, bobbed all around the top of her head, reminding Helen of an old-fashioned wobble toy. "Compassionate as ever I see, Irene?" She couldn't stop the snide remark jumping out of her mouth as she made her coffee. Irene slowly turned her head, not having seen Helen come through the door.

"I don't know why I turned my head, only you would come out with a nambi-pambi remark like that. You've no idea what it's like trying to teach when that boy's impudence is being flaunted in your face in front of the rest of the class. I have a duty to teach all the children, which is very hard when he disrupts the class on a daily basis."

"You've no idea, Irene, what Connor is dealing with at home. At least he managed to get to school. And you have a duty to be supportive to the needs of all your pupils."

Irene's face contorted and Helen knew that if she were a cartoon character steam would be cascading out her ears.

"Well I don't need to worry as you're going to come in and show me how it's done, aren't you, Helen?" The sarcasm didn't just ooze out Irene's mouth, it flooded with every syllable spoken.

Helen sighed. "Irene, I think we both know that is not what Rosie said, but you know I'm always happy to share and help any of my colleagues, especially you." This time Helen liberally smeared cynicism thickly over her words. The rest of the staff squirmed in their chairs listening to the two teachers, deciding that keeping their mouths shut was the most sensible option.

"Don't you just love it when the young, fresh out of college staff think they know it all, Donna?"

Irene's sole and debatable ally didn't even provide Irene with a full nod of agreement, restricting it to a line across her lips, not that bulletproof Irene noticed or cared.

Helen had had enough and, instead of wasting her breath, gave an eye roll and shake of the head and concentrated on gulping down her coffee to beat the bell.

40 Connor

Hayley was in her element as she regaled the 'Hayley and Connor Cop Story' to her gossip-hungry audience.

"Aye, two polis picked us up. They stopped the motor right in front of us like they do on the telly. I think they left big black tyre marks all over the road, didn't they, Connor?"

Sitting next to Hayley, his back leaning on the crumbly sandstone wall, Connor shifted his bum from one cheek to the other, trying to find a wee bit of protection from the solid seat. His attention had drifted miles away from her story until she dunted him in the ribs; he had been no part of her performance. She took the grunt he made as an affirmative and carried on.

"Aye, and Speedy Gonzales here bolted off into the night. Meanwhile, I had to go in the back of the polis car."

"Did you get cuffed?" Ben asked excitedly.

"Eh, well nearly, but I just told them that I wis'nae wearing them and they locked the door instead," Hayley expertly lied.

"Did your pappi no go bush? Ma mum would have grounded me for a year if I got brought home by the polis," Chantelle said.

"Aw, he'd been on the whiskey so he wis'nae too bad. I got ma arse skelped and then sent tae ma room. But he wis fine the next day. Probably could'nae remember."

"Wis that why the polis was up at the school this morning?" Kerry asked.

At the mention of this, Connor tuned in like a radio on high frequency, ears pricked and mind focused.

"What were the polis at the school the day?" Connor asked, trying to act nonchalant.

"Aye, when I wis taking a message up to the office, I saw them going intae the heid's room," Kerry explained.

"Hmm. Does nae body know why they were there?" Connor inquired.

The gathered group stayed silent.

"So what did your maw say, Connor?" Hayley asked.

"Nothing. She wis'nae bothered."

"Gawd, you's are both lucky. Ma arse would have been red raw," Gary said.

The group looked upon the pair with newfound respect. Having had a run-in with the law and survived, definitely warranted it. Hayley enjoyed her new elevated status, particularly when it meant everyone wanted to play with her. Connor couldn't have cared less, but appreciated the shares in snacks he got, though they made little impact in the gaping cavernous hole in his belly. The bell went and everyone jostled to stand beside the new heroes of the day.

Connor had never hated anyone as much as he hated the 'Gallows'. Everything about her annoyed him. He sat in the class despising everything she did and said. He listened to her talking to her golden group that did no wrong, her words floating gently down into their ears like petals. He imagined her smiling at them as she spoke. As he watched, all he could see was her massive arse that jiggled as if it were attached to a washing machine on spin. His thoughts then wandered to his mum and the task he had stupidly got himself mixed up in. How he was going to get his mum to school was beyond him. Miss Kane had freaked him out when she spoke about going down to the flat. It was bad enough the head knowing where he lived, but Miss Kane knowing was just a step too far. Imagine if she saw inside the house. He could feel his face tinge with embarrassment at the thought of her seeing where he lived. The mess on the floor, the stink of pee, the fog of smoke. It was going to be bad enough that she met his mum, who was …

"Boys and girls, we'd better be nice and quiet. It seems as though Connor here is lost in a dream."

At the mention of his name, Connor snapped out of his wee dwam to be met with the sneer of the 'Gallows' bearing down on him. Shuffling backwards in his chair to try and regain focus, he heard the others giggling. A flush washed over his face as the hackles rose up his back.

"You've decided to join us, Connor? How kind of you. Deep in thought as usual. It's a wonder you are not top of the class with all that deep thinking you do. Care to share any of it with us?"

Connor sat forcing his rogue tongue to stay still.

"I thought as much. A head full of cotton wool is not going to give us any insightful ideas. Now if it is not too much trouble for you, COULD YOU KINDLY SWITCH YOUR BRAIN ON AND GET SOME WORK DONE?" Her words arrived accompanied by a shower of spit that Connor distastefully wiped away, much to the delight of his audience who laughed louder than they should have.

Slamming her hands down on his desk, her colossal frame-caused shockwaves that made Connor's chair shake. Her eyes came level with his and he matched her stare while his snarl that flickered the side of his lips. He could see beads of sweat popping out on her forehead like bubbles on a cooking pancake. He let his stare slip as his eyes followed a bead rolling to its death down her cheek. The smell of her stale sweat filled his nostrils and he could feel the heat from her face reflecting back onto his. Still he remained unflummoxed by her desperate attempt to intimidate him. Remaining unfathomed by her stares, she changed tactics and swiveled round to address the class.

"Well, boys and girls, as you have all found Mr Jackson's antics so entertaining, I think it is only fair that I allow all of you to have a personal audience with him this lunchtime." Unsure of exactly what she meant they sat quietly as she continued; "You are all going to be joining Connor for lunchtime detention."

The mention of detention caused an uproar of 'unfairs' to ricochet round the class. Connor fizzed inside, but managed to calmly say, "I cannae."

"PARDON?" Gallows bellowed back. "PARDON?"

"I cannae."

"I cannae? I cannae? Who exactly do you think you are speaking to and what exactly is it you think you cannot do? Because I'll tell you, something boy, if I tell you, you are on detention, you damn well, will be on detention!"

The class were in shock now. Their teacher had used the 'damn' word and had risen her voice to shrieking level, a spectacle that demanded their full attention.

Connor sat looking as calm as a sheep in a meadow then, thinking he needed to reply to his teacher, said, "I cannae do detention."

Breathing rapidly now, the Gallows tried to recompose herself before she opened her mouth. Speaking through gritted teeth, her voice could just be heard. "Tell me why you think you CANNOT do detention?"

"'cause I have tae go hame and get ma mum for Miss Kane."

"PARDON?"

Thinking she must be really deaf he spoke in a louder voice, repeating the same information but slowing his words down.

She opened her mouth, but words failed to come out at first. Instead, she pointed towards the door, then at Connor then back to the door. Connor remained rooted to the seat. Then her gasket blew.

"GET YOUR SORRY LITTLE ... BACKSIDE OUT THAT DOOR. I CAN NO LONGER BEAR THE SIGHT OF YOU IN HE ..!"

Before she managed to complete her sentence. a chap came on the door followed by Miss Kane's face.

"Sorry to interrupt, Mrs Gallows …" She stopped mid-sentence as she sensed something going on. "Erm … is everything ok?"

"Is everything ok? I'm so glad you asked, Miss Kane, and I'm so glad you are here. I've just put Connor on lunchtime detention as a result of his atrocious behaviour and he tells me that he 'cannae' do it as he has to go and get his mum for you. You can now put him right and explain that he will have to do his detention instead."

The whole class were lapping up the afternoon performance, moving their heads from speaker to speaker like Wimbledon spectators.

"Ah, I'm sorry to hear that you've had some difficulty following the class rules, Connor. It sounds like you've been giving Mrs Gallows a hard time. I'm sorry, too, Mrs Gallows, that you've had a difficult morning. Normally I would be insisting that Connor completed his detention, but I'm wondering if this once it could be postponed until tomorrow as the job he has to do is really important?"

"Pardon, are you trying to undermine my authority, Miss Kane? I think you are missing the point here. Connor's behaviour needs to be dealt with today and I'm sorry you can't see the importance of that."

Utterly embarrassed at being spoken to like that in front of the children who were sitting with gobs wide open, Helen continued, "I do absolutely …"

Miss Kane's voice was drowned by the lunch bell. The quiet corridor erupted with voices as children were dismissed from classes. One or two ignored the steam puffing off their teacher and began to pack up, while others were unsure what to do as the unsteady atmosphere had knocked everything off-kilter.

"What do you think you are doing? Nobody gave you permission to pack away," Mrs Gallows roared at the presumptuous few that had used their own initiative. Thumping round to her desk, she sat down and folded her arms in front of her heaving chest, her short arms just managing to cross over one another. Miss Kane stood, still with the door slightly ajar also unsure of the next move. The class slowly got the message that lunch would not be happening until they sat down quietly.

Allowing the door to close, Miss Kane made her way over to the teacher's desk, bending her head low to speak to Mrs Gallows. Despite their quietness, nobody could hear what she said, but they heard the response loud and clear.

"ABSOLUTELY NOT! HOW DARE YOU COME IN HERE AND SUGGEST SUCH A THING!"

They then watched Miss Kane walk red-faced towards the door, stopping on the way to whisper to Connor.

"Please don't worry about anything, Connor. I will sort this out."

Connor couldn't help but grin, gloating over the fact he had such a powerful ally against the Gallows, and this final act by Miss Kane was the final nail in the coffin for her. There would be no coming back for Miss Kane now. She had well and truly crossed the line in the eyes of Mrs Gallows.

Once the door slammed shut, Mrs Gallows furthered the atmosphere by silently sitting, watching them all. Unable to stay quiet, a few tentatively put up their hands to ask to go and complete lunch duties. Their requests were denied. Eventually, she stood up and commanded their full attention.

"This is what's going to happen. Everybody has lunchtime detention today. If for whatever reason you do not turn up to my class at 1 pm, you will have lunchtime detention for the rest of the week. Understood?"

Twenty-eight heads nodded. One remained still.

41 Lucy

Proudly wearing her 'special' badge, Lucy walked with her head a little higher to collect her lunch. Flushing with embarrassment as Elsa commented on her adornment, she quickly picked up her tray, just managing a quick flash of a smile in return.

Amazed at how little lunch the kids sitting at her table actually ate, Lucy watched the rigmarole of 'not eating' they carried out every lunchtime, in between her mouthfuls. First, they picked delicate pieces of meat off their plate with their fingers. Then they examined it before they tested it with their tongue. Then they finally put it back on their plate to push it around some more. Lucy cleared her plate and moved on to her cake. Before devouring it, she had an idea. Using her knife, she cut it in half and ate only one piece. Collecting a paper towel from the end of the table, she carefully wrapped the remaining piece up, then stuffed it in her pocket. Mum would be so pleased with her bringing something home for her to eat. She hoped this would put her in a good mood and stop her shouting at her.

Standing up, she carefully picked up her empty plates and took them over to the clearing area; she dropped her cutlery into the bucket of soapy water and saw some of the bubbles jump onto her shoes, making them glisten. Reaching up, she stacked her plate onto the pile then rushed outside, holding her hand carefully over her pocket, guarding her special cake.

Walking out of the dining hall, she noticed a swarm of children from Connor's class huddled round the headteacher. Lucy noted the loud voices they were using, all talking over one another. If that had been her old school they would all have been roared at, she thought. This brought a smile to her face as she thought about how good this school was and how nice the teachers were, and she skipped off down the corridor, one hand swinging and the other clutching her pocket.

Rain plummeted from the sky preventing outside play. Lucy went into her class and picked up a piece of paper and some pens. The noise level was much higher than usual with pent up energy being confined to the class. The dank smell of 'wet' seemed to go unnoticed by the children. Shutting out the giggling and carrying on, Lucy concentrated on colouring a beautiful flower. On its completion, she slowly wrote 'Mum', drew a love heart and then signed it 'Lucy', encircled it all in one encompassing heart. Trying to be careful, she rolled it up, but one end rolled up tighter than the other and she started again, first trying to smooth out the wrinkles made by the unsuccessful first attempt. Once satisfied, she stuffed it into her bag along with the cake, which had largely disintegrated into a pile of crumbs that trickled out the corner of the paper towel.

Before lunch, Lucy had quietly and somewhat jealously watched Alan enjoy juice and cake with his gran. Alan had enthusiastically introduced his gran to the whole class and then chosen three friends to play a game. No matter how hard she tried, Lucy could not imagine how it would be if her mum did come up to school this afternoon as Connor and Miss Kane had said she would. Lucy felt the faint tingles of butterflies in her tummy as she sat waiting for the bell to go and waited patiently to see if her special day turned out to be really so.

42 Helen

Sneaking into Linda's room, Helen slammed the door closed. Her friend lifted her head at the sound and immediately saw from her face that something was wrong.

"Fucking hell. That fucking woman is nuts!"

"I take it, it's Irene you're referring to?" Linda inquired. "What's happened now?"

"She's fucking nuts. I went in just before the bell to get Connor, who is going to get his mum for Lucy's special day and she said he couldn't go because he was on detention. Which I know he should do, but we spent the morning in at Rosie's office discussing the fact something was going on at home and that we needed to tread lightly. *She* was advised to be supportive and then puts him on fucking detention!"

"What for?"

"Aw, she didn't say ... probably for breathing the wrong way, you know what she's like. I then suggested that she postponed the detention to tomorrow."

"You've got balls, Helen, I'll give you that. Did she go nuts when you suggested that?"

"Well, aye, she did, in front of the class, who were all sitting like butter wouldn't melt. So, then I went up to whisper to her without the audience and reminded her of what Rosie said and suggested that she cut Connor a bit of slack."

"Jesus, Helen, you wanting trouble? What did she say then?"

"Aw, she only roared at me in front of everyone. So, I walked out, stopping first to quietly speak to Connor. Fucking bitch that she is."

"Ha, ha, I love your style. I can see her point being pissed off at you trying to re-arrange her detention, but I know she probably dealt out the detention without much reason."

"We've been trying to get in touch with the mum all week and I know if she comes up to the school we'll get so many questions answered. I'm just pissed off she can't see the bigger picture. I'm determined not to let this pair slip beneath the radar again."

"So, what you going to do now?"

"I'm going to calm down then go and see Rosie."

"Good luck."

"Do you think I've overstepped the mark?" Helen asked, suddenly worried about what she'd done.

"Honestly? I think you are very passionate about the welfare of your kids and you're just trying to do the best for them, even if it means pissing off a few along the way. Your heart is in the right place and that is something I can't say for everyone. I admire your balls. Now go and get to Rosie before Irene does."

Not waiting to be told again, Helen made her way towards the dining hall and spotted Rosie in the middle of a group of Irene's kids. Making her way over slowly, she tried to get her words right in her head before speaking them out loud. As she reached them, she heard the kids moaning about Irene. Catching Rosie's eye, she indicated she wanted a word.

"Ok, boys and girls, it sounds as though I need a little more time to look into this. Thank you for coming to share your information. I will get back to you as soon as I can. Go and have your lunch and sit on the bench until I tell you otherwise, ok?"

A collective nod went back before they rushed off to get their lunch trays. Ushering them out of her way, Rosie made her way over to Helen.

"They look annoyed about something," Helen said, nosing for some more information.

"That they are. Apparently, Irene swore in class and has put them all on detention for nothing," Rosie said with raised eyebrows.

"Swore? Really?"

"Shit, I really shouldn't have told you that. They are all very indignant over the matter."

"My lips are sealed. I'm sort of here for the same reason?" Helen continued.

"What? Irene swore at you and put you on detention?"

"Ha, not quite. Did Carol tell you about Connor going to get his mum after lunch?"

"Yes, she did. Do you think she will come?"

"I really hope so and Connor seemed quite convinced that she would."

"Yes, I think you are right. So, the problem is, he is now on detention?"

"Correct. I did suggest that maybe she could postpone it until tomorrow, but that didn't go down too well," Helen said, with a wry smile on her face.

"No, I'm sure it didn't. Ok. This once I'm going to overrule Irene and allow Connor to get his mum. I'm sure I won't be winning any popularity contests with that decision, but the greater good and all that. If you tell Connor, I will go and speak to Irene."

"Thank you so much, Rosie."

Rosie never got the chance to reply as a gaggle of primary two girls were busy tugging her skirt to inform her of something. Helen scanned the dining room, then her eyes found Connor. Scooting in between the tables, she made her way over to him. Along the way, she smiled at random children, that waved at the familiar face not usually spotted in their dining room. Connor sat with his back to her, concentrating on demolishing the pile of food in front of him. She touched him on the shoulder.

"Only me, Connor," Helen said in a quiet voice. "Ok ... once you've finished your lunch you can go home and tell mum about Lucy's special afternoon, but you've got to promise me you will be as quick as you can. I'm putting a lot of trust in you to do this, ok?"

"Eh, aye," Connor said, slightly bemused by the turn of events.

"But Mrs Gallows told us that if we did'nae turn up the day we'd have detention the rest of the week. Connor, you don't want that do you?" Hayley, butted in, unable to keep her nose out.

"Hayley, do you mind? I was having a private conversation with Connor, not you."

"Sorry, miss, but the 'Gallows …'"

"Mrs Gallows, Hayley," Helen corrected.

"Mrs Gallows put us on detention for nothing and she swore. I'm going tae tell ma pappi and he's going tae go mental."

"Right, Hayley, I think Mrs Gallows will know exactly why she put you on detention."

"Miss, we did'nae do anything. She's trying to blame Connor then blame all of us. It's no fair."

"I'm sure it will all get sorted and explained to you. Anyway, Connor, is that you finished?"

"Aye, miss,"

"Well off you go and be as quick as you can and thank you, Connor."

Helen plonked herself down next to Linda in the staffroom, balancing her lunch tray on top of her knees. Carefully she stabbed the minuscule straw through the tub that housed the mouthful of juice within. She knew Linda wanted to hear how her chat with Rosie had gone, but hunger prevailed. Linda knew better than to interrupt this. After a second bite of her wrap, Helen turned her head to Linda. "Done!"

"Satisfactory outcome?"

"Yup, he is away home. Has Irene been in?"

"Not whilst I've been here. Anyone seen Irene?"

"Nope. Not seen hide nor hair of her, which is not like her," Donna said in between mouthfuls of apple crumble and custard.

"Oh, I hope she's ok. Like you said, it's not like her to miss lunch," Helen said, trying to sound convincing.

"I think she has got a lot on her plate at the moment, not that she would admit it to anyone. It's terrible really," Donna let on, then stopped suddenly as she realised she'd said way more than she should have.

"Really?" Linda inquired, desperate to hear more. "Do you mean at school or home? Not nice either way, though."

"Oh, I probably shouldn't have said anything, but it's more at home."

"That's a shame. We are a team. We all work to support one another. Hopefully, things will sort themselves out. I hope it is nothing serious," Helen added, trying to sound supportive, but finding it very difficult. Not wanting to give anything else away, Donna put her head down and returned to shoveling her dessert. There was a quick chap at the staffroom door and then Carol's head appeared. "Sorry to interrupt everybody, but Rosie would like to see you, Helen."

"Now?"

"Yes, if you don't mind. Bring your lunch, I'm sure that will be fine."

Popping the last piece of her wrap in her mouth, Helen held her hands up. Following Carol out the door, she grilled her.

"So, do you know what it is about? Am I in trouble?"

"Not sure, but Irene has just left with a rather puffy face. She looked really upset," Carol advised her.

"Left Rosie's office?"

"Yes, and school. I think she is away home, but that is all I'm saying."

"Really? The Gallows crying? Shit."

The pair walked the remaining length of the corridor in silence, a myriad of excuses and justifications going through Helen's mind. Taking a deep breath Helen chapped the head teacher's door then walked in.

"Sorry for dragging you away from your lunch, Helen, but I need to ask you a favour. Irene has had to go home unwell. Can I take your pupil free time off of you this afternoon so Jack can cover Irene's class?"

"Sure, absolutely," said Helen somewhat relieved. This had not been one of the fifty scenarios that had gone through her head on the short walk to the office. But it was by far, much more favourable. "Is she ok?"

"I hope so. It sounds as though she is under some amount of stress at home and I think it has been carrying over into the class."

"Oh, I see. I'm sorry to hear that. If there is anything else I can do to help, just ask," Helen advised.

"Thanks, Helen. I'm not sure how things will go, but she seems quite upset."

"That doesn't sound good. Is it serious?"

"Not in terms of health as such, but I really don't want to say anymore."

"I understand. Ok, if that is all I will go and get organised."

"Thank you, Helen. Is Connor back yet?"

"Not that I've heard. He was a bit later leaving."

"Well if mum turns up please let me know. I would like a chat with her too, though as I said I'm not holding my breath."

"Sure, I will let you know either way."

43 Connor

Jumping down the flight of steps at the front of the school, Connor landed in a puddle, drenching his shoes and the bottom of his trousers so that they wrapped themselves closely around his ankles. The playground was unusually quiet as the rain fell noisily into puddles that formed in the ditches created by the broken tarmac. Swinging one-footed on the gate, he swung it open then skipped down the road, trying to think how he was ever going to succeed in getting his mum to school. He broke into a sprint, remembering his promise to Miss Kane.

He opened the door praying that his mum would at least be awake. Bounding into the room, then the bedroom looking for her, he shouted, "Muuum! Muum!" Confused he sat on the couch. Then he heard a creak and his mum peeked out from behind the couch.

"Jesus, son, I near had a heart attack there. I heard the door and knew it wis'nae home time; thought he had found us. What you doing back from the school? You in trouble? Thought you liked this school?"

"I do. It's Lucy's special day … mind she said you were tae go up for a cuppa tea with her the day?"

"I cannae go, son. Look at the state of me. I cannae go out there."

"Her teacher wis going tae come doon and get you. I said I would get you instead. Lucy really wants you to go. And this teacher is cool, no like any other teacher you've ever met. You'll love her."

"Aw, I know, but I just don't think I can, son. Lucy'll understand."

"Mum, please, a told the teacher I would get you. Please. Come on," Connor got his mum's coat and took it over to her. "Please, Mum. Just this once. I promise you, you'll like this teacher. If you don't come she might come and get you. You know what might happen then …"

"Gawd, Connor, do you think she would? I could'nae cope with a visit from the social. They might take the pair of you away."

"Aye, maybe. So that's why you need to come."

Seeing her mind being pushed into going, he started moving. He helped his mum put on her coat and found her trainers and pushed her feet into them, just like she used to do when he was younger. He could feel her trembling and it wasn't from the cold. She sat down on the couch and shook her head again at Connor.

"I cannae, son."

Not taking no for an answer, he continued as if she hadn't uttered a word. Doing his best to heave her off the couch, he pulled with all his might. But, despite being a skinny thing, he couldn't budge her.

"Mum, you need to come. You cannae have them coming here." Tears rolled down his mum's face. He could feel his brimming too. She put her hand down by her side to assist herself getting up and he knew they were going. Hauling her up, he guided her to the front door, his hand planted firmly on her back.

"Son, I look terrible. Let me at least brush ma hair."

Connor waited patiently as his mum went back to the mirror in the bathroom and tied her lank hair into a ponytail. Once she was done, she grabbed hold of his arm and they made their slow descent of the stairs. The rain fell slower as they opened the closed door as if someone was taking their time turning off a tap. Every now and then the sun made a concerted effort to be seen, then just before it popped through, a cloud would swirl pass as if sending it to the back of the class again.

Connor tried to keep a good pace, but struggled with the weight of his mum on his arm – she just couldn't keep up with him. He heard her foot scrape along the pavement and when he looked back he saw the streaky pattern it made on the wet ground. It never occurred to him how painful it might be as his mum never once complained, only dug her fingers deeper into his arm. Still a fair bit from the school, they heard the bell go. Connor swore to himself and gave his mum a tug, trying to quicken her pace even more.

Stumbling on her good leg, she shouted out; "Son, I'm no gonnae make it. Go ahead. I don't want you getting intae trouble for being late."

"In what'll you do? You cannae walk yourself. Come on, it's fine."

"I could just sit in this close doorway till the school finishes and then you could come and get me."

"Naw, Mum, just come on," With determination driving him on, he gripped his mum even tighter than before, put his head down and battled forward. The street was quiet, the indecisive weather keeping folk at home. As they neared the school, Connor was spurred on and couldn't quite believe he'd managed to get his mum this far. He reached out and pushed the gate open but was yanked backwards as his mum came to a complete standstill. He tugged her forward, but she didn't move.

"Mum, come on."

"I'm sorry, son, I cannae."

"How no?"

"What will they say? What will they think of me? I cannae, son."

"Mum, we're here. Please. Lucy wants … needs you. Miss Kane wants to meet you. I want you to. Please." He continued to pull her arm and she couldn't help but make progress towards the school. Connor felt her hand trembling and when he turned to look at her, he could see how scared she was.

"It's ok, Mum, I promise." He gave her hand a wee squeeze and helped her up the stairs as she painfully lifted her dodgy leg up each step. He pressed the buzzer and felt his shoulders relax as he saw Mrs Barr's face come to the door to let him in.

"Connor, you made it back and in good time. Good afternoon, Mrs Jackson. I'm so pleased you could make it and I know that Lucy will be even more delighted. That was so kind of you, Connor, to go home and help mum along the road. You are such a good help. Ok, Connor, off you go to class and I will take mum down to see Lucy, ok?"

Connor stood with his head down, reluctant to move, afraid of what his teacher might say as he was late and hadn't turned up for detention.

"On you go, son," his mum said, letting go of his arm, pushing him gently on the back with her other arm. Refusing to go, he stayed put.

"Connor, is something wrong?" Mrs Barr inquired.

"I wis meant to be on detention today."

"Yes, I did hear about that. I'm going to come along to the class later to talk to you all. Mrs Gallows has, unfortunately, had to go home as she is not well, so Mr Hay is taking you this afternoon, now off you go."

With that delightful news, Connor went on his way, looking forward to what the rest of his day would bring as he knew it would be good.

"Son," his mum called after him, "will you help me home?"

"Aye. See you out the front after the bell."

"Right you are, son."

44 Lucy

Since the lunch bell, Lucy had been sitting watching the door like a dog waiting for its master. But nothing. Miss Kane had spoken to her a few times about concentrating and getting her job done, but she just kept drifting off, imagining what it would be like if her mum walked through the door. A chap at the door brought Lucy's head sharply back, belly full of anticipation. It quickly sank, as she saw Mrs Barr coming through the door. She dropped her head to the table as she felt the last drops of hope vanish.

"Well, good afternoon, Primary Four."

"Good afternoon, Mrs Barr," the class chanted back.

"Good afternoon, Lucy," Mrs Barr said as she noticed Lucy with her head on the table. At the mention of her name, Lucy sat upright, terrified she was about to get into trouble.

"Well, Lucy, I've got a very special visitor to see you." Moving towards the door, Mrs Barr beckoned her finger at whoever was outside. Lucy watched and saw her mum come shuffling into the class. Totally shocked at what she saw, Lucy froze. Only her lips moved as they turned upwards into a smile.

"Hi, hen," her mum said. "Are you no coming tae give me a hug?"

At the invitation, Lucy slowly pushed her seat back, causing it to screech across the hard-plastic flooring and maneuvered her way between the seats and tables then threw herself into her mother's arms and hung on like a baby chimp.

"Wow, what a welcome, Mrs Jackson. I will leave you in the capable hands of Miss Kane and Lucy for the afternoon. I know you will have an amazing time." Before leaving she patted Lucy's back and glanced over at Miss Kane, putting her hand over her heart.

"Boys and girls, please say good afternoon to Lucy's mum. What would you like the boys and girls to call you? Mrs Jackson ok?" Lucy's mum nodded in agreement and the class welcomed her. "Lucy, why don't you take your mum over to our couch and you can have some of the special biscuits you've made."

Lucy released herself from round her mum's neck and took her mum's hand and led her over to the biscuits. The class followed their movements, captivated by the awkward, slow limping progress made by Lucy's mum as she dragged her leg across the room. Kids dramatically moved bags and chairs out of her way as if what she had was catching. Lucy held fiercely onto her mum's hand, still in shock that her mum was here. Reaching the chairs, she fussed over her mum, helping her sit down; she gave her a biscuit and drink of juice, smiling the whole time.

Lucy could hear Miss Kane setting work for the rest of the class and looked up and watched them follow her instructions. Lucy nestled herself on the chair next to her mum and gave her a hug. This was *the best day ever!*

"Thanks, hen. Did you make these?" Lucy nodded. "They're tasty. Your teacher seems nice. Nae wonder you like the school. Never had teachers like that when I wis wee."

Lucy munched into her biscuit and sipped her juice and felt really important getting all this special treatment with her mum when the other kids had to work. She watched as Miss Kane made her way over to them with a big smile on her face.

"You two look cosy. Are you enjoying your biscuits?"

"Aye, they're lovely. Did Lucy really make them?"

"Yes, she did, didn't you, Lucy?" Lucy smiled shyly. "Sorry, in all the excitement I forgot to introduce myself – I'm Helen Kane, Lucy's teacher and it's a pleasure to meet you." Miss Kane extended her hand.

"Hi."

"Lucy is a wee gem, a great wee girl who always tries her best."

"Aw, she is great; she does nae talk much, though does she?"

"Eh, no she doesn't, but we've been making some great progress with a few signs that she uses. Anyway, I'm not going to ruin her special afternoon. Maybe I could chat for a wee while later?"

"Eh, aye."

"Great. Lucy, do you want to choose some friends to play a game with you and your mum?" Lucy eagerly nodded. "Why don't you go and pick them and I will get the game set up."

Lucy stood and went over to her friend Jane and then Chloe, gesturing for them to come over with her. Lucy held her two friends' hands and felt so happy inside. She decided she felt just like the other boys and girls in her class and it was a long time since she had felt like that.

"Hi," Jane said when she met Lucy's mum. "I live out the back from you."

"Aye, I remember you from that time Lucy was playing with you and we lost Connor," Lucy's mum replied. "What's your name?"

"Chloe."

"Nice tae meet you. Well, I hope you know how tae play this game 'cause I don't."

"Don't worry, I know," said Jane, taking charge.

Lucy sat in between her mum and her two friends, joining in the game as best she could, giggling every time it was her shot; her excitement bursting when trapped by the cage on the game board. Every so often she snuggled into her mum, smiling and not wanting the day to end.

45 Helen

Helen had felt somewhat nervous when she returned to her class after lunch. Her children, unfortunately, received the brunt of her emotions and were told to work like mice as she battled with her mood. She had noticed Lucy lifting her head every time someone came to the door and realised that she too probably felt the same. Praying that Connor had at least returned to school, she fiddled with things in her desk, trying to calm down.

Seeing the shape of Rosie at the door, Helen's heart froze as she waited to hear what news she brought. Relaxing as she heard the chilled tone she used, Helen felt sure good news was coming. Her breathing returned to normal as she glimpsed the wee woman shuffling behind Rosie and knew it was Lucy's mum. She struggled to watch the slow and painful movements of the mother as she hobbled into the class, clinging onto Rosie's arm. Helen tried hard to stifle her gasp of shock as she took in the bedraggled picture in front of her. Even her class were silenced by the sight. At first, all eyes were drawn to her leg, which even in a stationary position caused some amount of consternation at the way it bent and leaned against the good one. The thin material of her leggings provided little disguise for its mangled shape. It was then hard for Helen's eyes to make sense of how such a tiny frame could actually support itself. The woman's thighs were thinner than Helen's arms and, even though her baggy jacket covered her upper body, it was evident there was not much beneath it. Her lank hair, pulled tight to the back of her head, smothered her tiny skull. Heavy creases crossed her sunken cheeks, ageing her well beyond her years, she was sure. Dark eyes burdened and sad had locked fearfully on Lucy, afraid to look elsewhere. A recent gash on her forehead could just be made out. This sent Helen's mind racing, wondering if the dark marks beneath her eyes were more than just dark circles.

Helen watched Lucy's mother's hand move from her pocket to the desk, her fear exposed as her hand shook until it met the hard surface of the desk she reached for. Helen began to panic and worry thinking about scenarios that may have caused this poor lady to become so scarred and dejected-looking. Giving herself a mental slap, she stopped the express train in her head and remembered the class in front of her.

But as she watched Lucy engulf her mother in a hug, her throat tightened and the tears caught her eyes. Their embrace was not just comfortable but emitted a strength undetected as they stood as individuals. Helen had hardly noticed Rosie leaving, so intrigued by the pair in front of her and the story they kept.

Dragging herself away from her thoughts, Helen forced herself to take control and direct her attention to the rest of her class. Desperate to talk to Lucy's mum, but worried about being too enthusiastic, Helen remained at the other side of the class, pretending to be busy with her remaining kids. Whenever she could, she studied the interactions between Lucy and her mother, fueling her bid to gain some understanding of what was going on. Helen had never seen Lucy so relaxed and so obviously happy. She positively glowed.

Helen felt all fuzzy inside when she watched the two of them and couldn't be more grateful at how things had turned out. She observed how the mum even seemed more relaxed, her shoulders no longer up around her ears. Glancing at the clock, she decided to make a move and go and chat to mum before it was too late.

Setting a task for the rest of the class she made her way over and smiled again as she watched Lucy laugh along with her mum and friends as they played their game.

"Well, it sounds as though you guys are having fun," Helen

smiled.

"Aye, miss. Lucy cannae stop laughing and that's making us all laugh," Jane informed her teacher.

"Well, it certainly sounds funny. Now it is nearly home time. Do you think the three of you could go and wash up your plates and cups?"

"Yes, miss," Chloe and Jane said in unison whilst Lucy nodded.

"Off you go then, girls." Once the girls were out of earshot, Helen continued. "It is so lovely to hear Lucy sounding so happy. She is delighted you came into school today and so am I. It is so nice to meet you," Helen said, gently touching Mrs Jackson's shoulder in what she hoped was a warm and friendly manner.

"Eh, it's nice tae be here. It's no often I hear her laugh ma self," Mrs Jackson said, looking down at the table to avoid eye contact.

"We've been trying to obtain some information from her last school. I'm wondering if you would be able to help us out?"

Helen watched as Lucy's mum visibly squirmed in her chair, glancing round as if to check for an escape route. Sensing her unease, Helen tried to reassure her, "I'm just wanting to make sure I have the right information so I can provide her with the best education. Has she ever been able to speak?"

The two sat in silence as Helen waited for mum to answer. Eventually, she did.

"Aye, she did used to talk ... would talk the hind legs off a donkey, but one day she just stopped and has nae talked since."

"Do you know how long ago that was?"

"Aye, it must have been about two years ago."

"Any idea why she stopped?" After these words left her mouth, Helen wished she could eat them back up. Tears began to well up in the mum's eyes and it wasn't just one hand that shook now. "Oh, my goodness, I'm really sorry; I seem to have upset you. I really didn't mean to."

Putting her arm round her shoulders, Helen could feel just how desperately thin she was, the childlike proportions making Helen feel like a mother. Finding a tissue, she gave it to Lucy's mum and hoped Lucy would be busy for another wee while with the dishes. Once her shoulders stopped shaking, Helen spoke again: "You know that we are here to help Lucy and if you want we will help you to find the help you need. You just need to let us. Both Lucy and Connor are great kids and I can see that you really care for them. It might be helpful to chat with Mrs Barr. I could take you along?"

"No, no it's fine. Me and ma weans will manage. Thanks for being so kind to Lucy. I don't think either of them have ever wanted tae come tae school so much."

"You don't need to thank me – it is my job to help and I want to help. Look, please just come along with me to the office and we'll get a wee cuppa and you can sort yourself out. I'll make sure Lucy and Connor wait for you after school. What do you think?"

"Aye, ok a wee cuppa would be nice. Are you just going tae leave the class by themself?"

"Yes, but I'll get someone to watch them. Don't worry. Give me a minute while I sort things out." Relying on her trusty messenger, Helen organised for a classroom assistant to watch the class and, after warning the class within an inch of their life, helped Mrs Jackson down the corridor to Rosie's room.

46 Connor

"Connor! Connor!"

Turning, Connor desperately tried to find Hayley through the crowd of jostling kids battling their way down the corridor to escape from school. Jarring against the crowd, he eventually saw her wee arms pushing school bags out of the way then she popped out, like a fish from water.

"What you doing?"

"I'm going to get ma mum from the office."

"Aw right, well I'll come with you," Hayley said, not allowing him to give no for an answer.

Before they had gone very far they heard the Irish tones of Mr Ford inquiring about their direction of travel. "Guys, I think you both know by now that we exit the school from the bottom door. Come on, let's go."

"Eh, he's going tae get his mum at the office," Hayley kindly answered for them both.

"Is that right, Connor?"

"Aye, sir."

"Are you going to hold his hand, Hayley?" The pair blushed at the romantic reference to their friendship, Connor stunned for words. Luckily Hayley's mouth was still working.

"Well, I wouldn't want Connor tae get lost. He is new to the school, sir." Hayley flashed her biggest smile and knew she'd won this time. Smiling, Mr Ford waved them on.

"Get on with the pair of you before I change my mind."

Hayley giggled and Connor smiled back and they quickened their pace in case he really did change his mind. Reaching the front office, there was a hoard of kids milling around asking questions at the office, waiting for taxis. Connor couldn't see his mum amongst any of them.

"Where is she?" Hayley asked.

Connor replied by shrugging his shoulders. Taking the matter into her own hands, Hayley pushed past the throng of kids and marched into the office.

"Hi, Mrs McLean. Connor's here tae get his mum and she's no here?"

"Well hello there, Hayley. I hear you've been giving your pappi a hard time?" Mrs McLean replied.

"Oh, how did you hear about that? Aye, he wis'nae too happy."

"I bet he wasn't. Don't you be doing anything like that again."

"No, I won't."

"Now, Connor, your mum is still in with Mrs Barr along with Lucy. So, take a wee seat and I'll go and see to it in a wee minute. Should you not be getting home, Hayley, so your pappi isn't worried?"

"No, I'm going to Connor's today." Hayley's lies rolled off her tongue, like a marble down a hill.

"Are you sure?"

"Aye, I am."

"Well, you'd better have a seat too."

Returning to Connor, she pulled him over to the two comfy black chairs, where they sat swinging their legs, waiting, their bags dropped at their side ready to be tripped over by anyone passing. After what seemed like forever, the door to Mrs Barr's room opened and their headteacher emerged.

"Ah, you remembered, Connor. I was just about to send out a search party," she said, smiling. "Have you had a good afternoon?"

"Aye, great," he replied.

"Aye, that's because Gallows was'nae in," Hayley piped up, unable to control her tongue.

"Eh, excuse me, young lady, that is not how we speak about people in this school and certainly not your teacher. What are you doing here anyway? Were you sent up to my office?"

Connor couldn't look at his friend, embarrassed on her behalf, but Hayley continued with her story making: "Eh, I'm walking Connor home. I'm going to his today for a play."

"Is that right?" Mrs Barr asked, looking at Connor.

"Eh, yip."

"Well, we'd better get your mum and Lucy then. Hayley, I'm needing some help tomorrow, at lunchtime sorting out some files, I will see you at 1 pm."

"What? Miiissss," Hayley moaned as she realised her errant comment had gotten her a job.

"What? You would like to do Wednesday as well?"

"No thanks."

"Good, I will see you tomorrow then." She stuck her head into her office; "Mrs Jackson, Lucy, Connor is here to help you home. Thank you again, Mrs Jackson, for coming to school. I think I can safely say that Lucy loved having you here, am I right Lucy?"

Connor could just see Lucy nodding her head whilst she sat in Mrs Barr's office. She floated in and out of view as Mrs Barr waved her long drapery sleeves backwards and forwards as she spoke.

"Please remember all we have discussed and if we can help we will do our best. So, on Wednesday, the school nurse will see both Connor and Lucy here, ok?" Mrs Barr continued.

"Aye. Thank you very much. I don't quite know what tae say," Connor heard his mum reply. He wondered what had been spoken about. Then he heard Miss Kane, "You don't need to thank us, it's our job to help. Connor and Lucy are such lovely kids too."

He watched his mum shuffle out of the room, holding onto Lucy as she went. Despite her usual uncoordinated movements, Connor thought his mum somehow looked different as she left the head teacher's office. He studied her, trying to find what it was. Her clothes were the same, her hair was the same ...? Whatever it was, he decided his mum somehow looked better.

Lucy flashed him a smile, her dark eyes twinkling, her head sitting a little higher on her shoulders than usual. Connor rose and took over from Lucy. When he turned round, he noticed Hayley sitting, her mouth wide open, lost for words for the first time in her life as she watched his mum.

"Right, Hayley, make use of yourself and take Connor's bag for him," Mrs Barr instructed. Hayley came to her senses and grabbed the two bags and stood up, still staring.

"That was very kind of you to invite Hayley back, Mrs Jackson."

"What?"

"Come on, Mum," Connor said quickly, trying to divert the conversation and hurry his mum out the door. With one hand on the metal rail and one on Connor's arm, they moved together down the flight of stairs. Cars lined the street as parents came to collect their children, causing the usually quiet street to come alive with the noise of opening and closing doors. Engines hummed as they sat with their heaters on to demist windows. A hoard of parents huddled under a tree waiting for their children to appear from round the back, taking shelter from the remnants of the rainy day.

Connor heard his mum's breath begin to quicken as she moved along the path. Lucy had skipped on in front and now stood swinging on the gate, waiting. Hayley lingered just ahead, wanting to walk with Connor, but unable to slow her pace enough. Connor felt as though everyone stared at him; the mums huddled under the tree, Mrs Barr standing at the top of the stairs, the kids still roaming around the playground. He felt the words 'fuck off' tickle the tip of his tongue, but managed to keep them at bay. As they neared the gate, he was sure he heard someone talk about nits and his hand went straight to his head, smoothing his mop down.

As if sensing his unease, Hayley came to the rescue with her tongue: "So did you have a good day, Lucy, being the special person?"

Lucy nodded furiously, her head whipping back and forth like a ball on a piece of elastic.

"And did you?" she asked, looking at Connor's mum, who walked head ducked down looking at the ground. Connor gave her a dunt in the ribs and pointed his head in the direction of Hayley.

"What, hen? I wis miles away?"

"I said ... did you have a good day?" Hayley slowly and loudly repeated the question.

"Aye, I did, hen. It was good. No wonder you both like going tae the school. What nice teachers you have."

"Aye. Miss Barr and Miss Kane are good, but that Gallows is something else, isn't she, Connor?"

"Aye, she's a witch," Connor agreed. Hayley chatted the whole way down the street, not needing much encouragement from the other three to continue. Connor felt just the tiniest bit envious of his friend's natural ability to chat, even though at times he wished she would shut up. He watched Lucy jump over the cracks on the pavement ahead of them and he felt his mum's grip on his arm relax a little as they neared home.

"What are you smiling at?' Hayley asked Connor.

"Nothing,"

"Nothing? Aye right, look at you,"

"Just turned out to be a good day, that's all."

"Aye, 'cause we didn't need to do detention and we had Mr Hay for the afternoon. It wis'nae a bad day, wis it? She wis so out of order putting us all on detenti… Oh my gawd, your Lucy is peeing herself," Hayley said, pointing ahead to where Lucy stood at the kerb. Knowing he was not really listening to what she was saying, Hayley tugged at Connor and pointed: "Connor, look at your Lucy. The pee is running doon her leg. Boak. Could she no have told us?"

This time both Connor and his mum looked up, their gaze drawn to where Lucy stared, not at the pool gathering at her feet. Connor pushed his mum down behind a parked car then dived forward and knocked Lucy down out of sight. Hayley, not sure of what was happening, ducked down to be on the safe side.

"Eh, do you fancy tellin' me what's going on?"

Connor couldn't talk. He couldn't believe he had just seen him … coming out of their close. He sat shaking, one hand over Lucy's mouth, terrified she would start with her weird noises, giving the game away. He didn't need to turn round and look at his mum to know she would be in a worse state than all of them. Ignoring Hayley, he edged forward and watched as his so-called dad walked down the street in the opposite direction.

Connor watched the figure disappear out of sight, though the picture of his dark beady eyes and skin that never seemed clean never ever left him. The buried smell of fags and stale breath returned, along with the rattling fear those words and images had gouged into his body. His monsters were all of a sudden real. Connor rooted to the spot, Hayley jabbering away in his ear, but he couldn't hear her. It was his mum that he heard.

"Son, we need to go. We've no got much time, Connor."

Automatically, he stood up, pulled up his mum and hauled his sister up. Looking up and down the street, he crossed. He heard his mum telling Hayley to go home and he turned to look at her;

saw her face full of questions that he couldn't answer. He pushed the close door open and helped his mum up the stairs.

The door had been stamped with a large footprint that covered the letterbox and beyond. Their shuffling up the stairs had alerted their neighbour of their arrival and she came down, poking her head just round the corner, over the bannister.

"I told him that nae body stayed here. I know it's none of ma business, but he did'nae look very happy and I don't want any bother here. So, you had better sort it out or the next time he comes in here kicking at doors, I'll be phoning the polis."

Her message delivered, her head retreated and the three of them went inside the flat.

47 Lucy

Sitting huddled in her corner, Lucy watched as her mum hobbled about the flat checking windows and doors were locked, while Connor paced up and down, repeating the phrase: "I cannae believe he found us, Mum. What are we going tae do? What are we going tae do?"

The smell of her mum's fag drifted over and filled Lucy's nose, the familiarity of it strangely giving her some comfort. Slowly, she slid her body round so that her head was on the floor, her arms still firmly locked around her legs. It was easy today to drift off into her happy place. So many happy thoughts that afternoon at school to take her away.

In her mind's eye, Lucy floated back to the start of her day – walking into class and the smile Miss Kane had given her; the class clapping at her as it was her 'special day'; the extra cake she received at lunch from Elsa; the hug from mum; playing the board game with Jane and Chloe; laughing and squirting each other with water as they cleaned up; hearing Mrs Barr tell her mum she would get the nurse to help them with her nits, then walking home with her mum for the first time she could remember. Then it went black. Lucy stopped then replayed this loop in her head over and over, reliving each moment. Feeling the tingles in her tummy, the warmth lingering every time over, the hug from her mum. Oh, how she wanted that now.

48 Helen

Helen's jubilant mood gave her the courage to phone Ed, eager to share her happiness with someone that made her happy. "Hey, how are you?" she asked when he answered.

"I'm good. How are you? You sound very chirpy for a Monday."

"That I am."

'Oh, yeah … want to share?"

"Well I do actually, and that is why I'm phoning … to see if you would like to come round and share a wee bottle of red?"

"Sounds like the best idea I've heard all day. I could be round in an hour or so, I'm just finishing up here."

"Sounds perfect. Want me to try and cook something?"

"Erm, you don't fill me with confidence when you say 'try'," he laughed.

"I'm afraid I'm not known for my culinary skills, but I'm sure I won't kill you with cheese on toast or I could be really adventurous and do beans on toast?"

"Ok, I'm thinking I will stop by Crust and pick up a pizza, as long as you don't get too offended."

"I was kind of hoping you would say something like that. Ok, see you in an hour."

"Looking forward to it."

Helen hurried round tidying up and then jumped in for a quick shower after giving her oxters a quick sniff and deciding that she really didn't want to anaesthetise Ed. Emerging from the shower, she looked in the mirror and sighed at the panda eyes reflected back at her. Removing all traces of her day makeup, Helen thought about the time, money and effort women had to go through every day to make themselves look better and decided that she was going to go *au naturale* for her date tonight with Ed, this bold statement quickly retracted after blow-drying her hair and the mirror reflected a belisha beacon. Plastering on foundation to counteract the redness, Helen groaned as her face became the antithesis of *natural*. Faffing in front of the mirror to try and achieve a less troweled on look, she shrieked when the buzzer went, as she wore nothing, but a towel. Hopping on one leg as she put her knickers on, she bounced through to the hall and buzzed Ed in. Before she'd even got back to her bedroom, he chapped on the door.

"I'll be there in a minute," she hollered back, hastily pulling a pair of jeans up over her legs, and halting as they reached her hips. "For fuck's sake," she moaned, pulling and sucking in as much as she could until the two sides of the zip finally engaged.

Rummaging through her wardrobe, she pulled four tops off their hangers until she found the one she wanted then ran to the door, quickly stopping for five seconds before she opened it to achieve a slightly chilled expression.

"Hey, how are you?" she asked, smiling as their eyes met.

"Everything all right? You look as though you've just run a marathon."

"What? Really?"

"Well, your face is a bit red, but you're still gorgeous." He winked. "Hungry?" he asked as he moved into the flat heading straight to the kitchen, not giving Helen a chance to reply.

"Aye, I am, actually," she said, following him, kicking the door shut with her heel. "Ready for a glass of red?"

"Am I ever! What a day!" he said as he carefully organised the pizza. "I forgot to ask what you liked so I got half meat and half veggie, just to cover all bases."

"Aw, you know me ... I eat anything. Sounds like you had a

tough day. Busy?"

"It's just been non-stop. I think they just want to see how much we can cope with in a day before we crack. I'm exhausted but glad I'm here. You're making me feel so much better."

A smile cracked over Helen's face and she leaned across to give him a kiss as she handed him his large glass of red.

"God, is that the whole bottle in my glass?"

"Nearly, but don't worry. What I lack in culinary expertise, I make up for in the wine department. My cellar is well stocked. Do you want a plate?"

"For takeaway pizza? No, fingers are fine. A seat wouldn't go amiss though."

"I think I can manage that. Come through to the fine dining room, sir," Helen joked. They sat down across from each other and munched through the pizza.

"Good shout. I was starving."

"Me too. How was your Monday?"

"You know today was one of those days that reminded me why I became a teacher."

"Really? It was that good?

Helen nodded emphatically. "Well, you know the wee girl and boy I was telling you about?"

"Yip, the nitty one that doesn't speak and the one that hates Irene as much as you hate Irene?"

"Check you – top marks for listening," Helen joked.

"Well, what can I say?" Ed said, feigning modesty.

"Well, basically, the mum, who we have been trying to get in touch with for over a week came to school and has agreed that we can get the psychologist on board to investigate Lucy's elective muteness and the school nurse to sort out the infestation of nits."

"Wow, that is good going. Does that mean you'll stop scratching your head as much?"

"What? Do I really?"

"Only every time you mention the wee girl with the nits. Which since we've been out has been quite a few times," Ed said with a wry look on his face.

"Oh gawd, how embarrassing. I really honestly don't think I've got them. It is just habit, I promise."

"It's actually quite funny. It's like an automatic reaction. You mention nit, you scratch your head. Ha, look you're doing it again."

"No, I didn't!"

"You so did," Ed said laughing.

"Fuck, this job is a nightmare," Helen said, scratching her head all over messing her hair up.

"Here, have some more pizza. Take your mind off those things. What was the mum like?"

"Oh my god, Ed, she was a soul if ever I've seen one. Even the kids were lost for words."

"A soul in what sense?"

"Every sense. She was tiny, like skin and bone and she had some sort of foot deformity. The leg just dragged behind her and she needed help to walk, though had no stick or crutch, just relied on her kids. Connor had to go home at lunch and help her to school. I thought he was just wanting an excuse to get out of school when he said he had to help his mum, but he was right. She just looked … I don't know, burnt out maybe? No idea what age she was, but her face had chiseled in lines and a good few scars on her face – one that looked fresh."

"That doesn't sound good. Is there a husband?"

"I don't think there is one on the scene. I made a right fool of myself as I started greeting in front of all the weans. Lucy ran up and gave her mum this hug that just melted my heart. Despite all I've said about the mother, there was definitely a bond. The love shone from the two of them. Aw, I'm going to greet again,"

Helen said, dabbing her eyes with the kitchen roll.

"Aw, come here," Ed said, pulling her off her chair and onto his knee. "You know, she is a lucky wee girl having a teacher like you."

Enjoying his big strong arms wrapped around her, Helen nestled her head into his chest.

"You couldn't not help a wee girl though, could you?"

"I think we both know it doesn't always happen like that."

"True. I'm just happy I can do something. I can't wait to see them both tomorrow. Have you got cramp in your legs yet?"

"Legs? What legs?"

"You cheeky shite. I'm as light as a feather. Here, your wine needs topping up." Helen filled his wine glass then picked his hand up and he followed her over to the sofa.

Arriving at school the next morning, Helen hoped no other teachers would be in the car park as Ed dropped her off in his flash BMW. But no, Linda and Carol were both walking in past the gates as his car stopped.

"Aw, I was so hoping not to see anyone this morning," Helen groaned.

"What are you embarrassed to be seen with me?" Ed said, half-joking.

"Absolutely not, but I'm now going to get a total slagging. Though I have to say it will be worth it."

"Glad to hear it. Now off you go and make those kids smile some more today."

"Ok, here goes." Helen grabbed her bag and pulled the door lever to open the door.

"Eh, think you are forgetting something," Ed said.

"Yeah, what? Oh," Helen said and scooted across to give him a kiss. "Are you just trying to make sure I get a total slagging?"

"Absolutely," Ed said, winking. As he roared off he woke the neighbours up with his horn.

"Good morning, Miss Kane. You seem to have a little spring in your step this morning. Sleep well?" Carol mocked.

"Carol, do you think she got any sleep last night?" Linda said, winking.

"Very funny, ladies. He actually just popped round this morning to give me a lift," Helen said with the biggest smirk on her face.

"Aye, right," Carol and Linda replied in unison.

"He is gorgeous, Helen. You've landed yourself a dancer there," Linda commented.

"Thanks. He does seem pretty special."

"Well, come on, let reality smack you in the face as you set your foot in here. Though I heard you had a pretty successful day yesterday?" Carol said.

"Aw, I did, Carol. Yesterday was one of my best days ever at work and at home," Helen said with a wink, running up the stairs before they badgered her for more information.

Getting ready for her day was much easier than usual and her bright mood exuded to all she came into contact with. This made her smile even more. The janitor came in to help her move some furniture.

"Aye, something making you smile the day?"

"Ah, you could say that. How've you been?"

"Aye, no bad. Did you hear about Irene?"

"Irene? No?"

"It turns out her man's been cheating on her with a wee lassie?"

"Really? I never heard. What a shame."

"Aye, I suppose it is. But I could never imagine taking a broken pay packet home to that one. Jings! She's a roaster, is she no?"

"That is one way of putting it, Tam. Thanks for your help."

"Nae bother, hen, any time. Have a good day."

"You too, Tam."

Helen had just finished writing the day's work on the board when the bell went. Her class filed in, sorting their things out for the day and Helen noticed that Lucy hadn't appeared. Usually, this would have sent her heart plummeting, but after the successful meeting yesterday she was sure she was just late. She continued with her morning routine and when the door burst open she lifted her head expecting to see Lucy. Instead, it was Hayley looking flustered and agitated.

"Miss, I need tae talk to you right now."

"Good morning to you too, Hayley. Have you left your manners at home?"

"Miss, it's really important."

Seeing the distress on her face, she left her class working and escorted Hayley out the door.

"What is it?"

"Miss, it's Connor. I think something bad has happened."

"Why would you say that?"

"'Cause you know I wis going to his house last night? Well on the way home he made us all duck down beneath a car 'cause they saw some guy coming out their close. Lucy was peeing herself she wis that scared."

"Woo. Hold on and rewind. Lucy might just have been caught short and maybe Connor was just kidding on."

"Naw, miss. I seen his face. He wis shit scared. Sorry for swearing, but he wis. Gawd, I wis even shaking."

"What was the guy like that came out the close?"

"Aw, he wis mean looking. Big. Bigger than Mr Hay. Though I never really got a good look at him."

"Ok, maybe it was someone they knew or maybe it was just a stranger. We don't know, do we?"

"But I went tae his door this morning and naebody answered.

And they're no here, are they?"

"No, they're not here. Ok, I will pass your information on to Mrs Barr. But they might just be sleeping, so don't worry, ok?"

"I'll try no to, miss."

Helen's feelings of despair rose within her that something was very, very wrong.

49 Mum

The Wednesday

It took me a while to work out where I was. I remember earlier Connor leaning over me saying something. What, I'm no sure. I was just starting to come to after one of my wee episodes. No sure how long I was out for. I heard a door bang somewhere and then it was quiet. Letting my eyes open slowly, I reached out for my fags. My nerves were rattling. I could feel my lungs about to explode with coughing. Fag will sort it.

Slowly, slowly my head got thigither and I tried to make sense of what I saw and where I was. Looking at my phone I saw it was Wednesday. My fuddled brain tried to think how I ended up where I was. Shaking like a leaf, my mind began to flash back.

It was a bit of a jumble. An itch on my face drew my hand up. I felt a burny bit as my fingers traced over the top of a newish cut. Then I remembered:

My phone had went, and I picked it up. I said, "Hello," but got nothing back. Hanging up, I thought it was just a wrong number. I hadn't recognised it. Thought it was one of those stupid call centre folk. Checking the time, I saw it was half two in the morning. No being able to sleep I had turned the telly on. Then it went again. This time I froze. Slowly turning it over, I saw it was the same number. Answering it, I got nothing again. Listening hard I could hear muffled sounds and that deep, angry breathing. It was him.

My brain went into overdrive. Screaming, I jumped up. Ran to the window and checked outside. Then ran to check the two back rooms that looked out over the close. Connor was awake and I shouted at him to get ready, we had to go, he had found us. It was definitely him this time.

He began to argue, telling me I was off my head. But he knew the drill. He knew what I was like when I had him in my brain like this.

Reluctantly, he pulled on his clothes and chucked stuff into a bag. I was near hysterical. Rushing around trying to get stuff together. My arse was making buttons right enough. I remember bashing my face on the bathroom cabinet. Blood gushed down my face. I grabbed a wee face cloth off the side of the bath. I must have let out a loud yelp, as the next thing I knew Connor was at my side trying to calm me. I got my wee stash of money and phoned a taxi.

I heard the horn. I told Connor to go and get his sister and get in the taxi. I would be there in a minute.

Grabbing the last few bits and bobs I could manage, I hurried down the stairs as best I could and got into the front, hauling my gammy leg in with my hands.

I must have had a sixth sense something was going to happen again, as I had read the paper the day before and seen bedsits for rent. Fishing in my purse, I found the scrunched-up piece of paper with the number on it. With my fingers trembling, I dialed the number.

I got an unamused woman on the other end. I better have money she said as she 'didn't like being woken in the middle of the night'. I assured her I did. I spent the drive looking behind me. Looking in front of me. Looking out the window beside me, as if his face was going to appear out of nowhere. The weans in the taxi with me, I knew they were safe. But as usual I was wondering, for how long? How long could I keep running like this?

Reaching the address, I let a sigh out. The woman was waiting in a red motor as promised. I knew it would be a shitehole, but it was far enough away. I hoped. Locking the doors, we all collapsed on the sofa. The weans conked out. Being up to high do-doh, I couldn't sleep. I sat awake listening to the new sounds. I must've fell asleep at some point because when I woke up I could tell it was morning. Checking my phone, it was nearly lunch time.

Having spent most of my money on the rooms, I had to get the weans into school. I knew they didn't like the school, but they got fed there. And my weans, like most weans liked their chow. I remember shuddering at the thought of having to go up there and face all those people. Having to deal with all that stuff and all they teacher types. They all thought I was shite. Fuck, they were probably right. I was just trying my best. I think I spent the next few hours running back and forth to the toilet. My guts churning with the thought of it. Eventually I knew I had to go or else it would be shut.

I remember the look of happiness on wee Lucy's face when I told her we were going out. She looked like the cat that had got the cream. In between fighting with Connor to get him to come with us and me walking like a ninety-year-old, we made it to the school.

It hadn't changed much from when I had last seen it, when I was a wean. Glad to get that nightmare of talking to those hoity toity teacher types over and done with, we went to the shop. I bought a few sleeping tablets as I thought my head was going to explode.

I was seeing things that weren't there I was so tired. I knew my head wouldn't let me sleep if it didn't get some help. And that was about the last I could recall.

Since leaving that bastard I've no been right. Come to think of it, I couldn't have been right in the first place thinking that wanker was the one.

Silly bitch I am. I can't sleep or I sleep all the time. Voices in my head. Seeing things that aren't there. Feeling that folk are watching me. When it gets really bad, I just lose it. I've heard folk say it's like the lights going dim. For me, it's more like I'm locked up in a windowless cell, straight jacketed and injected with an over dose of sedatives. It's no nice. I can hear the weans sometimes. Fuck, I sometimes even feel them clambering all over me. Just nothing I can do about it. Go to the doctors and they try and fill you with shite. Makes you like a zombie twenty-four seven. Mouth full of cotton wool and a head like mince. I take my chances being lost a few days here and there, then end up like that. Not that it's easy on any of us. Worst for Connor. Poor buggar. Lucy just seems to accept it. Not that any of us know what goes on inside her head. Doesn't creep up on you either. No warning. Just bam and your down.

Looking about the place I see it's no great. But it's all we've got. I saw the empty packet of sleeping tablets amongst the shite on the floor. I must've gubbed more then I should've. Praying my weans were at the school, I got up and did a few dishes to stop my mind going nuts worrying about them. I decided to give them till half three then I would panic.

I heard their feet thunder up the stair. My belly stopped its flipping nonsense and my breath got back to normal. Thank fuck they were ok.

To say I was shocked when I saw the state of Lucy's head was an understatement. I near could have gret. With everything that had been happening she kind of got forgotten. I must have been out for longer than usual for it to get so bad.

The Thursday

I could see he wasn't happy when I asked him to go with me to the postie. But I just couldn't go down the street without him. He's never bothered before. Usually glad to get a day off the school. My nerves were just shot to pot since the other night and all the fracas that happened. Then last night had been torture after the visit from the nurse. I mean was she really a nurse? Was she maybe sent by him to come and get my weans from me? She looked awful dodgy. No nurse's uniform to be seen and I don't remember no message from the school telling me she was coming. Some folk might call me cautious, but after all I've been through, I just can't help it.

After the wee nursey woman had left, I got Connor to help me close all the curtains. Then I had to lock the doors and wedge bits of paper down the sash of the windows so nobody could jemmy them open. I scrubbed and combed all our heads for ages, getting the wee beasties out. Lucy was yelping with pain. Her hair being so long it took ages to comb it all out. No having any proper shampoo or conditioner didn't help. But I couldn't have sent Connor out just in case. Besides I'd no money.

Afterwards I wanted us all to sleep in the same bed. Connor was having none of it. He told me, in no uncertain terms, was he sleeping with his mum. So, I had Lucy curled up next to me on the couch. She snuggled in quite the thing and she fell fast asleep as I stroked her hair. She's like a wee angel when she's like that. My gorgeous wee lassie.

After midnight I went through and checked on Connor. I panicked at first because I couldn't see him, no wanting to turn the big light on. I snuck forward my heart in my mouth and slowly, slowly I saw his outline under the covers. Flat as can be. Sound asleep. I stared down at him. Swept the hair off his wee face. So peaceful looking. How different from the scowling face that I see so often. A wee tear crept into my eye and I let it fall. Quickly, I stopped moping. Worried that if I started I wouldn't stop. I couldn't afford for that to happen. Inwardly giving my face a good slap, I went back through and squidged back in beside Lucy to continue my sentry post.

I was awake for most of the night. Keeping an eye on my

babies. I must have smoked about twenty fags, trying to stay awake. All night I battled with myself over things I thought I could hear and things I thought I could see. Folk staggering past the window home from the pub nearly sent me off on one. But I managed to steady myself and they made it past my window without incident. Being one stair up, I don't know what I thought they would do. It really is no wonder folk call me nuts.

I then became fixated with a thumping noise. Holding my breath for ages to try and hear it better. My mind was racing. Then it stopped which was almost worse as I thought it was him playing with my mind. Somehow, he had developed evil super powers adding to his armory. I covered my ears and hummed a wee tune to myself, keeping my eyes shut. Then when I saw the sun come up, I could breathe again. I shifted Lucy over a bit and settled down for a wee kip.

My heart was pounding as I stepped out the close. I grabbed Lucy's arm and held on tight. Feart to let go. Connor was raging, but he had to come. We needed food and money and I needed them both. It didn't help that he wanted nothing to do with us, and walked away behind. But I kept glancing back and knowing he was there made it just about bearable.

I'm not the fittest of folks. My fags have done my lungs in and I have a pain in my leg from a 'fall' I had when I was with that bastard. Most I'm sure would've said it was deliberate, he on the other hand said it was just an accident. Called me a liar for trying to suggest otherwise. And that got me a slap to the jaw. I don't know if it was broken or not, there was no way he was letting me go to the hospital to find out. He told me to stop being such a woose. He'd had worse, when he was half my age, apparently. He got a beer out and told me to get his dinner on or I would find out what sore was really like. It's just never been the same and I walk with my leg trailing behind me like a collie dog.

I was doing no bad. I hadn't had to get Connor to help me

once. Then we walked past the wee cafe and I swear it was him I saw inside. It was the black coat with the parky hood that I saw first. Then he turned his head and I swear it was the same rodent eyes and snarling creep of a smile on his face. Hands like shovels, wrapped around his coffee mug.

Connor must have been watching me after all. As no sooner had my legs began to buckle from beneath me he was next to me. Hands under my arm, whispering into my ear; 'it's no him, ma. It's no him. Come on.' It was too late: I was gone.

He had me by my hair pulling it till my scalp was tight over my head. His head in my face. The smell of his breath filling my space, as he growled into my face. The sneering, snarls he spat at me. Words whirling by my ears, walloping my heart with each cutting remark. The stammering of my heart waiting for it to end. The snap as he slammed my nose off the door, another time.

Then it was Lucy rubbing my back and Connor hushing me that brought me back. Blinking I saw where we were and let Connor lead me past the cafe. He found a wee bench and we had a wee breather. My heart was still bouncing in my chest. But I was here with my weans. Not with that evil son of a bitch.

After I had a fag for my nerves, I told Connor we had to go home. I couldn't go any further. He heard none of it and told me we had to go to the postie. He pulled me up and put his hands under my arms and we walked like an oddly married couple to the shop. Money in hand I treated the pair to a wee sweetie. I got a wee smile from Connor and a hug from Lucy.

Their wee lives are shite, I know that. It's no right a boy of his age having to do so much, know so much and have seen so much. But if it wasn't for him and Lucy I wouldn't be here.

So, I have to be here now. I need to keep him away from them. He said he would get me. Then he would get them. And believe you me, when that bastard says he is going to do something, he doesn't lie. So far, I've managed to keep them out his reach and

I pray each and every day that I can continue.

We donner back up the street, stopping in at the frozen food shop and we get some supplies. I'm so caught up keeping look out that I near walked out the shop without paying, trolley and all. Lucy pulled my arm and looked at me then pointed to the cashier. I slapped my head and unloaded the trolley. Connor had waited outside, making it twice as hard to keep tabs on him. He's got something bugging him the day. I mean aye, his face is usually scowling, but today he's got a fucking stinking mood to go with it.

I'm always relieved when we get back to our house, wherever that might be. I stuck the wee mince round into the oven and put the tatties on to cook before opening the tin of peas.

Connor was like a caged tiger all afternoon pacing back and forth and just no settling. I put his tea out and that seemed to soothe him a wee bitty. I tried to get him to talk, tell me what was wrong. Stupid, when it is bloody obvious what is wrong I suppose, existing and not living. All he came up with was school, which is no like him. He's either ill or he's in bother at school again and is trying to butter me up.

Happy as a pig in shit comes to mind when describing how delighted my wee Lucy was, being allowed to go and play with her wee friend. They words Connor said fair whacked a sair punch though. And he's right, the wee lassie was just wanting to do what I did every day when I was her age; go and play with her wee pal. It just made me feel uneasy.

After they had bolted out the door, I made my way through to the back room and onto the bed to look out the window. I saw them all outside chatting. What good weans they are really. Wondering what I should do with myself, I took a look about and decided some house work wouldn't go a miss.

Someone had dumped clothes everywhere. Whilst picking

them up I found a wee trail of krispies and this sent me in the search for a Hoover. No luck. Instead I found a wee dust pan and brush and did the best I could. The place was mingin.

Stains on the carpet that I would rather no think about and a lovely big damp spot that loomed above me. We had been in worse. Just had to make do to protect my weans. Having got money for the gas I decided I would treat myself to a wee bath. I would be able to hear the weans playing out the back whilst in the bathroom.

I filled the bath and got a fresh towel out the bag. Having money meant we were able to do a wee bit washing at the launderette. Nothing beats the smell of a fresh towel. I found the new bar of soap and eventually after I found the wee red bit, got the thin plastic coating off.

Dipping my toe in, the water was roasting. Slowly I lowered my body in, having to hover just above the water, hanging on to the sides till I got used to the warm water hitting my arse. Lathering up the soap I blew the wee bubbles off then gave myself a good scrub.

Body covered in soap meant you couldn't see the scars from the fag burns on my chest. Some days they didn't half itch. They were one of my permanent reminders. They had faded over time, but they were still there. Lying, I closed my eyes and let the warm bath soothe my weary body, careful not to let the water go any deeper than my chin. I still couldn't wash my hair without bending backwards over a sink. I still couldn't bear the water touching my face. For some reason that wanker had a sick fascination for watching others thrash and scream as their head was forced under water. I just couldn't get over it. It still surprises me that the weans could have water on their faces. Being his weans didn't make them immune from his sickness, oh no.

I started to shiver, my thoughts making me uneasy and that

was me, up and out. I rubbed the towel quickly over me. There was no one bit I liked about it; not my mangled leg, not my scrawny chest, or jelly belly. He was right about that; I am an ugly sow.

I pulled on a pair of leggings and a baggy t-shirt. Still able to hear the weans, I settled down with a cuppa tea, fag and the telly on, and by all accounts felt quite relaxed.

It was then I realised it wasn't the weans being outside that really bothered me, it was being alone. Being alone meant I had time to think. Thinking wasn't good for me as it always led me to the same place. And that was a place that brought nothing but trouble for us all.

Getting restless I stuck my head out the back window to check on my weans. Looking down, I saw my wee Lucy happy as Larry playing with her wee pal. I stood watching her for a wee minute, taking myself back to when I was a wean, playing in the street with my pals and I felt a smile creep on to my face. After a wee minute or two it suddenly dawned on me that, that wee buggar Connor wasn't anywhere to be seen.

Hollering down the stairs, I got the lassies' attention. I was panicking by this point and without thinking made my own way down the back close. It took me all my time, as I held onto the bannister for dear life. Not liking to go out myself, I stood at the door and shouted Lucy to get up the stairs now. Her wee pal told me Connor had just gone and she set off to find him.

I gave Lucy an awful roasting for letting her brother go off. It wasn't really the wee soul's fault, but I was so angry. She just stared back at me with those big, puppy, brown eyes, boring into my heart. Once we were both safely back in the house, I gave her a cuddle, glad nothing had happened.

Next thing I heard him thundering round the corner, throwing his self nearly straight into me, giving me his excuses. I roared at him and clouted his lug, then immediately felt awful. The way he swung his arm back I thought he was going to hit me and I ducked. But he stopped and locked himself in his room for the night. I could feel the colour drain from my face. The look he gave me was just like his father's. One of him is more than enough for this world. No feeling myself as my head started to burl, I took a wee tablet to help me sleep.

The Friday

The weans were up early and without me saying anything, they had dressed themselves and had decided they were going to the school. Must be some school, the pair both so eager. My wee pill the night before let me sleep without wakening with my terrors. I felt a wee bitty groggy, but no too bad. I managed to make the weans toast, using the last of the butter. Three cups of sugary tea and we were all good. Last night's fall out forgotten, I told Connor to watch his sister and walk her to school and home. He replied with his usual, "Aye, Mum," and the pair set off.

I watched the two walk up the street, Lucy trying to keep up with her brother as he strode in front. I smiled as I remembered me doing the same with my big brother when I was wee. Thinking of my brother brought back memories.

They all disowned me eventually; sick of me covering up for him. Lying for him. They had warned me no to get involved, but I was fooled.

First it was his gift of the gab, he could sell ice to an Eskimo when I first met him. A real charmer. Or so I thought. He swept me off my feet, bought me flowers on the way home from his work, for no reason, took me out for dinner. He even paid for me to go on holiday with him abroad. I'd only been out the country once before, so that was a real treat. Or so I told myself. I seemed to blank out all the shite that happened. Nobody I knew saw him stay out at the pub all night. Nobody knew he left me to walk in the dead of night alone, back to wherever we were staying.

Nobody I knew saw him have beer for breakfast. Nobody I knew saw me cower and cry when he forced himself upon me. He didn't care. He'd paid for the holiday. He'd do as he damn well pleased. Then he must have felt bad at some points as he apologised and would buy me a wee present. And that was me fooled again.

He must have got fed up trying to buy my love as he soon changed tactics, this time to blackmail. He used to sob like a wean, telling me about his life growing up. His dad used to beat him, his step mum never fed him. The list went on. I felt sorry for him. Thought I could help him. I convinced myself his behaviour wasn't really his fault. I should support him. So, I did. He went to the pub. Got shit-faced. Staggered home. Gave me dog's abuse. Repeat. I never once told anyone. I put on the face. Everything was fine. If anyone ever came round, the house was always tidy. If he was at the pub, I'd make up excuses. If he was in the house, I made excuses so the guest couldn't stay long.

There were times when he didn't drink too much, when he'd try and make it up to me. Somehow, they negated all the shite times in my brain. Those were the ones I hung onto.

I suppose I didn't know how he was affecting me at first. I didn't realise that, when he was out at the pub and I was sitting watching TV, I was actually sitting waiting to see what mood he brought home with him. Filtering through every possible scenario that might occur when he walked through that door. That I was running about trying to make things the way he liked it. Trying to make him in a good mood. I put on the clothes he liked. Cooked the food he liked. Had the house tidy.

I kept telling myself that if I helped him more, he would get better quicker.

Eventually everything I did was in consultation with him. Sometimes the discussion was only in my head: *If I buy this, what will he say? Will he be happy? Will he approve? If I say this to my mum, will he hear about it?'*

It's no wonder I've ended up as mad as I am, constantly having an imaginary two-way conversation in my head, trying to predict his actions and the outcomes of his mood every second of the day.

Things stepped up a gear or two when I was pregnant with Connor. The name calling escalated. The belittling. He liked to tell me no one else would have me. I was lucky to have him. I believed him. I mean who would have someone that looked as ugly as he said I was?

Control. Not something I was aware of. I was too busy trying to make things smooth at home. Too busy trying to keep him happy. So, when he started checking my phone or checking up on where I went, I didn't think anything of it.

Though one day I must have had a moment of clarity as I told him I was leaving. He dissolved into a blubbering mess. Like a wean, holding onto my legs, begging me not to go. Threatening he would end it if I left. Well, that was it. I couldn't have him die because of me. Plus, for him to beg like that, must mean he really loved me. I shudder now at my stupidity. He must've seen me coming. A right push over.

Then he started getting a bit handier. It just went bush from there. All the hiding I thought I'd been doing, blown out the water. They all knew. They would have to have been blind no to. Black eyes, bruises, never joining family get togethers for the fear he would go off on one.

They couldn't understand why I stayed. Then probably when I needed them most they had, had enough and told me if I chose him again I was on my own.

They never understood how he had me captured. He had me well and truly under wraps. I just couldn't say no. it was like I was on a merry go round that was going so fast, I couldn't jump off for fear I'd kill myself. I was trapped on board, come hell or high water.

He persuaded me to move up the coast away from my family. The worst thing I ever did. I was all his then. Even if they had wanted to see me, he would have made sure they didn't.

I ended up being a prisoner in my own home. He never let me out on my own. Never let me speak to anyone. When we walked the weans to the school, he would be nice as nine pence chatting away. I was known as the quiet, wee wifey. When we went to the school for anything he turned on his charm as if butter wouldn't melt. The weans knew better than to utter a word.

He threatened me; threatened the worst things ever about my precious weans.

Then one day out the blue he started on the weans. I could only do so much to stop him. He's a brute of a man. They were terrified. I was too. My beautiful weans and I couldn't protect them. He's a sick, sick bastard. He used to laugh as he messed with their wee heads. Played Russian Roulette with their dinner. One would be the food he was eating. One would be nothing. One would be dog food. The three of us prayed that my wee weans never got that one. Because, aye, they had to eat it. Every last drop of it. On their hands and knees, out a bowl like a dog.

Despite ma praying, Lucy got it. I couldnae believe it. I told him I would take it. She could have my tea. But nope, I got a slap across the jaw for suggesting that. I think I must've been knocked out. When I came to Lucy was dry boking. Greeting her heart out. Connor was bawling too, begging his dad to stop. His face red with a hand shape, prominently pulsating on his cheek.

He was sitting like he was a fucking king, watching the best comedy show on earth. He shoved her wee face in it. Picked a handful up smearing it over her wee mouth. In her wee mouth. Wouldn't let her hair go till she had finished what was there. The three of us were greeting. But that brave wee lassie did it. He threw her outside like she was a dog. We didn't get her back in till he had crashed out in his chair. Snoring like a fucking train. Whiskey bottle by his side.

Once he started on my weans, it was like a thunderbolt from the sky – I had to leave. I schemed in my fuddled, weary brain how I would escape. It took me months and far too many incidents with him until I had it all sorted and for the right opportunity to arise. But it did come.

I had told Connor about my plan and I could see in his eyes that he was scared, but we both knew we had to do it. I never worried about telling Lucy as I knew she would do whatever we told her. I had managed to squirrel away some money from the odd time he'd sent me to the shop to get more drink when he couldn't be arsed.

We had next to nothing on us, just the shoes and the clothes on our back. And it wasn't till the day arrived, did I know that *that* was going to be the day.

It was pay day and as usual he had bought an extra big carry out on the way home from work. I think he was coming down with the flu as he'd also got himself some flu remedies. Which would mean he was probably taking a sickie the next day. Another kick up the arse to get away pronto. Being stuck in the house whilst he was 'ill' on top of him being crazy was a whole new level of torture for us all.

The mixture of the alcohol and flu tablets must have made him drowsier than usual and by 9 pm, he was out cold in his chair in front of the telly. I poked him a few times just to make sure he was out of it, shitting myself as I did it. Not a peep. He'd left the house keys on the table next to him. I was like a wean at school playing the 'who's got the keys game?', though the stakes if I got caught were much more than having to be out of the game.

I put my hands over the keys and slowly picked them up, praying they never made a sound. Connor was watching me and I could see him holding his breath the same as me. The wanker grunted in his sleep and I thought that was it. We both looked at each other then he let out a ripper of a fart, shifting his arse cheeks, but keeping his eyes shut.

I made a 'move it' motion to Connor. He had his sister by the hand and we crept like thieves in the night out the back door. Once down the back stairs we bolted onto the main road and we didn't stop moving until we got to the train station. We didn't look back. We didn't say a word. We jumped on the first train. Then on another. Then on another until we were far away. Only then did we seem to breathe normally.

I don't think any of us could believe we had done it. Connor took the wanker's keys from me and, opening the train window in the middle of nowhere, flung them out. The wanker would be raging when he woke up. No wife and kids and no keys for his prison or his precious fucking car.

I thought we would be free once we were away. But his taunts and threats followed us. I just couldn't settle. The threats he had made were too much for me no to take heed. We weren't in that house locked up, but we certainly weren't free.

I hadn't seen or heard from any of my family since he took me out the town. I did try a few times, but that wanker always somehow had a sixth sense that I wis trying to make contact and would find whatever letter I had written and took great delight in throwing it in the fire. Well, no really him throwing it in the fire. He would make me hold it and put my hand in the fire. No quickly either. Lucy went ballistic when she saw him doing that to me and I had to pretend that it didn't really hurt. The scars on my hand tell another story.

I thought I might have bumped into one of my brothers or sisters, but I haven't seen hide nor hair of any of them. Fuck they might all be dead for all I know! No really been up the town I suppose to bump into them.

My belly was full of the usual nerves. Always worse when I

was left alone. I had, had to do everything in my power to stop myself from begging the weans to stay at home. I know they should be at school, usually they are quite happy no going, but I can see they are both happy to go and as much as I wanted to, I just couldn't stop them from going.

I managed to keep myself busy for the first wee while. Tidying up after the pair. I pulled the covers over the bed Connor had slept in. Rinsed the dishes under the tap. No washing up liquid left. Then I folded the covers from the make shift bed Lucy and I were sharing. That was me knackered.

Sitting down, I lit a fag and watched the goings on out in the street. Mothers happily walking to the shops with their weans. Pushing buggies loaded down with bags. Old men walking along with their pals chatting, smoking fags, laughing.

Here was me, locked in my house. Terrified of the outside world. Terrified of all the folk out there. Terrified I might bump into that one man again.

Giving myself the spooks, I got up. I checked my front door. It was shut and locked. I looked in the bathroom. Nobody there. I looked in the bedroom. Nobody there. I looked behind the couch in the sitting room. Nobody there. I still couldn't settle. I was always waiting. I was always watching. I was always listening. He wasn't even here and he had complete control of me. Holding me in complete fear and terror.

Slowly I felt it creep up on me. Slowly, slowly to start this time, my mind just wandering down the well-trodden paths. I managed a few turns off before being back on it. Then it gathered speed, my mind racing this time, hurtling towards that dark destination, my mind's favourite place. Always drawing me in.

Rasping breath. Words to kill. Drowning me in stale smoke and booze. Body shaking. Pinned at the throat. Struggle. Slap. Weans screaming. Growling. Roar. Glint of knife. Still. Metal against skin. Blood oozing. Laughter. Hair clenched. Dragged. Scalp burning. Screaming. Kick to head.

Door locked. Weans screaming. Weans screaming. WEANS SCREAMING. Quiet.

Sobbing and hugging myself, I curled into a ball. My weans. My beautiful weans. That bastard. My beautiful weans. I fell into my dark place head first. Happy to drown. Trying to get lost. Trying to forget.

From my depths I heard Connor shouting me. I was struggling to get back. I didn't want to come back. He is a persistent buggar at times. Eventually I sat up.

'Ma the heid teacher is at the door. She'll no go away till ye come and talk tae her.'

Hearing that I gave myself a shake. I didn't need the social on me. Take my weans away then I couldn't protect them. I wandered through to the front door. And right enough there the head was, standing smiling at me at the door. I can't really remember what she said, my head being mince. Something to do with Lucy getting hassled by a parent. My poor wee lassie. The woman was nice, telling me she was going to do everything she could to sort out the matter. I grabbed Lucy who was standing staring up at the woman like she was god. I gave her a wee hug and sent her into the room. Connor was standing watching and the teacher told him to go and check on his sister, which he did.

The woman touched my arm, rubbing it gently. I yanked it away no used to any of that sort of thing. I remember her voice. Soft, soothing, kind words. She told me she wanted to help. I was to trust her and she would do what she could. I thanked her then closed the door to my fortress my weans safe inside. I felt tears well up in my eyes. I couldn't remember the last time anyone had been so nice. I wanted her to help me. I wanted her to make things better for my weans. But I was just too feart. I couldn't take the risk. He was just too evil. He was just too determined.

The feeble facade I had put on for the teacher vanished. I was back in my gloom. I curled up on the couch and let myself drown again. I wanted to hug my weans. I wanted to be the good mother I had seen earlier walking with her weans down the street. I just couldn't do it. The draw to my dark place was too much. It smothered me. I could hear Connor on the outer edges, shouting at me. I just couldn't come back.

The Saturday

My gloom consumed me all day. Relentless was the hammering my thoughts gave my mind. My head was bursting. A pain shot through it that lingered all day. Keeping my eyes open was just torture. Trying to blank out the world, I curled my body up on the couch and shut myself down. I never remember much when I'm like this. Memory, rational thought goes out the window. I do remember throwing my gorgeous wee lassie to the floor and I still can't believe I did it.

She was bouncing up and down on me, pulling my arm, rubbing my face. I just snapped. The pain in my head, my dark thoughts just too strong for me to have patience and be who she needed me to be. A split second and then she was on the floor. I could see her cowering; didn't look to see the distress in her wee face, but I heard the quiet tears and the pain she felt. I didn't even get up to cuddle her. I was tethered to the spot, rendered useless by the demons within me, my deadness making my self-loathing even worse. I skulked away from my mothering duties, climbed back into my dark space and tried to escape.

The Sunday

I never thought I'd get a breath again after that coughing fit. Every time I went to breathe the roar of my cough came back strangling the breath out of me again. What a fright I got. Stars swirled in front of my eyes after I finished. I was a bag of nerves and when I found out I hadn't fags left. It was panic that set in making me set off on poor Lucy again.

If she just didn't jump in my face all the time it wouldn't be so bad. But if she's not stuck to me like a limpet she's clambering over the top of me, knocking the wind from me. I think I felt worse because I knew there wasn't any money. No just for ma fags, but for the weans too. What kind of mother am I? I can't give my weans food. I lose my temper with them. I'm shit scared of going out my front door. My weans were living in a shit hole. The stench of pish made me Noam, but never drove me to really do something about it. I'm just a fucking useless piece of morose shit.

And yes, I had seen the filthy wee creatures on her head again and suppose I took this out on her as well. Though it wasn't as if it was her fault. Anybody can get them, I know that. I was scared of the backlash she would get from all the weans at the school. They never half got on to her at her last place. Connor told me what they had said and my heart was smashed. No being able to do anything to help made it worse. Every time I went to go up to that last school, I bottled it and I never made it over the door.

I just couldn't settle in this house. Something kept me on edge. Coming back to my old haunts maybe wasn't the best decision. But I was desperate and I was pretty sure he wouldn't be around. But that feeling I got was strong. I badly wanted to be wrong so my weans could have a wee bit of a normal life. Fuck, so I could be a mum. That headteacher had made things worse, all those kind words she told me made me remember there were some good folk.

He had warned me that nobody would listen to the likes of me. I was fat. I was ugly. I made him want to slit his wrists. I was so depressing to be around. I was stupid as fuck. The services would see me for the useless mother I was and take my weans off me.

They were my world and if that happened I don't know what I would do. I was thinking maybe they would be better off without me. Imagine they had a mother like that head teacher? If I could be sure he didn't get them, then I would maybe think that was the best answer. I could feel tears rolling down my face as I thought of anything happening to my weans, as I thought of leaving them. Broke my heart. I sat watching the pair; Lucy was sitting on the couch curled up like she was when she was a baby. Connor stretched out on the floor, hands behind his head, getting so big. My tears just tumbled down my face, I couldn't help it.

I was glad I had found a sneaky wee fiver in my stash and I sent Connor out to buy me fags to get me through the night. Told him to ask the wee guy at the shop for singles ... couldn't afford a packet ... Tae buy fritters with the change to fill their wee bellies. I lit a wee fag then dragged the duvet from the bedroom and chucked it over the top of Connor.

Then I snuggled next to my wee lassie, giving her an extra tight hug and hoped I would sleep.

The Monday

I've never moved so fast in my life when I heard the front door going in the middle of the day. I was like speedy Gonzales. I used my arm to pull my crappy leg to where it should be. I never had time to think about how scared I was; I just knew I had to hide. Diving behind the couch I knew if it was him he would find me in ten seconds flat. But it was all I could do.

Holding what breath I had left, I never moved. Then when I heard him shouting 'Mum', I moved forward and looked round the couch, just to make sure it was just my boy. If it wasn't for the look of terror on his face, I think I might have murdered him. I don't know where he thought I would have went.

I wasn't expecting him to ask me to go up to the school. My face must have said it all, because he started to beg me. Knowing me well, once he told me about the teacher coming to the door I had to say aye. I looked like shit. More shit than usual. I had limited time and resources, but even so I doubt a team of makeup artists could've fixed my fucked-up face.

I pulled my hair back into a pony tail and limped out into the hall and grabbed my boy's arm. Despite having grabbed his arm a hundred times before, it was only now I realised how big he was getting. I could feel his muscles tight beneath his wee jacket. Giving him a hug, I watched as he pulled the door open, holding it for me, before he helped me down the stairs.

My heart was pounding. The thought of having to go into the school in front of all those teachers; judging me, telling the social I'm no a fit mother. I'd been through it before. God, even when I was a wean they were on my back telling me I would never amount to anything. That one mean teacher telling me I was a waste of space. I hated school and the school hated me. I got bullied because I never fitted in. Never had the right uniform. Never had the right trainers. The right snack for break time. Mum did the best she could, but she was always skint. Once dad left, we really struggled. Four weans in a tiny wee house. We never had much, but she did her best.

I could feel my mouth all dry and my hand start to shake as we crossed the road. Connor was walking at an awful pace. My leg was gawping as it trailed behind me and was about as much use as a chocolate teapot. I just gritted my teeth.

But then it got too bad and I tried to tell him just to leave me, but he would have none of it. As we neared the school I could feel myself slowing down even more. Connor ploughed on and I had no choice, but to follow.

I'm sure the head teacher must've heard my heart belting against my ribs as she opened the door. I think it is the first time in my life a head teacher has ever spoken to me so nicely. Well actually, make that the second, as she spoke nicely to me the other night at the house door. She even took my arm walking down the corridor to give me a wee bit help; told me it was lovely to see me at the school and how good it was that I was supporting my weans. Nobody has said anything like that to me before. And I know it doesn't look like I care, but I do with all my heart. When she said that, I could feel my eyes filling up.

The school is definitely a different looking place from when I was at it. Gone were the dark, depressing corridors. Instead all the weans work was up, bright and cheery. Even the weans we passed in the corridor looked happy to be there. I can see now why my two like it so much. And my wee Lucy, what a hug I got from her. Melted my heart it did, even though she nearly pulled me over. She is a wee darling. My own wee darling. She had a lovely teacher too. I must be getting old, as I'm sure I'm old enough to be her mother. Pretty, young thing and nice with it.

I felt like such an arse when I started to greet when she was asking me about Lucy and her talking. That bastard has so much to answer for and my tears were more full of rage for what he has done to my wee lassie and Connor.

Yon teacher was awful nice though, and I felt totally relaxed, even when we went up and had a cuppa in the head's office.

I think things might just be ok. The head's going to get somebody to help her with her speech and she told me that the nurse would come round and help with the nits. I told them that I'd rather they did that at the school and she said it wasn't any bother. I have just to keep in touch by phone. And if there's anything else, they would do their best to help me. They never asked me too much which was good, because I couldn't really tell them. But sounds like moving back here's not been such a bad move after all. The weans seem happy and the teachers seem to be doing all they can to help.

Early Hours Tuesday

It's strange you would have thought that if I ever saw that bastard again I would go and freak out on the spot. But this strange calm came over me. I knew deep down somewhere it was just a matter of time before it happened. I just didn't know where or when. As soon as I saw him coming out the close, I knew what I was going to do – there wasn't any other option.

Once we'd got back in the flat, I told Connor I had to go a wee message. He just looked at me as if I was crazy, yelling at me that I couldn't leave them now, of all the days. I promised I would be as quick as I could. I went to the bottom of the stairs and waited. I knew it wouldn't be long until a jakey-type walked by. I hollered one over, gave them the last of my money and told them they'd better be back in 5. Mentioning the ex's name still worked as I saw the fear in the lad's eyes and off he went like a shot. He returned quicker than I expected with the goods I required. I just prayed it was enough.

The tears ran down my cheeks as I held my weans, an arm round each. I kissed them both, told them how much I loved them. They were both so peaceful lying sleeping like babies. I picked up my wee pills, swallowed them, then snuggled down next to them on the bed. He was never going to harm us again.

50 Helen

Finishing her marking at home, Helen still wondered if there really was a sinister reason for Lucy and Connor's absence that day. Rosie had said they were probably just off. Helen couldn't help but feel disappointed after the great day and the progress they seemed to have made the day before. The TV was on in the background, the news headlines rattling through.

Helen's ears tuned in as the local news started to speak about her town:

'Police are treating the death of a woman and two children found in their flat in the Ross area of town as suspicious and are urging anyone with any information to come forward …'

The cup of tea fell from Helen's hand as she screamed.

About the Author

Suzie is a Scot through and through, having been brought up in a wee Ayrshire town with her two brothers Nicky and Nathan.

She is currently living down under in Perth, Western Australia, learning the lingo and testing a beer or two.

Her biggest source of inspiration are her two kids; Lullah and Hamish, whom she loves to travel the world with.

Having been a teacher in both hemispheres, Suzie has had an array of interactions with kids and all things school-related.

When she's not writing or teaching, she can be found pulling a few coffees in her café, *La Chiquita's* in Fremantle, with her partner David.

Her love of books is indebted to her parents, Margaret and Ken, both voracious readers.

Lightning Source UK Ltd.
Milton Keynes UK
UKHW011826110522
402841UK00001B/88